CW00865701

Rack & Ruin

A Victorian Crime Thriller

Carol Hedges

Little G Books

For Avalyn and Edward

About the Author

Carol Hedges is the successful British author of 16 books for teenagers and adults. Her writing has received much critical acclaim, and her novel Jigsaw was shortlisted for the Angus Book Award and longlisted for the Carnegie Medal.

Carol was born in Hertfordshire, and after university, where she gained a BA (Hons.) in English Literature & Archaeology, she trained as a children's librarian. She worked for the London Borough of Camden for many years subsequently re-training as a secondary school teacher when her daughter was born.

Carol still lives and writes in Hertfordshire. She is a local activist and green campaigner, and the proud owner of a customised 1988 pink 2CV.

The Victorian Detectives series

Diamonds & Dust
Honour & Obey
Death & Dominion
Rack & Ruin
Wonders & Wickedness

Acknowledgments

Many thanks to Gina Dickerson of RoseWolf Design for another superb cover. Also to my two patient editors: Martyn Hedges and Archie Young.

To those wonderful individuals who have urged me to give Stride & Cully another outing: Terry, Barb, Shelley, Liz, Cathy, Rosie Amber, Jo, Val and so many others too numerous to mention. This book would not have been written without your encouragement.

Finally, I acknowledge my debt to all those amazing Victorian novelists for lighting the path through the fog with their genius. Unworthily but optimistically, I follow in their footsteps.

Rack & Ruin

A Victorian Crime Thriller

'Babylon was a great city.
Her merchandise was of gold and silver
Of precious stones, of pearls, of fine linen.
Sheep, horses, chariots, slaves
And the souls of men.'

Belshazzar's Feast

'I am no bird; and no net ensnares me; I am a free human
being with an independent will.'

Charlotte Bronte: Jane Eyre

London 1863. It is the month of May, and the city is in full bloom. Green leaves unfurl, yellow celandines peep from their lowly beds. Violets beckon coyly. Pink frothy waterfalls of blossom cascade from park cherry trees. Birds and bees go about the purposes for which they were created and everywhere from crook to cranny, in garden bed or bow pot, warmth returns and nature reasserts itself in song, hum, bud and flower.

Except here.

Here there is only the shrill roar of escaping steam, the groans of machines heaving ponderous loads of earth to the surface, the blasts of explosives, and the clack of pumping devices as the future arrives in lines of steel rails and a thundering in the blood.

Here, carcasses of houses lie untenanted. They rot, their windows gaping like the mouths of corpses, empty of teeth. Here, no sellers of fruit or flowers huddle over their baskets. No newsboys shout the day's headlines. No sleek cat creeps through the area railings.

For this is Hind Street, scene of the latest encroachment of the great iron railway. And while not a dead end, Hind Street has been seriously wounded by its present change of circumstances.

Eight houses at one end of the street have been pulled down already, leaving the occupants who rented rooms on a day to day basis scattered to the four winds to shift as best they can.

The rest of the houses still stand on the brink of destruction, clinging precariously to their foundations with the spectral lines of demolished ceilings, staircases and floors imprinted on their remaining walls.

Only the houses at one end of the street, numbers 12 to 18 are still occupied. We shall return to number 18 later on.

For now, let us peer through a slat in the unpainted wooden hoardings that surround the area and watch as Fred Grizewood, the young civil engineer in charge of the demolition gives his team of contractors careful instructions on placing the explosives around the base of number 9.

The fuse is lit. The men jump clear. There is an almighty bang like the loudest clap of thunder you have ever heard.

Followed by a long echoing crash and the crumble of falling brick and timber. The ground shakes underfoot.

When the noise has ceased, the dust has settled and the men have stopped coughing, everybody re-gathers around the hole that was previously surrounded by number 9 Hind Street.

They stare down.

There is a long, puzzled silence.

One of the contractors jumps into the hole, and stirs something with his boot. He bends down and pokes it cautiously. Then he looks up at Grizewood and says quietly.

"I think you'd better send for the police."

****

Inspector Lachlan Greig of the Metropolitan Police Force, recently promoted to 'A' Division makes his way up Bow Street towards his place of work. There is a lot to be said for being based at the *'oldest and most celebrated Police Office in London'* (Bradshaw's Illustrated Hand Book to London and Its Environs).

Inspector Greig says it quite a lot, usually under his breath as he elbows his way through the groups of tourists who stand gawping outside the handsome police house on the east side of the Covent Garden piazza and requesting officers who emerge to 'do a runner'.

Greig is an imposing man, thirty years old and well above the regulation five feet seven inches. He is handsome, with a clear complexion, broad shoulders, bright chestnut hair and beard of a slightly lighter colour, and a certain glint in his eye. Life had taught him, sadly, that being gifted with a high degree of intelligence didn't always play out well with those of his colleagues, and those of the criminal fraternity, who were not equally gifted.

He enters the building, whistling his favourite air: *The Bluebells of Scotland*, slightly flat, and is greeted by the desk constable who has a worried expression and a piece of paper. He passes Greig the latter.

"Railway site back of Hind Street, sir. Bodies discovered. Police presence requested. Sergeant Hacket and a couple of constables have just left."

Greig rolls his eyes. There are always drunken fights breaking out between the various tribes of navigators swarming like tiny black ants all over the developments that have transformed London into one gigantic ruined, dust-laden brickyard.

Frequently the fights end in fatalities. A lot of police time is spent trying to sort out who was responsible.

"On my way," he says resignedly.

He spins on his heel and heads for the door.

****

There is nothing resigned about Daisy Lawton's progress. Daisy Lawton is positively *skipping* along the pavement. Why shouldn't she? It is a fine sunny day after all. She has a new cherry striped dress and a straw bonnet with matching cherry ribbons. She is young and pretty and in love. And it is Spring ... lovely lovely Spring, when even the noxious city streets seem to smell sweeter.

Daisy approaches the Burlington Arcade where, to complete her happiness, her best friend Letitia Simpkins is waiting for her.

"Tishy! Oh Tishy - what a perfectly splendiferous day," Daisy exclaims, throwing her arms around her best friend's neck.

Letitia Simpkins gently frees herself from the exuberant embrace, straightening the rather plain bonnet that has been knocked cockeyed.

"You are in high spirits this morning," she says.

Daisy's expansive gesture takes in the uniformed beadles, the shoppers, the brightly lit plate-glass shop windows and, were it able to stretch that far, the whole of the city itself.

"It is Spring!" she cries. "The sun is shining and Papa has paid my allowance, so I can treat us both to tea and cakes."

She links arms with Letitia and steers her up the elegant colonnaded thoroughfare and into a small tea-room, where a smiling waiter directs them to a table by the window.

"Oh good. We can watch people passing and quiz their clothes," Daisy says.

Letitia sits, carefully placing her leather satchel on the floor beside her chair. Daisy eyes it and frowns prettily.

'What have you got there Tishy? Please don't say it's books."

"Then I won't."

"Books are for the schoolroom. And we left Putney and Miss Chadwick's Academy ages ago."

"I think it was only last Christmas."

"Oh. Was it? Well, it seems like ages ago. And how tedious it was. All those French verbs and times tables and what to do in a thunderstorm. I can't remember a single thing. And I certainly have no intention of opening another book - unless it is a novel about love or mysterious happenings."

The waiter places two tiny porcelain cups of coffee on the table, together with a plate of cakes. Daisy dimples her thanks.

"Now Tishy, tuck in. My treat. And I want to know everything you've been doing since we last met."

Letitia sips her coffee, reflecting how their two lives have diverged since those days of girlish confidences and whispered conversations in the dormitory they shared. Back then the two girls were inseparable, comrades in arms against a world of rules and regulations and the spiteful girls who took out their frustration at the pettiness of a girls' boarding school by bullying the other pupils.

And now here they are. Beautiful, loved and adored Daisy living in a world of romance and silk dresses. And she, plain as a pikestaff Tishy, the clever one whom no man courts and no man ever will.

For Letitia Simpkins has few illusions about her attractions - her nose is not retroussé and her mouth is not rosebud - she is entirely lacking in r-factor. Plus, there is a set to her jaw and her figure is so flat you could use it as a plank. Only a good-natured liar would call her attractive.

"Oh, I haven't been doing much," she says, putting down her cup. "Just reading a bit and walking and looking after Mama."

"Is she still unwell?"

"She manages to come downstairs sometimes. Most of the time she stays in bed."

"Poor you. I remember she was ill while we were at school. That was why you didn't go home in the school holidays, wasn't it?"

Letitia looks out of the window, where women in the latest bonnets and shawls flit by like brightly coloured butterflies. She prefers not to think about those long dreary holidays in the company of the school servants and the French mistress who was too poor to return to her village and used to sob in her room at night.

"It was. But enough of me and my humdrum days," she says. "Tell me about your life. Is there a new beau? I expect there is. Where did you meet him?"

Daisy rolls her eyes and sighs ecstatically.

"Oh Tishy - there are several. But one I like in particular. I met him at the house of Mama's friend, Mrs Osborne. She had a five o'clock tea and Mama let me go as there were going to be a lot of young people there. He has the bluest eyes you can imagine, and the dearest moustache in the world."

"Sounds divine."

"Oh, it is. He was standing by the French window when I came in and our eyes met across the crowded room and ... well ... that was that. He is a Dragoon Guard."

Letitia smiles to herself. Daisy and her various beaux have been a source of amusement since they were both thirteen and she fell madly in love with the art master. Still it is pleasant to be sitting here, enjoying her harmless chatter.

Listening to Daisy rattling on takes her mind off the more pressing problems: her mother's sickness, the doctor's bill that arrived today, and whether her father is going to be sufficiently in temper to be asked for the money to pay it.

Letitia often wishes her family life was less tense and complicated.

"What do you think, Tishy?"

Letitia blinks. She has been so wrapped up in her own thoughts that she has failed to focus on Daisy.

"Oh - I think ... well, it's what you think that's the important thing?"

"I think pale pink spotted tulle, with puffings and a heart shaped berthe."

Letitia stares at her. For all she knows, Daisy could be speaking double Dutch, not that the subject was ever taught at school as far as she recalls.

"Well then, I agree."

"I knew you would!"

Daisy finishes her coffee, runs a wetted finger round her plate and licks the crumbs before signalling the waiter to bring the bill which she settles, brushing Letitia's protests aside.

The two friends put on their gloves, make their way out to the street, kiss each other fondly and go their separate ways. And there we shall have to leave them for the time being. For we have a far more important, though far less pleasant elsewhere to be.

****

Inspector Greig has served in the police force since he was eighteen. Therefore, he has seen and heard things that would turn the stomachs and harrow the souls of lesser men.

It takes a lot to move him, but as he scrambles into the hole where number 9 Hind Street formerly stood, and looks down on the small bundles that are being carefully examined by two of his men, he feels an unexpected surge of emotion.

"What have we got?"

Sergeant Ben Hacket stares at him, his youthful face white and stricken. He is a country lad, new to London and to the Metropolitan Police. He hasn't yet developed the hard carapace needed to survive the horrors he will encounter.

"Eleven dead babies, sir."

A couple of contractors watching proceedings from the edge of the hole, turn their faces away. Greig nods, takes out his notebook and begins the laborious procedures necessary whenever a dead body - or bodies - is discovered. Upon these notes will depend the report that he will submit to the authorities and the sort of inquiries that he may be requested to undertake as a consequence.

He writes down where the tiny bodies are lying, drawing sketches of their exact position and relation to each other. He makes notes on the old rags and newspapers covering them, and checks for any objects that may be in the vicinity that might have contributed to their deaths.

He works swiftly and in grim silence, watched by his colleagues and the shocked group of contractors. At last he closes the notebook and glances at Sergeant Hacket.

"There will have to be a coroner's inquest."

Hacket nods, his mouth a thin, tight line.

"Poor little beggars," he murmurs. "Barely had time to draw breath."

Greig reopens his notebook, scribbles a few lines, then tears out the page.

"Run over to University College Hospital. Ask for a couple of porters to move the bodies to the morgue as quickly as they can. Don't take no for an answer and don't accept 'later'. If there's any quibbling, explain what we've found and say that the coroner will want a post-mortem examination and full report as soon as possible. I'll notify him when I get back to the station."

All this time Fred Grizewood has been standing some way off, nervously passing the brim of his hat between his hands. Now he approaches the edge of the hole.

"Officer, once you have removed the ... the ... corpses, is there any reason why I cannot order my team to continue working?" he asks.

Greig gives him a stare so hard you could bounce rocks off it.

"I'm sorry sir, there will be no further work done here until my men have finished examining the site and the inquest has ended."

The young man flinches under his gaze.

"But the men are paid a day rate. If they do not work, they will not get paid," he persists.

"At least they are alive. Unlike those poor little creatures," Greig says flatly.

There is a silence. The engineer's face flushes. He studies his boots, which are caked in damp yellow London clay.

"I was not meaning to be disrespectful to the dead."

"No. I'm sure you weren't."

"Mr Wandle won't like the men stopping."

"That is of no concern to me. It is highly possible that a crime has been committed here and until the inquest jury has reached a verdict, no further work will take place. Is that clearly understood?"

The engineer bites his lip, fiddles with his watch chain and looks away.

"Now I suggest you secure the entrances," Greig says. "Once word gets round, you'll have the mob at your gates. Not to mention journalists from the popular press, which is probably even worse, in my experience."

The engineer nods dumbly.

Greig beckons to his constables.

"Go and talk to the navigators. They may have come into contact with the people who lived in the house. See what they can tell you about them. A name, a description, anything."

As he returns to Bow Street, Inspector Greig thinks about what he has just viewed, and how these infants and their sad deaths are all part and parcel of the great city he now works in.

Greig has been living in London for some time. He started his career in the Leith Police as a newly qualified officer and moved up the ranks, before making the decision to leave his home town and come south.

London. The overwhelming vastness of it still has the power to both amaze and appal him. The immense tangle of streets, courts and alleys. The filthy crepuscular interiors of the poorer houses with their wooden beams and crazed confusion of staircases. The hard, unyielding noise.

It doesn't seem beautiful to him any longer, as it did briefly when he arrived. The smog washes over it, darkening its brick and ashlar stone. A city of fog and darkness. A bricken wilderness, barren and wild. Pagan and savage. Babylondon.

****

Meanwhile Letitia Simpkins makes her way back to the rented house in Islington where the family currently resides. In her sixteen years the family has occupied various properties in various locales.

Some have been quite grand houses, some rather less so, as the quality of the Simpkins living quarters is dependent upon Mr Simpkins securing employment, which is dependent upon his temper. Which is unpredictable.

But currently her father has secured a well-paid job and here they are in a newly built terraced house with tessellated tiles on the path leading to the front door, which has smart modern acid-etched upper glass panels.

Letitia pulls the house key from her pocket and opens the green painted door, which is the same colour as all the other doors in the street. She wrinkles her nose at the familiar smell of unappetising meals which seems to follow them wherever they go.

From upstairs, a frail voice calls out, "Is that you, Letty?"

"Yes, Mama," she responds, hanging up her bonnet and placing her bag on one of the hall chairs.

She climbs the stairs and enters her mother's bedroom. The air is close. Her Mama, white faced and reduced, lies helplessly crooked amidst a heap of pillows and untucked sheets.

"My pillows ... please," she whispers.

Letitia crosses to the bed and slips an arm under Mama's shoulders, raising her in the bed. Then she rearranges the crooked pillows. She refills the glass of barley water from the jug.

Mama has been like this for as long as she can remember. Letitia has never been told specifically what it is she suffers from, but she gathers that it started with her twin brothers' births and has been getting worse with each subsequent pregnancy, all of which have ended in miscarriage.

Now her mother has given up on life. She languishes, confined to bed or on better days, to the downstairs sofa. Letitia gathers her father is not sympathetic to his wife's condition. Sometimes, if she wakes in the night, she hears arguments through the thin walls. Her father's voice hard and insistent, her mother's feeble protests. Her small wretched cries of pain.

"Would you like me to open the window a little, Mama? The tree in the garden is in blossom and the air is so mild and warm."

Her mother sighs and shakes her head.

"No thank you dear. It would fly straight to my chest and I have barely recovered from my winter cold. Can you go down to the kitchen and find out what the cook is preparing for dinner? Your father has not been happy with her efforts over the past few evenings. I fear we may have to apply to the agency for a new one."

"I shall see to it at once," Letitia says.

"And ask her to make a cherry cake. William and Arthur do like a slice of cherry cake when they come in from school."

Letitia goes downstairs. She would have enjoyed a slice of cake after her long day at school, she thinks grimly. But such luxuries were never offered to her. Other boarders got parcels from home containing fruit and cake. She never did.

But, she reminds herself as she prepares to do battle with the latest incarnation of truculent kitchen staff, Daisy always shared her good things generously, so at the end of the day she did not go short.

Letitia reaches the ground floor and heads for the basement. Much as she loves her brothers it is hard not to feel some resentment at the way the house revolves around them.

She has only been back for a couple of months, but already she has noticed how Mama's eyes light up when the boys are around - however noisy and rough they are. Mama always tries to make an effort, questioning them about their day in the way she never does her daughter.

And there is something else preying on Letitia's mind. No mention has been made of her future. It seems that she is just supposed to stay at home, acting as Mama's amanuensis, nurse and general household manager for the rest of her life.

Nobody has asked her whether this is actually what she wants to do; whether it is the kind of life she envisages for herself. It has been taken for granted that it is. But it is not. And as each day passes, Letitia is feeling increasingly incarcerated, like an eagle in a cage.

Having dealt firmly but diplomatically with the cook, she climbs the stairs back to the ground floor. Her satchel lies where she left it, propped against the coat rack. She picks it up and takes it into the small cramped parlour, also known as her father's study.

It is the only room to contain a desk. It is her father's desk. But her father is at work, so Letitia rolls up the lid and seats herself in front of it. She opens the satchel and takes out a notebook, a pencil and a book. The book is by Mary Wollstonecraft and it is titled *A Vindication of the Rights of Woman.*

It is not her book. She has been lent it by one of the new friends she has made. Friends she has kept secret from her family. Even from Daisy. Now, with the house quiet and nobody to disturb her until the twins return from school, she opens the book, and begins to read.

****

To understand why Letitia Simpkins, newly released from the stifling confines of a Girls' Boarding School and now facing a future of drudgery and servitude, is avidly devouring a text so revolutionary and scandalous in its day that if her parents knew what she was reading, her father would throw it upon the nearest fire, we must go back to a rainy Saturday in early March.

Driven out of the house by the squabbling of her two brothers, the ire of Mr Simpkins and Mama's querulous demands, Letitia was walking along Regent Street. It was raining, a slow persistent rain that was falling as if it had all day. Rain dripped off the rim of her bonnet and ran down her face.

Her thoughts were dark and bitter. Like the water that was seeping through the thin soles of her boots, the realisation that she was of very little significance to her family was slowly and uncomfortably seeping into her soul.

Unlike Daisy, there had been no party to celebrate her return, no newly decorated bedroom awaiting her arrival. Instead, it had been made clear to her that the end of her education marked the beginning of her life as unpaid house staff.

On her first evening back, she had been handed a basket of her brothers' socks, and told to darn them, as Mama was too frail to ply the needle. It was also suggested that she listened to them repeat their lessons, and should help them with their homework.

Other domestic duties pressed in thick and fast: supervising the servants, running errands for Mama, writing her letters, fetching her many medicines and pills from the chemist. Now here she was, stalking the rain-soaked streets, and trying to hold back the tears that came unbidden to her eyes.

Letitia paused under a shop awning to wipe her face but as she stepped out, the awning suddenly buckled under the weight of water, spilling its contents all over her. She was soaked to the skin. It was the last straw. She buried her face in her hands and burst into tears.

A light touch on her shoulder made her look up. A young woman had drawn alongside and was regarding her solicitously from a pair of very blue eyes.

"You poor, poor girl," she said. "What a thing to happen!"

Letitia stared at her in dumb tear-streaked misery.

The young woman took her gently by the arm.

"If you'd like to come with me, I can supply you with some fresh clothes, and a cup of hot coffee to warm you up."

She led the unprotesting Letitia towards the top of Regent Street, pausing in front of a big white painted house fronted by black railings.

"Here we are," she said, guiding her up the steps. "Come in and get dry."

Letitia pauses in her studies, recalling that first meeting with Sarah Lunt, the sweet-faced librarian of the Regent Street Ladies' Literary & Philosophical Society. How kind she was. How kind they had all been.

Clad in dry clothes, and provided with a steaming hot drink and a saffron bun, all the hoarded woe and misery of the past months had spilled out and she had found herself confiding in her rescuer in a way she had not done with anybody since dormitory days.

But miracle of miracles, instead of chiding her for being undutiful and selfish, or reminding her of the debt she owed to her parents for feeding and clothing her and giving her a roof to shelter under, the young woman had sympathised.

She had even gone further, intimating that in her opinion, bright young women ought to be able to access higher education and receive training for some profession where they could fulfil their innate potential and earn a living, rather than being expected to fritter away their valuable time and their precious health in household pursuits.

The visit had been an eye-opener. Letitia had not realised there were other women who loved learning as she did; who thought that she and they deserved a future of their own. Women who believed that there was more to life than just waiting around for some man to turn up.

From thereon in, whenever she could get away, Letitia had sneaked out, making up various excuses for her absences, and had returned to the Regent Street house. There she got to know some of the other ladies who ran the group. And as the weeks passed, she absorbed more and more of their thoughts and ideas, finding in them an answering echo to her own.

So now here she is reading this book in preparation for a public lecture by one of the group's founders, Miss Sophie Jacques. The topic, *How Higher Education Could Change Women's Lives* is most pertinent to her situation, though she is not sure how she will ever get any more education herself, much as she longs desperately to research and explore and study.

For her, the door to more learning seems to have slammed shut, leaving her on the outside looking in, like a hungry child pressing its nose to a sweetshop window. As if to mock her thwarted ambitions, Letitia is currently supervising her brothers, who are about to sit the entrance exam to a minor public school.

They are struggling to master the Euclid theorems, the Latin, the Greek and Religious Study needed to pass. She, on the other hand, is soaking up all the new knowledge, painfully aware that were she a boy, she could probably sit the same exams and pass with flying colours.

She reads on, pausing occasionally to note down her thoughts or copy a quotation. But Time, that normally moves so slowly, is fleeting by on airy wings. All too soon the front door crashes open and the loud imperious voices of her brothers fracture the tranquillity of the afternoon.

Letitia sighs, closing the book and her notebook. For now, scholarly pursuits must cease and household chores begin.

****

Almost as soon as Inspector Greig and his men leave Hind Street, a draggle of onlookers, gawpers and people with nothing better to do with their time start to arrive, word having got out that Something Nasty Has Happened.

Thus, by the time the two male lodgers at number 18 Hind Street return, the street is almost impassable, such is the press of people, dogs, carts, and itinerant street sellers of ham sandwiches, fruit and ginger beer, who have spotted an opportunity to make a few pence on the basis that a non-ambulant crowd always requires feeding at some point.

Edwin Persiflage and Danton Waxwing elbow their way through the throng until they reach their front door. They are both bank clerks in the same private bank. They are earnest young men with well-oiled hair, cheap gaudy waistcoats and big ideas.

They have been discussing them (the ideas) over a lunchtime chop and a glass of porter at the Lamb and Flagon, a quiet backstreet pub where food can be consumed and ideas discussed without the rest of the world wanting to know your business.

Mr Sprowle, landlord of number 18 Hind Street, views their arrival in his hallway with an air of pursed-mouthed disapproval. He doesn't like clerks. He likes their rent, but regards them as cheeky young upstarts. Especially these two. Mr Sprowle was educated in the School of Hard Knocks, leading to a Degree in Resentment.

"Home early, ain'tcha?"

"Half-holiday," Waxwing says airily.

"Ho. Nice. Wery nice. For some. I never had a half-holiday when I was your age. Nor a whole holiday neither. Had to work fifteen hours a day and -"

"What's afoot?" Persiflage asks, gesturing over his shoulder at the crowd.

"Twelve inches, last time I checked. Hur, hur, hur," says Sprowle, who is to comedy what bricks are to opera.

The two clerks roll their eyes.

Luckily Sprowle cannot resist imparting information to which he owns the exclusive rights, especially to people who need reminding that in this life there are those that rent and those that rent to them.

"They found *bodies* in the cellar of number 9,' he says. "Dead bodies," he adds with lugubrious if tautological relish.

"Bodies - plural?" Waxwing asks, raising his eyebrows.

"'S what I heard. Babbies too. Pore li'l mites. What's the world coming to?"

Sprowle takes off his cap, revealing a bald crown patchily covered by greasy strands of thin grey hair.

"Of course, them what has been living here for some time, like myself, will be *aiding the police in their enquiries*," he says self-importantly.

The two clerks exchange a quick look.

"Will the police be visiting the house?" Persiflage asks with feigned nonchalance.

"Nah - I has to go down to Bow Street in the next few days to talk to ..." Sprowle fishes around in his tattered coat pocket, finally producing a small card. He squints at it: "In-spector L Greig. Yeah. That's the cove."

For some reason, both clerks look relieved.

"Well - we must get on," Persiflage says. "Ledgers to write and so on."

"So on," Waxwing echoes, nodding.

They mount the uncarpeted stairs to their small room on the first floor, but do not speak until they are inside with the door closed.

"Rum," Persiflage remarks.

"Very rum."

"Could have been worse," Persiflage says. "At least the police aren't coming to the house."

"Not that they'd search it," Waxwing says, removing his jacket and hanging it on a bentwood chair. "And even if they did, what would they find?"

"What indeed."

"Precisely."

"Even so ..." Persiflage says thoughtfully.

"Quite. Exactly what I was thinking."

"We don't want anything to go amiss at this early stage."

"No indeed. That would be ... most unfortunate."

"Most."

Persiflage goes to the window and looks down.

"So you'll ..." he says, not turning round.

"I will. I'll do it now."

Waxwing kneels by the bed. Slowly and very carefully he brings out a small wooden box. He puts on his jacket and quits the room, taking the box with him. There is the sound of footsteps descending on the stairs. Then the front door slams.

Persiflage continues to stare out of the window, his eyes following his fellow clerk until he is lost amidst the crowd. Some time later Waxwing will return to the lodging house. Still carefully carrying the small wooden box.

****

Daisy Lawton, having sounded the opinion of her dear friend Tishy, (which was her own opinion to begin with) returns to the department store and spends some time trying on the pale pink spotted tulle day dress, with puffings and a heart shaped berthe.

Being fussed over by sales assistants is very soothing to the spirit. As is being told how pretty she is. And twirling in front of the big gilt mirror admiring her neat waist and pretty white shoulders.

Having pins stuck into her side by one of the store's dressmakers is less so, but if she wants to wear the dress to the next tea party in a few days' time, she must suffer. In silence - though with a few little squeaks.

Finally satisfied that the dress will fit her to perfection, she chooses matching ribbons for her hair and the dearest pair of satin slippers. She arranges for the whole outfit to be sent to the house the following day, along with the bill which Papa will settle, though she may have to prepare him in advance. There have been many such purchases since she returned home.

Daisy checks the time on her little silver and pearl watch, a present from Mama and Papa on the occasion of her sixteenth birthday. Oh dear - she is late. She is supposed to be meeting Mama outside Daleys.

Mama is going to instruct her how to select the best linen and china. It is important to know this for her future home. Nothing marks out a lady more than the pattern of her china and the thread count of her sheets. They will then go home in a cab and she will practice the piano for an hour so that she can perform her waltzes at the next supper party.

Playing the piano gives one the opportunity to show off pretty wrists and dainty fingers. Last time Daisy entertained, the young men were positively elbowing each other out of the way to turn the pages of her music.

She smiles to herself, remembering how a certain handsome Dragoon Guard won, and as a result stood all afternoon at her side, turning the pages. It was a pity he couldn't read music and occasionally turned too late or too many pages, but a girl can't expect everything in a beau. Fine dark eyes and silky moustaches win over musical accuracy any day.

Daisy hurries along the pavement, aware that she is the cynosure of many male eyes, but schooled to keep her own eyes demurely lowered. She is only too aware of the whores in the doorways. Even at this hour she passes brightly dressed women in low cut dresses, smelling strongly of cheap perfume and perspiration.

Mama has dinned it into her ever since she was old enough to understand, that a young girl's reputation is the most precious thing she owns and once lost, it cannot be retrieved.

Daisy does not intend such a thing to happen to her. All her life she has waited for this moment: her entry into society. The mantelpiece in the drawing room is stacked with cards and invitations. Her wardrobe is stacked with pretty dresses and accessories. She is primed and ready to conquer every young and eligible male heart in London. Nothing can possibly go wrong.

****

Inspector Greig has a reputation also. In his case it is for keeping a cool head in times of stress. It has been hard won, and right now it is being sorely tried by the director of the Bayswater, Paddington & Holborn Bridge Metropolitan Railway Company, who has hastened hot foot from his office to harangue him.

Montague Wandle is a very large man in a very loud suit with a very shiny top hat and a grievance. Which he is currently airing. Young engineer Fred Grizewood, reluctantly dragged along as ballast, hovers uneasily in the background.

"Now, you look here," Wandle says, thumping Greig's desk with a large fist. "I have a timetable. One week to complete the current works. Cut and cover and move on. And right now, thanks to you, I shall fall behind schedule. Now then - what do you have to say!"

The Inspector says nothing. His expression is almost as wooden as his desk.

"I'm sure the men will be returning to work tomorrow," Engineer Grizewood says from some outlying part of the room in an effort to defrost the conversation.

"Will they though?" Wandle snaps. "With policemen swarming all over the site, and asking questions of everybody? Hardly conducive to putting in a full day's hard graft."

"Perhaps it may have escaped your notice *sir*, that the bodies of eleven infants were discovered on the site this morning?" Greig's voice drips icicles.

"Well, they ain't there now, are they?"

"So, what is it, exactly, that you wish me to do?"

Wandle glares at him.

"Call off your men of course. Leave the site. It's clear that none of my navvies had anything to do with it and I want them to get on with what they're paid to do."

The young engineer gives Greig a beseeching glance.

"WHEN my officers have completed their inquiries and WHEN I am satisfied with what they report, and WHEN the coroner has delivered his verdict, I will let you know. Sir. And now good day to you," Greig says coldly, rising to his feet to indicate that the interview is over.

Wandle gapes at him.

"This is your final word?"

"It is my final word indeed."

Wandle also heaves himself to his feet, his face mottled with anger.

"Then I shall be writing a stiff letter to the Home Secretary," he splutters as he heads for the door.

"That is your choice."

Greig wonders why people always think a letter to the Home Secretary is such a terrible threat, given that said letter will probably languish unread for weeks in a pile of others on the desk of one of the many under-secretaries, before being discarded into the nearest waste paper receptacle.

But that is not his problem. His problem is the upcoming coroner's inquest and the outcome resulting from the decision reached. If the deaths are recorded as accidental, or debility from birth, as they so often are in these tragic cases, then there is nothing more he can do.

****

A bright May morning a few days later. The sun shines down upon the hansoms, growlers, vans and bumpers crawling at twelve miles an hour along the traffic-filled streets. It shines down upon old women squatting in the gutters with their herbs, apples, matches and sandwiches in trays around their necks.

It shines down on the carts of costers selling coals, flowers, fish, muffins, tea and crockery. It shines down upon a bare wooden table in a side room of the Cat and Salutation pub, where eleven small and emaciated bodies lie ready for viewing by the jury of the Westminster coroner.

If death had a smell it would be this mix of stale ale, tobacco and sawdust, Greig thinks gloomily. He stands by the open window awaiting the jury's arrival. Proximity to the dead, even on a warm sunny day, leads to a lowering of the spirits and a sense of finality.

The total absence of sound makes the whole occasion even more depressing. Usually there are at least a few sobbing relatives in the vicinity. Even if they are faking their grief. He glances across at Sergeant Ben Hacket who is clenching and unclenching his fists and trying not to focus upon the pitiful naked bodies with their bashed in skulls, broken rib cases and tiny limbs bent out of shape.

The door opens, and one by one the members of the jury file in to view the bodies. Greig scans their faces as they pass by him. Their expressions vary from detached interest to pity. Silently they stare, silently they file out. When the last juror has gone, Greig nods to Hacket and they leave the temporary mortuary, closing and locking the door behind them.

Crossing the road, the two police officers enter the coroner's court, where the jury is just taking its places on the row of chairs provided. One side of the big central table is occupied by reporters from the main London newspapers, already busy scribbling and sketching the witness box and the coroner, who sits at the head of the table, perusing a summary of the case.

To Greig, who has attended many inquests, it is a familiar scene, as is the noisy presence of members of the public, the idlers and curiosity-mongers, who always turned up at a court hearing, a crime scene or a hanging. The air is already fragrant with the smell of oranges and unwashed bodies.

What is unfamiliar is the speed with which this inquest has been arranged. Somebody has been pulling strings behind the scenes he thinks, as he takes his place. Fairly important strings. Though he notices they have had to bring in the Middlesex coroner to do it.

Sergeant Hacket clears his throat, shuffles his piece of paper nervously. Greig nods encouragingly.

"You'll be fine, Ben. Speak slowly and clearly, and answer any questions as truthfully as you can."

It is the young man's first public inquest hearing and as he was also the first officer at the scene, it is his duty to present the police report to the coroner. Greig has come to support him. He has decided that young Hacket has the makings of a good officer.

Once he gets used to the way of life, and stops seeing spelling and punctuation as optional extras.

The inquest opens with the autopsy report, read out in the flat, detached tone always adopted by pathologists everywhere who are called upon to deliver a medical analysis of the dead.

Greig listens intently, focusing on the implications of the words. Upon this will depend whether the jury decides a criminal act has taken place. Upon that will decide whether he has a case to investigate.

"I have been working on the remains of the infants that the police brought in three days ago," the surgeon says, his face devoid of any expression. He could be reading out a washing list. "There were eight females and three males. After making a study of the ossification of the skeletal bones, I was able to assign ages to each cadaver."

"Given the non-fusion of the petro-mastoid bones, I predicate that nine of the infants were in their first year. This is confirmed by the still separation of the two halves of the frontal bone of the skull. The other two were in their second year - as witnessed by the lack of jointure of the arch and body of the vertebrae."

"Well, well. You can tell all that just from looking at the bones," the coroner marvels.

The pathologist gives him a tight-lipped stare.

"If you doubt my opinion, I am happy to lend you a copy of Quain's Osteology, where you can check the ossification tables for yourself," he remarks tartly.

Wisely, the coroner decides not to rise to this.

"Is there anything else you can tell me?"

"What do you want to know?"

"How they died."

The pathologist consults his notes.

"Impossible to say precisely, though the protrusion of the ribs would suggest that insufficient nutrition may have contributed. Eight bodies show evidence of damage to the spinal column and various breakages to the lower and upper limbs, from which I assume human intervention, accidental or deliberate, caused their demise."

"Can you give any indication as to the times of death?"

"All the deaths occurred recently, that is within the last six to eight months. Several of the bodies were found to have been wrapped in old copies of the Telegraph, so it was possible to date their demise pretty accurately."

The press scribbles, the coroner makes notes, the onlookers whisper and point. Hacket is called to the witness box and makes a very competent job of giving his report. All this time Greig studies the jurors intently.

Do not come back with a verdict of accidental death, he wills them silently. Do not think for a moment this is chance or accident, or that there is insufficient evidence. It is murder, and you must find it so.

He thinks of the tiny bodies lying broken and un-mourned upon the pub table. I will hunt down whoever did this to you, he promises them. I will track your murderers to wherever they are hiding, and I will get justice for each and every one of you.

****

Next morning Inspector Greig enters Bow Street police office to discover a small selection of Hind Street residents lurking in the waiting area. They have turned up to be interviewed after the inquest jury returned a unanimous verdict of murder.

Also in the group is the Metropolitan Police's arch-nemesis Richard Dandy, chief reporter on *The Inquirer*, the paper that prides itself on speaking for 'The Ordinary Man in the Street'. He has turned up on the off chance of obtaining a story, and is already deep in conversation with one of the residents.

"Morning Inspector," Dandy calls out. "Did you read this morning's headline? *'The Barbarity of the Brutally Butchered Babies'*. My readers are going to be Very Shocked and Disgusted."

Greig folds his arms and glares.

"These are police premises. And I'll thank you to vacate them."

Dandy gets out his notebook, removes a stub of pencil from behind one ear and licks the end.

"I'll just write that down, if you don't mind."

"I forbid you from writing anything down while you are here."

Dandy pauses, pencil mid-air.

"Would you like to explain to my readers exactly why not?"

"I don't have to explain any of my actions to you."

"Can I write *that* down?"

"Certainly not."

"Can I write down that you said I shouldn't write down that you said -"

"Just. Get. Out!" Greig says between gritted teeth.

The small crowd of residents stare from Greig to Dandy. They understand that a fight is going on, although they can't see any blood. Dandy tosses Greig an evil grin, tips his hat jauntily to the audience and saunters out, humming.

Greig glowers at his retreating back, then turns to the desk constable.

"Where is everybody?"

"Inspector Atherton's got a couple of Mary-Anns in the interview room. Night patrol picked them up at the top of the Haymarket. Bold as brass and wearing women's clothing. Constable Davis is in with him. Sergeant Hacket and Sergeant Williams are getting the prisoners ready for court. I don't know where anybody else is."

Greig sighs.

"Right. I'll use the charge room. Can you get it ready, please."

As the constable hurries to do his bidding, Greig beckons to the small group of residents, who have quickly morphed from Interested Bystanders to Upright Citizens Here to Aid the Police in Their Inquiries.

"Good day, ladies and gentlemen. Who would like to be interviewed first?"

Lunchtime finds Inspector Greig in the Superintendent's office, reporting back on his morning's work.

"The first person I saw was Mr Bracegirdle Hemyng who lives at number 16. He says that as far as he was aware, the occupants of number 9 were a respectable couple who took in washing. Says that he frequently saw baskets being delivered and there was always washing hanging in the back yard."

"Baskets can be used for many things, though."

"Indeed. His wife says she occasionally passed the couple in the street or saw them buying food in the market, but they were not on greeting terms. Liked to keep themselves to themselves, is how she put it.

"Then there was the Irish family in number 12. They lived the closest. The man calls himself Baron Coleraine, though I suspect that isn't his real name. He and his three sons work for the company building the railway. The wife and two daughters sell whatever is in season in the streets around the area.

"He says both he and his wife regularly heard babies crying in the house. They saw a steady stream of young women arriving. And others with bundles that could have been babies. They assumed these were delivering washing, or handing over their children to be minded while they were at work.

"He also saw the man feeding small bloody lumps to his cats. He thought they were lumps of meat. I now wonder whether they were aborted foetuses."

"Does he know the names of the couple?"

"He thinks they were called Mr and Mrs Hall. Mr Sydney Sprowle who rents out rooms at number 18 was able to give us a pretty good description of them. I've left him with the police artist to see if we can get a likeness."

"You know what this is about?"

"I believe the couple were indulging in the crime of baby minding for financial gain and panicked when their operations were about to be disturbed by the notice to quit.

"I believe they deliberately murdered such infants as were still alive and in their charge, and then fled the area. I also think it likely that more infant deaths may have taken place at number 9 Hind Street - the amount and whereabouts of the children we may never know."

"And you still want to investigate it? I'd say your chances of success are practically nil. Cases like this crop up regularly. It is almost impossible to track down the perpetrators and even if you do, they always claim the children were ailing when they died. It's not worth pursuing. Besides, I'd have thought a nice murder was more up your street."

Greig breathes in sharply.

"And is this not murder? Or do the deaths of innocent babes not count in this great city of ours?"

The Superintendent looks at him sharply. Nine months ago, Greig arrived from the Edinburgh Police with excellent references. His conduct since joining Bow Street has been impeccable - more than can be said for his predecessor, who was known for taking bribes and letting off prostitutes in return for 'favours' of a fourpenny upright nature.

An honest man. An upright man. A good thief-taker too if his record is to be believed, the Superintendent thinks. A man to be relied on. Yet not a man he warms to. And right now, there is something in Greig's voice and in the set expression on his face that he can't define, but it is making him feel uncomfortable.

He shrugs.

"Then the case is yours."

"Thank you. I shall need an assistant - may I ask for Sergeant Ben Hacket. He was at the building site when the bodies were uncovered, and he gave a good account of himself at the coroner's inquest."

The superintendent nods.

"He could do with being taken under someone's wing and it may as well be you as anyone else - there are some here who'd teach him the wrong way to go about things."

"I'll be on my way then."

As the strains of the *Bluebells of Scotland* whistled slightly flat fades into silence, the Superintendent reminds himself that Inspector Greig is practically a foreigner, coming from where he does, north of the border. Thus, allowances have to be made.

Meanwhile Greig makes his way up to the first-floor recreation room, where Sergeant Hacket is enjoying a brew and a gossip with a couple of day constables.

"I shall be at the Lamb & Flag having a bite of luncheon. Report to me in the charge room in an hour, sergeant. We have matters pertaining to the investigation that we need to discuss."

The Lamb & Flag Public House and Dining Rooms has served as Greig's preferred watering-hole since his arrival in

London. Not just for the food, which is hot, plentiful and seems to originate from recognised farm animals, but for the ambience.

The Lamb & Flag is an off-the-beaten-track, spit and sawdust, slap-bang sort of establishment, patronised by the sort of people who show no interest in anything beyond their plate of dinner. This suited Greig. He didn't want to be bothered with badinage, police or otherwise, while he is eating.

Nor did he want to be recognised as belonging to the forces of law and order. Occupying the same seat in a corner box, he always keeps his head down and his street coat buttoned up while he busies himself with his meal and a copy of the *Daily Mail*.

After finishing his lunch, Greig returns to Bow Street, where Sergeant Hacket is waiting for him in the entrance. Greig walks him away from the station.

"I have decided that we shall be working undercover, sergeant," he tells the young man. "Our story will be that we represent the railway company and are seeking to trace the couple who lived at number 9 Hind Street. We will not mention what we uncovered. The minute they get an inkling of police interest, they will be off like the wind and we will never track them down."

"Haven't they already gone?"

"Yes, but not far. My experience is that most people in their situation stay in the area they know, maybe moving only a few streets away only. They have their supply lines and their contacts in place. So, we will start by getting to know the local area, the shops and pubs, the places where people hang out."

A frown crosses Sergeant Hacket's open young face.

"Isn't what we're going to do ... well ... kind of lying, sir - given that there is no money and we don't work for the railway company. Not that I'm saying it's wrong," he adds hastily.

"The two pillars of successful detection are information and confession," Greig says. "These are the only things you need to concern yourself with. We're wading in murky waters, sergeant, and it's going to get a lot deeper and a deal murkier before we're done, believe me."

****

Daisy Lawton's world is a world away from both the Lamb & Flag and Bow Street police office. It is so far away that it could even be on another planet, or in another galaxy. It is a world of fans and flounces, of linens and laces, of button kid boots and sweetly trimmed bonnets.

And here is the heroine herself just coming up the front path of the nicely appointed house in Fitzroy Square. She is carrying a bouquet of hot house flowers. She pauses on the step to bury her nose into their sweetness.

Daisy enters the house, handing the bouquet to the parlour maid with instructions to put it in water and take it straight up to her bedroom. Mama does not approve of flowers in bedrooms, declaring that the scent gives one bad dreams, but Mama is out at a Ladies' Committee Meeting and won't be back until much later, so she won't know.

As for her adored and adoring Papa, who is probably operating on some poor person (Daisy pulls a face), he is completely at her mercy and can deny her nothing. She removes her bonnet, carefully fluffing up the feathers before hanging it up, then mounts the stairs to the first floor.

Daisy pushes open the door to her room, uttering a little sigh of contentment. How lovely it is: the pretty rosewood dressing table with its framed bentwood mirror and lace runner, the bright sofa cushions and striped Turkey carpet. And her soft little bed with its crisp white sheets, canopy, and quilted coverlet.

How nicely Mama has done it. When she left, this was a little girl's room, with bars on the window and toys on the floor. Now it is the room of a young lady ready to enter the world. Without taking off her outdoor shoes, Daisy throws herself onto her bed and laces her hands behind her head.

She is the luckiest girl in London, she thinks. She really is. She has everything she could possibly want. Wherever she goes, every male eye follows her - of course she isn't supposed to notice this, but she does.

And if she plays her cards right she might, eventually, be on track to receive that longed-for proposal of marriage. Her sails are set and her future is secure. Daisy daydreams of a lovely house, a handsome indulgent husband, a carriage with matching bay horses and a wardrobe full of dresses and bonnets.

Later, dressed in one of her new pink silk gowns and with her hair combed and curled, she makes her way downstairs to the sitting room, passing the open door of the dining room, which is set for dinner. The table sparkles with silverware and trailing ivy falls decoratively from vases.

Tonight is a special dinner, for it is Papa's birthday, and in honour of the occasion the best china and the nicest wines have been selected. A saddle of mutton with caper sauce is to be the centrepiece of the feast, with lemon syllabub and tiny ratafia biscuits for dessert.

Daisy is smiling as she enters the sitting room, where Mama and Papa are waiting for her.

"Now my Daisy-duck, what have you been up to today?" Papa says, rising from his armchair, his face brightening.

Daisy hurries over to him, leans forward and bestows a kiss on his whiskered cheek.

"Oh, I have been very busy doing lots of things, Fa," she says. "And I have learned a new tune in honour of your birthday - I shall play it for you after dinner."

"I should like that very much."

She dimples her thanks, then holds out a small parcel.

"Now what could this be?" her father says, feigning total astonishment.

"Oh Fa! It is my present to you. Open it at once!"

He sits, carefully unfolding the pretty wrapping paper to reveal a pair of slippers embroidered with purple and yellow pansies.

"Do you like them? I sewed the design myself."

"My favourite flower."

"Pansies mean 'loving thoughts', Fa."

"I shall be honoured to wear them."

He unlaces his shoes and puts on the new slippers.

"Oh Fa! You can't go in to dinner in your slippers!" Daisy scolds.

"As it is my birthday, I think I may be allowed a little indulgence for once - yes Florence, dinner is served? Then let us dine!"

He rises, offering one arm to his wife, the other to Daisy and together, they make their way to the dining room to enjoy the birthday dinner.

What is left of the mutton is congealing in its fat, the house still in semi-darkness, all occupants abed, when Daisy's adored father gets up, shaves and hurries off to University College Hospital, to perform the first operation on his list.

By the time Daisy rises, refreshed and radiant, he has already operated on four people. Life on the edge of a knife. And as in life, so in surgery: One tiny slip, and the future is altered forever.

****

It is a few days later, on a sunny Saturday afternoon in the merry month of May, and our two bank clerks are off on an omnibus ride. Edwin Persiflage and Danton Waxwing sit on the top deck and light their cigars. Smoking is their one vice. At least it is the only vice they think of as a vice. The rest are more job skills.

Persiflage and Waxwing do not think of themselves as mere friends, they are so much more than that. They are men who are going places. Men who make things happen. Their acquaintance began when Waxwing, the younger of the two, joined the London and County Bank in Islington as a junior clerk and was given the desk next to Persiflage.

It didn't take them long to recognise in each other the qualities that would make their partnership greater than the sum of its parts. Anger and resentment. In Persiflage, who has had his feet knocked off every rung of the ladder of life from the very beginning, anger had become so innate that it had become almost an art form of its own.

Now the omnibus carries them towards St James's Park where they have a date. Or rather Persiflage, who has superficial good looks and a predatory charm that appeals to a certain type of naive lower-class woman, is meeting a young lady.

They are not exactly 'walking out' in the accepted sense of the phrase, more just walking. Though if you asked the young lady, who is small, blonde and fluffy and goes by the general nickname 'Millie girl', she might tell you a different tale, being prone to referring to 'my young man who works in a bank'.

The two first set eyes on each other in the second gallery of the Royal Alhambra Palace and Music Hall where Millie was with a group of girls out for a good time, and Persiflage was in a similar position with some of the young bank clerks.

Having eyed each other up during one of the intervals, they edged closer during the next one and struck up a conversation. As you do on a night out.

As soon as Persiflage learned where Millie worked, he offered to buy her a glass of Bass's pale ale and one thing leading to another, a slightly tipsy Millie ended up being escorted home by a stone-cold sober Persiflage who couldn't quite believe his luck.

And now here they are, the two young clerks, spruce and brushed and carnation buttonholed. They alight from the omnibus and approach the park, where sheep safely graze and birds sweetly sing.

And here is Millie standing in the entrance with another young lady, rather plain and pale and thin, whom she introduces gaily as 'my best friend Affie'. Affie has come along to occupy Waxwing's attention.

The spare wheels eye each other in grim silence while the introductions are made. But proprieties must be obeyed and so Waxwing offers her his arm, which she takes, eliciting a lot of winking from Millie, who declares that "See, I told you. This is such fun, innit?"

The two couples, one slightly more uncoupled than the other, walk towards the lake. Millie keeps up a bright stream of chatter, occasionally glancing over her shoulder to catch Affie's eye and nod significantly. They reach the little stone bridge and halt to admire the view.

"I say Millie girl, that is a ripping bonnet you're wearing," Persiflage remarks lazily.

It is the first thing he has said since they greeted each other, not that he has had much opportunity to speak. Millie girl is not a great believer in silence, regarding it as a hole that needs to be filled.

"Oh - do you like it, Eddy?" she says, tossing her head. "I think it is ever so fetching. Soon as I saw it I said, oh, that is the bonnet for me. Lavender is the latest colour."

Persiflage, who couldn't really care less about women's bonnets, smiles vulpinely.

"What you think of Affie's bonnet, Mr ... umm?" Millie girl asks the hapless Waxwing, for whom all females are a mystery; the one he is currently squiring being no exception.

"Very nice."

"See, Affie! I told you he'd like it. Now then Eddy, I'm that parched I could drink up the lake," Millie throws back her head and laughs coquettishly. "A nice cuppa tea'd go down a treat."

They stroll to the tea stall and over a mug of hot and very sweet tea, Edwin asks Millie girl about life at the Palace of Westminster, where she works as a skivvy. So she tells him all the latest news and gossip, to which he listens very intently, never taking his eyes off her face for a second. Occasionally he stops her, and asks her to go over some piece of gossip, or enlarge upon another.

Eventually Millie girl runs out of news and tea and the two couples make their way back to the omnibus stop. There is a bit of amicable horseplay involving the lilac bonnet and a stolen kiss, but Millie girl is careful not to let things get out of hand, because she knows that a girl playing fast and loose is a girl who won't end up at the altar with a ring on her finger.

That evening, having dined on a plate of stewed eels at the Ratcatcher's Daughter, (the sort of public house that never features in any tourist guide to the city) Persiflage sits in one of the basketweave chairs and reflects on what they have gleaned from the naive Millie.

"I hate them all," he remarks, the words dripping sourly from his lips like unripe lemons. "The rich, the privileged, the MPs. Never done an honest day's work in their lives. Never got their hands dirty. Living on the backs of the starving poor. Faugh!"

"I must say, that stuff Miss Miller told us about the state banquet was interesting. We could dine well on what got thrown away, by the sound of it."

"Not just us. Whole streets could have dined well off it. It will not do."

"No."

"Somebody has to stand up and say: enough is enough."

"Yes."

"It might as well be us as anybody else."

"I agree."

Persiflage reaches under the shared bed and pulls out the small wooden box. He lifts the lid and extracts a note book, a pen and a bottle of ink.

"I must write up the day's events," he says.

"I shall go out for an evening constitutional then, and leave you to it."

Persiflage gives him a brief nod. Waxwing takes his hat from the windowsill and leaves. Persiflage turns to a blank page and writes in a neat clerkish hand:

Hind Street Anarchists. Information received May 10th 1863.

****

A short distance away Fred Grizewood is drowning his sorrows in a pint of warm, cloudy beer. The public house he frequents is called The Engineer, an irony that usually brings a wry smile to his face every time he crosses the threshold.

Since the gruesome discovery of the dead babies, however, Grizewood finds himself distinctly irony-deficient. Indeed, he has sunk into depression. Now he stares into his glass, wishing that Finding Dead Bodies on A Working Site had been covered by one of the many civil engineering courses he attended.

From that fateful day, the young engineer has had to deal with members of the public who have turned up in their denizens to gawp at the crime scene, totally ignoring all the prominently posted Danger signs.

He has had to engage new navvies, because the original ones refused to work in such a tragic place. And every day, about a third of the new ones say they aren't coming back either, having heard the gruesome tale from the previous gang.

He has seen articles in the popular press depicting the discovery in increasingly lurid and inaccurate terms. And to cap it all he has had to run the gamut of various religious crackpots who've stood and shouted at him and waved placards saying that Railways are the Work of Satan and All who Work on them are Trying to Break into Hell.

To add to his woes, the Board of the Bayswater, Paddington & Holborn Bridge Railway Company have been exerting constant and unremitting pressure upon him to finish the work on time.

Before coming out, he has written a desperate letter to his mentor Mr Joseph Bazalgette, addressed to his Morden home, seeking his advice.

Grizewood finishes his beer, and orders another. He is becoming an advocate for the curative powers of alcohol. Sober, he feels unhappy, inhibited. Drunk, he experiences a wild feeling of elation, of possibility.

He does not think his father, a senior cleric in the Church of England, would approve. Not that he approves of anything his youngest son does. Not that he knows. The estrangement between father and son has lasted years.

Back home, it takes him a long time to fall asleep. It always does. Time crawls, broken-backed. He hovers on the brink of sleep, unwilling to let go and allow himself to be gathered up into the net of dreams.

He knows that he will dream the same thing. He always does. He is standing on the edge of a trench, looking down. From the walls protrude tiny feet and hands. He staggers, falls to his knees, spreads out his arms.

In the small hours of the morning, he will wake up to find himself crying.

****

The approval of parents is something Letitia Simpkins is choosing *not* to think about as she sits in her night-gown on the bentwood chair in the small, stuffy bedroom that is just big enough for her but not suitable for her two brothers, which is why they occupy the bigger, nicer room that looks out on the garden.

You'd be hard put to swing a cat in her room. Not that she has tried - and anyway the cat decamped two houses ago, fed up with having its tail pulled and only being fed intermittently. Letitia remembers the cat with some regret. It was the only sentient being in the house who seemed pleased to see her.

She folds her hands in her lap and thinks about the events of the afternoon when she attended the first of the series of lectures at the Regent Street Ladies' Literary & Philosophical Society.

Miss Sophie Jacques, a young woman with bonfire-bright eyes, a determined chin and an intense expression spoke upon the topic *How Higher Education Could Change Women's Lives.*

As Miss Jacques mounted the dais, carrying her sheaf of notes, a shaft of sunlight suddenly lit up her hair so that she seemed to Letitia all light, glowing like some bird.

She started speaking, and suddenly the other women in the room disappeared. It was as if she was speaking to Letitia alone. She sat very still, very upright in her seat, her eyes fixed on the small figure on the dais, drinking in the words.

They still sound in her head. She can recall every one of them.

"We are bred for marriage, yet we cannot actively pursue it, but must sit passively and wait to be chosen. Everything we may wish to have or wish to be must come to us through a single channel and a single choice. Home, happiness, reputation, ease, pleasure yes even the bread we eat must come to us through a small gold ring."

There was much more on similar lines, delivered with fervour and conviction. Letitia had only ever sat through the monotonous drone of her teachers. She didn't know there was any other way to impart knowledge.

Afterwards, when the applause had died down and everyone converged on the table at the back where tea and biscuits were being served, Letitia remained in her seat, ice-hot with excitement. She felt that she had been given a present, wrapped up, something infinitely precious, a diamond.

On her return, she had gone straight upstairs, taken out her hairpins and rearranged her hair so that it resembled Miss Jacques. She tied a belt round her waist, as she had seen her heroine do also. Newly fashioned inside and out, she had marched downstairs to supervise her brothers' studies.

In her skirt pocket was - oh joy - Miss Jacques' visiting card, handed to her by the Great One herself as she was leaving the hall. She was to be 'at home' to visitors at her lodgings tomorrow. Her kind friend Sarah Lunt secured her the invitation.

Now Letitia sits and listens to the sounds of the night. Pipes gurgle. In the distance a church clock chimes two, the sound muffled. Sleep nags at her, but she can't give in to it, not yet. In the hazy region between sleep and full consciousness she sees herself with new clarity.

She has been given hope - the radiance of it burns through her like a religious feeling. Somebody recognises that she should have the same chances in life as her two brothers and is prepared to fight for her to have them.

Since she has returned home from school, all the colours have vanished from her life. She has been imprisoned in a world that was only black and white. She didn't realise it until now, when all the colours have come back.

Letitia isn't sure how exactly she is going to attain her life chances; it is enough to know that they are out there somewhere, just waiting for her.

****

Night is a time when street space simmers with peril and evil. You might call it superstition, or fear, but either way it is wrong to pretend that the night is like the day, but without light.

In the dark, sounds are more tangible than objects. Listen. You hear bells sounding the quarter-hour; the unsteady footsteps of faltering drunks. You hear the scuttling and squeaking of rats, bold and brazen in a street with a dead wall on one side. A man with no home and a chronic sniff bewails his lot. A woman sobs her misery to nobody but herself. A child, weakened by hunger and neglect, lies in a gutter and raises its voice to a pitiless sky in one final cry of despair.

****

The engineer wakes slowly feeling as if he is rising to the surface through a mud bath. Most days are like this. He opens his eyes. Morning light drips around the window blind, not getting far. For a few minutes, he lies staring at the stained ceiling as if amazed to find it there, or himself under it.

Then he slides out from between the grey patched sheets and splashes his face with last night's cold water. The tools of his trade lie scattered about. He stares at them without much recognition. His life seems to consist of things that he borrowed a long time ago but which it's now too late to return.

He raises the blind and looks out. He has got so used to seeing the city as a series of brick piles and rubble that from here it always seems like a foreign place, never before viewed. Sun sparkles on red roof tiles. Birds swoop and dart. Smoke rises straight up into a cloudless blue sky.

He could be someone else, he thinks. He is intelligent. He has had a good education. He speaks two languages. He read Hegel's *Philosophie des Rechts* in the original German while waiting for permission to access the site again.

If he had the will to change, a belief in his ability to accomplish what he set out to do, he could step out of this room and enter a new life, be a different person, more rational. He is only twenty-five, still a young man.

But every time he tries to change direction, it feels as if some giant hand has got him by the scruff of the neck and is propelling him through a network of pipes under a landscape he does not know until he surfaces back where he started.

The engineer shaves carefully and dresses in his work suit and a clean soft collar - he is after all a *skilled artisan*. (He can still see his father's face when he told him. Can hear the words being spat back at him like a curse).

Having done all he can sartorially to face the day, he heads downstairs and enters the dining room, where his landlady's drab of a maid is serving crisp bacon and watery eggs to the rest of the lodgers. He slips silently into his place and unfolds the limp, grubby napkin.

He still has not heard from Mr Joseph Bazalgette.

After gulping down his breakfast, he sets off for the site. The morning rush hour is underway. It is still early, but the population of Camden Town are afoot, also using the marrowbone stage to reach their place of employment.

An endless stream of spruce young city clerks in their pea-green gloves, scarlet braces and with roses in their buttonholes jostle the older counting house clerks who plod steadily along, head down, speaking to nobody.

Young seamstresses and milliners, their pretty faces pinched from want, their dresses shabby but neatly darned, slip in and out of the crowd like needles pulling thread. They all carry wicker baskets containing last night's candlelit home work.

Stopping only to purchase a stale tart from one of the bakeshops he passes, the engineer reaches his destination, where once more he runs the gauntlet of the crowd, who today seem slightly diminished in both noise and number, and slips through the gate.

He opens his satchel and takes out the sheaf of drawings he has made of the site, noting that the contractor has already started the navvies on their day's tasks. He seems to be fielding a full team. Maybe the 'curse' has lifted at last.

His train of thought is interrupted by the appearance of the onsite chemist, a laconic middle-aged man called Albert Noble. He wears ageing corduroy trousers and has yellow stained fingers and a hat that looks as if it has exploded a couple of times.

The chemist spends his time in a small wooden hut by the site perimeter, where his sole function is to make up the delicate and notoriously unstable concoction of nitric acid, sulphuric acid and glycerol that is used to blast the way through the urban jungle.

Now he hurries up to the engineer, a worried frown upon his face.

"Morning Mr Noble," Grizewood says, carefully tuning his facial expression to neutral.

"It may be for some."

"Is there a problem?"

The chemist holds up his hand, palm out, index finger raised.

"One can of nitro-glycerine and two blasting caps are missing from my shed. I always check the shelves every morning upon arrival and again before I leave. You cannot be too careful with an unpredictable chemical like nitro-glycerine. Dear me no. I had four cans last night. This morning, when I checked the shelves again, I found that one of them had gone missing."

"You are quite sure?"

The chemist gives him a look that says that if he (the engineer) thinks that he (the chemist) can't count to four, then he (the engineer) is the one with the problem.

"This is a very serious matter, Mr Grizewood," the chemist says. "Very. Serious. Indeed. Nitro-glycerine, even a small amount mixed with alcohol and sealed in a can is still a dangerous and unstable substance. Especially in the hands of somebody who does not know how to deal with it."

"Yes, I know that."

"I shall have to report it to the Board," Noble says crisply. "Unless it 'turns up', you will have to report it also."

He leans forward, lowering his voice and treating the engineer to a waft of foul morning breath.

"Just a hint to the wise - many of the navvies are Irish. Roman Catholics or Fenians I have no doubt. A place to start asking? Need I say more?"

"Yes. No. Perhaps," the engineer says unhappily. "You are absolutely sure that a can is missing? It couldn't have been used and ..."

His voice tails off in the face of the chemist's withering stare.

"I shall speak to the foreman," he says meekly.

"Do that. And if you get no satisfaction, I suggest you speak to the police inspector that was here a while ago. The Scotch one. He looked like he had his wits about him. Unlike some. Meanwhile I shall go and telegraph Mr Wandle. Good day to you."

His back bristling with indignation, the chemist heads for the gate. The engineer watches him leave, feeling his heart sink. Suddenly the light at the end of his mental tunnel is showing only more tunnel. Cursing under his breath, he goes to locate the foreman. It is going to be another long, difficult day.

****

Meanwhile just a few streets away, a small backstreet grocer's shop is opening up for trade. It is the sort of local shop that displays a variety of goods calculated to meet the needs of servants and the poorer classes generally.

The dingy shop windows are covered with advertisements for meat paste, boot polish and gentleman's relish. The sign over the door reads: *Pastorelli & Rifkin, Provisions.*

A small boy carrying a long wooden pole has just emerged from the shop interior and taken down the wooden shutters. Now he drags a trestle table out front, and begins to arrange boxes of broken biscuits, stale currant buns, and tea mixed with sawdust for the delectation of future customers.

The small boy wears a long grubby apron, once white, and a worried expression. He has heard his father (the Pastorelli of the sign) and his cousin (the Rifkin ditto) discussing the fall off in trade since the arrival of the railway.

He has learned that since the houses on wheels made their first appearance, followed by the wagons loaded with timber and the gravel-coloured men with picks and shovels, people have stopped patronising *Pastorelli & Rifkin*, which is now physically as well as ideologically on the wrong side of the tracks.

Even the troops of navvies who were the next to arrive do not shop here. And with the continued dissolution of Hind Street and the neighbouring streets to it, trade has dwindled to a few regulars.

The talk now is of relocation somewhere else. Possibly south of the river, a place that strikes fear into the boy's soul as he knows it to be a place inhabited by ferocious monster children who live in caves and will eat him alive.

The boy is just finishing garnishing the trestle table with torn up newspaper, when he is approached by two men. They are clean, well shaven and decently dressed, which immediately singles them out as strangers and sends a warning signal. The boy folds his arms and assumes a hostile expression.

The slightly older man steps forward.

"Morning, my laddy," he says. "Owner in?"

He has a slight (and therefore suspicious) Scottish accent.

The boy looks vague.

"Dunno."

"Mebbe we could step inside and take a look for ourselves?"

Something about the tone of the man's voice gives the impression that this is a statement of intent rather than a question.

The boy shrugs and stands aside.

The men enter the shop. The boy loiters in the doorway because he has finished his outside work and while the men are in the shop, he can't start his inside work sweeping it out.

The men approach the counter, where his father is arranging the sales book and filling the wooden cash drawers under it with coppers and threepenny bits. He stops, looks the two men up and down, and adopts a similar stance to his son.

"Gen'lemen?"

Once again it is the older man who speaks.

"Good day to you. Are you the proprietor of this establishment?"

The boy's father runs this past some mental translator for a minute, then agrees that he is.

"Then I'm hoping you'll be able to help me out. I've been asked to find the couple who used to live at number 9 Hind Street - mebbe you've served them - the man has a beard and walks with a stick. The woman is a tidy body, always wears a black knitted shawl round her head. Do you know them?"

"Might do. Why? Who's asking?"

"It's to do with the railway company workings and the destruction of the house they were living in. I can't say any more, because it's private business, you understand."

"You mean they're entitled to compensation?"

"All I can say at this stage is that there is something waiting for them."

The boy's father looks thoughtful.

"I may know the people you mean. They might have shopped here. Possibly. Haven't seen them for a few days. I could ask around."

His eyes stare greedily at the older man.

"I'm sure that would be appreciated. By all concerned," the man pauses, looks at him meaningfully. "Mebbe my colleague will drop by in a day or so."

"Yes ...?"

It is clear the man is already mentally pocketing his share of the compensation.

"So, we'll bid you good day and we'll be on our way."

The man touches his hat and they both leave the shop.

The boy inches in, his eyes wide. His father places a finger to his lips, then goes to the doorway and looks up and down the road.

"They've gone," he says.

"I know that couple," the boy chirps eagerly. "They were called Herbert and Amelia Hall. They used to come in on a Friday evening. They always bought a bottle of Daffy's cordial and a quartern loaf and some potatoes."

"Might be the same ones, yes," his father replies. "You could see if anybody knows where they've shifted to."

"Will there be a lot of money?"

The man shrugs.

The boy looks at him, eyes full of hope.

"P'raps there will be enough so we don't have to move?"

"P'raps there will. I don't know. First, we have to find them - and we mustn't tell anybody why we're looking for them. D'you get it? Stumm's the word from now on. Coz if there's any money in this, then it's our money. After all, we're the ones the railway gen'tl'men came to first."

****

Letitia Simpkins is also facing a dilemma. Mama has had another of 'her' nights and has another of 'her' heads, meaning Papa has one of 'his' moods. As a consequence, Letitia has had to supervise breakfast for Papa and the boys. Not a pleasant chore.

Papa consumes his bacon and eggs in angry glaring silence broken by angry glaring shouting when the boys make enough noise and spillage to awaken the dead. Then half-way through breakfast, the familiar sounds of a barrel organ filtering discordantly from the street reduces him to paroxysms of rage.

Letitia is forced to leave her breakfast and hurry to the street door, on the other side of which the scruffy man with the sad monkey on a chain is waiting to be paid to go away.

Placing tuppence in the animal's little tin cup, she reflects that now she does not have enough money to take the omnibus to Miss Jacques' lodgings, and will have to walk.

To add to her difficulties, it is also the day of the twins' entrance exams, so she has to accompany them to the venue, and accompany them back afterwards, treating them to a fruit tart on the return journey, (money provided by Mama) as a reward for all their hard work.

She toys with telling them she has no money for treats, and using the money for her bus fare instead. But she knows that the boys will expect something and will complain to Mama and her thievery will be exposed in all its meanness.

Oh, how she wishes she had money of her own - earned by the work of her hands, instead of having to go bonnet in hand to her parents. It is so humiliating. She has to ask, sometimes beg for the wherewithal to purchase anything for herself.

After the unpleasant meal is over, and Papa has slammed the door, she makes the boys recite their times tables, fractions and decimals, their science, sundry capital cities and the dates of the Kings of England. Then she brushes their coats and hats and they all sally forth into the blue-skied morning.

A short walk later, having wished them both good luck and promised to be waiting for them when they have finished, Letitia waves good-bye to her brothers and hurries off in the direction of Miss Sophie Jacques' lodgings, which are off Tottenham Court Road.

She knocks at the door and is admitted by her friend Sarah, who shows her into a neat sitting room fragrant with the smell of coffee. The walls are covered with a light paper panelled out with a design of birds and roses, and there are cosy chairs and a couple of small tables.

Every square inch of space is occupied, such is the popularity of Miss Jacques and the regard in which she is held. There are young women sitting on chairs, the carpet and even two young women perched precariously on the window ledge.

At the centre of the room Sophie Jacques, in a becoming green silk dress, her hair down and a morning wrapper around her shoulders, sits on a grey upholstered chaise-longue, dispensing coffee from a large silver pot.

She glances up at Letitia and smiles.

"Ah - Letitia, our newest and youngest member! Sarah has been telling me all about you. Welcome little one. Come, I have saved you a place."

Pink with embarrassment, Letitia picks her way round, over and across the seated bodies and sits down on the narrow end of the chaise-longue.

"This young lady represents all that we are fighting for," Sophie Jacques tells the assembled company. "She is barely seventeen and has just left school. And what does our great country deem that she is good for? Embroidering fire screens, planning meals and bearing children - pah!"

Letitia ventures timidly, "I enjoy helping my brothers with their lessons."

Sophia passes her a cup of coffee.

"I'm sure you do, little one, but that is not the point, is it? Ladies, this is precisely what I rail against - so many bright young women leave school barely knowing anything useful, and are then reduced to accepting a hand-me-down education from their brothers."

"I never went to school, though I had a series of governesses. I do not recall learning anything useful either," one of the window-sitters states, adding, "Other than what to do in a thunderstorm at night."

"Draw your bed into the centre of the room, commend your soul to Almighty God and go to sleep," her companion says, to much laughter.

Letitia sips her bitter black coffee. The conversation ebbs and flows around her. These young women seem so confident in their opinions, so assured. They speak in such well-bred voices. She wonders how many of them have ever had to darn socks and pinch pennies from the housekeeping to buy cambric to make themselves new drawers.

Time slips by on enchanted feet, until eventually Sophia Jacques announces that a light luncheon is to be served in the adjoining room. Suddenly Letitia realises that while she has been sitting here listening entranced, the boys will have finished their exams and be waiting for her to walk them home.

Horrified, she jumps to her feet, makes her excuses and stumbles out of the room. Guilt gives her feet wings but even so, when she reaches her destination, she finds no twins waiting for her.

Letitia goes into the exam hall. It is empty but for a caretaker sweeping up. Her only hope now is that the boys have somehow made their own way home without her. Breathless and lunchless, she tears through the city streets with the speed of an arsonist though a cornfield, elbowing people out of her path as she goes.

Reaching her home, Letitia pounds up the front steps, fumbling in her bag for the key. She flings open the door and tumbles into the hallway, one hand at her side, gasping for breath, hoping and praying that she will hear the customary sounds of two eleven-year-old boys squabbling over some toy.

But the house is loudly and terrifyingly silent.

****

To Inspector Greig, the floor of his office is the equivalent of a big flat filing cabinet. He has just augmented it with a report on the morning visit to *Pastorelli & Rifkin*, when one of the day constables knocks politely.

"Person at the front desk requesting to see you, sir."

Greig rises and follows him along the corridor. Leaning against the desk is the young engineer, fiddling awkwardly with his pocket watch. For one joyous moment, Greig hopes he has come to divulge the whereabouts of the couple who lived at number 9 Hind Street. Then he catches sight of the young man's woebegone expression and shelves the thought.

The engineer seems close to collapse. Greig signals for a chair to be brought and sits him down. He requests a glass of water. Finally, when the engineer's colour has somewhat returned, he inquires,

"Can I help you?"

The engineer swallows a couple of times, his hands tightening spasmodically round the glass.

"We seem to have mislaid a can of nitro-glycerine."

"We?"

"That is to say, the site chemist thinks it is missing. I have questioned the contractor and all the workmen and nobody knows anything about it."

"You are sure it is missing?"

"Oh yes, I'm sure," the engineer says bitterly. "Just as I'm sure the blame will be laid at my door."

"Where was it being kept?"

"In the chemist's shed. Which was locked."

"And who is in charge of the key?"

"I have one key; he has the other."

"And both keys are ...?"

"In their correct places."

"A mystery, then."

"But one with consequences. Do you know exactly how much damage one small can of nitro-glycerine can do?"

"I do not need to know. It is sufficient that you are concerned enough to report it. And what would you like me to do?"

The engineer wrings his hands.

"I do not know. I kept hoping that it would turn up ... as things do. But it hasn't. I thought I'd better tell somebody official ... in case ..." his voice tails off miserably.

Greig thinks rapidly.

"The other cans?"

"We used them today."

"So, there are none on the site at the moment."

The engineer shakes his head.

"Then you must hope that whoever has taken it realises what they have got before it is too late."

The engineer gives him a stricken look.

"I suggest you put some warning posters around the area."

The engineer nods.

"And maybe make the site as secure as you can in future, yes? I shall make a note of what you have told me. If you can throw any further light on the matter - such as the names of any suspects, do not hesitate to call by."

The engineer mumbles his thanks, rises and stumbles to the door.

"Keep me informed, won't you?" Greig calls after him.

He exchanges an exasperated look with the desk constable, and shakes his head.

"That young man seems to attract trouble like jam attracts wasps."

"That's the yoof of today for you, sir," responds the day constable smugly, who can only be a couple of years older than the engineer. "Is he in trouble?"

"He will be if what he has lost has fallen into unscrupulous hands," Greig says. "I only hope for his sake that it has not."

A few hours later Inspector Greig sits at his desk in his room on the second floor of his lodgings. He is writing his fortnightly letter to his widowed sister in Scotland. He dips his pen into the pot of ink, chews the end of it, then begins.

Dearest Jeanie (he writes)

I hope this letter finds you and the babes well. I am sending a little more money than usual as I know it is Ishbel's birthday next week, and I should like you to buy her something nice from me to celebrate her special day. I leave the choice of gift up to you, as you probably know what she would like.

The weather here continues to be clement, so I have managed to shake off the cold that plagued me for so many weeks and can now enjoy - if that is the right word, the various smells of the city.

Mainly this is horse dung, though it is said that around Temple Bar, the air smells of brown stout. That I have not noticed, but as I walk through Islington, I always smell odours of fried fish and damaged oranges. The worst place is Marylebone which stinks from all the back-street piggeries, though to me, everywhere smells of smoke and drains.

What would I not give for a few good lungfulls of pure Highland air! And some peace and quiet. Here, the noise is deafening; everywhere you go your ears are assaulted by it and yourself assaulted by all the people rushing past like maniacs along the streets.

Today has been a busy day as usual. My investigations are going well - except in one area: the mystery of the disappearing biscuits continues. Another one has gone from the box.

A bit of 'light relief' if I may call it such was provided by a young woman who turned up claiming her young brothers had gone missing. She was in quite a distressed state, having wandered across town and not had a bite to eat all day.

Luckily once we provided her with tea and a sandwich and then accompanied her back to her home where it turned out the two boys had merely stopped off to watch a Punch & Judy Show and were not lost at all.

Such is the life I lead in this great city, but it pays the bills - for us both. My dearest love to Ishbel and Donald. I expect they have grown since I left, and will soon forget all about their 'Uncle Lackie'!

My best and warmest regards to you,
Your devoted brother,
Lachlan

He blots his signature and sits back in his chair. It has been an eventful day, culminating in the dramatic appearance of Miss Letitia Simpkins. An interesting young woman, no great beauty for sure, but with opinions. He wishes her well.

Greig listens to the church clocks chiming the quarter hour. He does not like to admit it, but the young woman has put him in mind of another young woman, much prettier than her, who also had opinions.

But that is in the past and since she, whose name he no longer mentions, has made her choice and it is not him, he has put all thoughts of love and romance as far from him as possible. And as many miles distance as he can.

****

To understand how a small amount of the highly dangerous oily liquid explosive known as nitro-glycerine has managed to go missing from the railway construction site we must go back to a certain balmy May evening a short while ago.

The Hind Street Anarchists are holding a special meeting upstairs in Persiflage and Waxwork's lodgings. The minutes have been read and approved, and the business now turns to the welcoming of new members.

There is only one new member: a tall cadaverous young man called Georg Beckford Muller. His arrival is directly linked to a toothache suffered by Waxwing which has necessitated numerous visits to the local chemist for oil of cloves and other medicines and it was on one of these visits that Waxwing got into conversation with Muller, the chief chemist.

Neither can now recall how the existence of the group came up in the conversation, but somehow it did, and now here is Muller in a threadbare brown coat, tobacco stained trousers and a clay pipe, making himself at home in the second-floor bedroom of number 18 Hind Street.

It is Muller's opinion that the city is being overrun by foreigners and it is all the Government's fault for allowing them in. In particular, he objects to the presence of the Irish, who turn up at the chemist's shop regularly. They demand medicines and cordials and then haggle over the price.

As the evening wears on and the drink goes down, the talk turns to more pragmatic matters, namely the ways and means to bring their grievances to public attention. Persiflage's relationship with Millie is pored over. It is agreed that this is certainly the most effective way. But the means - ah, that's quite another dish of fish.

At which point Muller stands up, albeit a little unsteadily, and gestures towards the landing.

"And out zere, my good friends, is the means. Just sitting and waiting to be taken."

Seeing the clerks exchange puzzled expressions, he continues.

"I refer to the works taking place."

The clerks mentally contemplate the infinite chaos of timbers, shaft hole and winches with chains and buckets, all visible from the landing window of the lodging house, which itself has now been shored up with huge timber beams to make it safe.

"Ye-es, but I still don't see ..." Waxwing begins.

"Somewhere on the ozzer side of those tall boards is a small hut. That is where the chemist works and where they keep the explosives. All we need to do is to get our hands on some of it."

Persiflage's smile is thin and bitter.

"Yes. I see. Then we take it to ... and ..."

Silence falls. A silence that thickens and spreads, filling the room like a terrible dark fog. As if prompted by the same malign force, all three rise from their seats and go out onto the landing to take a look.

Below the window the construction site is a desert of clay, planks and piles of rubble. A line of picks and shovels leans against a cart. The whole area is a series of fortifications surrounded by huge scaffolds that resemble guillotines.

Overhead is a cheese rind moon and a sprinkling of stars, small and bright and pitiless. Muller points to a small wooden hut, dimly visible, perched on a wooden platform.

"Zere, my fellow comrades, is our quarry."

Waxwing eases up the window.

"If we had some rope, we could tie it to the bannisters and climb down," he says thoughtfully.

"A rope, a basket and something to remove a couple of planks from the side of the hut," Persiflage says. "A crowbar or jemmy would do the trick."

"Gentlemen, I see you are already making a plan," Muller says. "I will be on hand to help transport the explosives back - for I must warn you, any jolts or shocks or bumps and BOOM!"

Waxwing's eyes widen.

"We are extremely grateful to you, Mr Muller," Persiflage says smoothly. "Let me think this out a little more. Then, when we are ready to act, I will write to you."

"I will await your instructions," Muller nods. "And now I sank you for your hospitality and I bid you both goodnight."

He touches the brim of his hat before descending the stairs. Waxwing follows to let him out. Persiflage remains on the landing, staring dreamily out over the construction site.

"And then ... Boom!" he murmurs softly. "Boom."

****

Hatton Garden is, according to a contemporary handbook of London: *a place where cheap barometers, thermometers, mathematical and philosophical instruments produced by Italians can be purchased.*

You can also purchase books, artificial flowers, confectionary, optical instruments, croquet mallets and false teeth made from hippopotamus ivory. If you so desire to.

Alas none of these commodities, fascinating as they are, have any attraction for Daisy Lawton. Here she comes tripping along the pavement, straw bonneted and sprig-muslined, and as fresh as her name suggests.

Here too is her Mama, also got up in new spring clothes. For 'tis the Season, and there are parties and balls in the offing - indeed the Lawton's drawing room mantelpiece positively *groans* with invitation cards, because if one moves in the upper echelons of society, and one's husband is a surgeon of some repute, and one is in possession of an eligible daughter, this is how it is. And invitations to balls and parties require new clothes and new clothes require new jewellery, as everybody knows.

Daisy and her Mama are here to look for a necklace - something simple but good, to adorn Daisy's swanlike neck and draw the young men's eyes to her. Daisy secretly hopes that the eyes of a certain handsome Dragoon Guard will be drawn to her.

This is her plan.

Mama however, has pinned her hopes on the son of an MP, although she hasn't spoken of this to Daisy. She will do, after she has met and talked with the young man's mother (an old school friend) and they have reached an understanding.

This is *her* plan.

It is a bright morning and the streets are alive with people. Little children swarm in and out of courts crowded with human life. A boy with a red fez and long black tassel lounges against the window of a print shop. Women with bright shawls stand in doorways gossiping in a strange language. They pause and eye Daisy curiously as she goes by.

Daisy's Mama holds her by the elbow and steers her carefully along the street. Many of the shops have strange exotic names painted above the door: *Ortelli & Primavesi*, *Negretti & Zambra*. It is like being in another country.

At last they reach a small jeweller's shop. They pause to admire the window display of diamond rings and finely worked gold chains and bracelets.

"This is the shop, my love. Your Papa has always bought my jewellery here," Mama says.

They enter, to be greeted by the dark-eyed jeweller. Mama is offered a seat by the counter. She explains the purpose of their visit. The jeweller studies Daisy with a professional eye.

"For such a pretty young lady, I would recommend a simple gold chain, finely worked, with a pearl flower pendant. Nothing fussy that might detract from what Nature has already endowed her."

Mama nods.

"May we see what you have in stock?"

The jeweller unlocks a drawer behind the counter and lifts out a tray. Daisy's eyes shine with delight as she stares at the delicate gold necklaces with their tiny pendants, some heart shaped, some like dainty flowers or tiny cameos.

"Oh Mama!" she breathes. "How lovely!"

The jeweller picks one necklace out from its velvet bed. It has a narrow gold chain, intricately wrought with tiny gold hoops and daisies and at the end, a minute seed pearl flower, each petal set in gold.

"If your Mama would permit me," he smiles coming round the counter. He places the chain round her neck, not letting his fingers touch her skin.

"Would the signorina like to view herself in the mirror?"

Daisy trots over to the gilt mirror, peers closely, turns sideways and sighs.

"Oh yes - it is lovely."

And it is. And she is.

"This is the one I want, Mama," she says, twirling away from the mirror and touching the chain with her slim white fingertips. "I have seen one similar in Godey's."

"The young lady looks charming, does she not?" the jeweller smiles, and Mama nods her agreement, for who would not agree with such a compliment paid to their daughter.

"We will take it," she says, producing her card. "Please have the bill made out and sent to my husband."

Later, when she is alone in her room, Daisy takes out the necklace from its little corded bag and places it round her throat. Her eyes sparkle as she imagines herself waltzing in the arms of her Guardsman. In a few days' time, she is going to her very first ball. It is all too exciting for words. She can hardly wait.

****

In the early morning, before the chimneys of factories and houses have begun to fill the air with smoke, London is a different place altogether. The city looks clean. Smells clean. The morning sun rises, lovely and genial, gilding roof tiles and steeples with pure light, whitening arches and the pillars of bridges and buildings.

Sweeping machines travel in rumbling lines down the street, removing any last traces of dust and dung that have not been scavenged during the previous day, for very little goes to waste.

After them come the great market-gardeners' carts and wagons, moving briskly along to be in time for early buyers. Brewers' drays and coal wagons lumber in, followed by the light carts of butchers, fishmongers and hoteliers, all after the best and freshest on offer.

Covent Garden on market day is a sight to behold. Children prowl about the place, their naked feet pattering on the pavement as they dive for offal or vegetable peelings or anything they can lay their hands on.

Look more closely. As the streets lighten and the church spires stand out against the clear sky with a sharpness that will be soon obliterated by smoke from a million chimneys, here come the coffee-stall keepers, ready to set up on street corners.

In Covent Garden, close by Bow Street police office, there are no less than three coffee-stalls. Here, early coffee is to be got and toast to go with it. The stalls consist of a springbarrow on top of which are four large brightly polished tin cans full of tea and coffee.

Beneath each is a small iron fire-pot, fuelled by charcoal to keep the drinks hot during the day. There is a tub under the stall where the cups and saucers are kept and there are wooden compartments for bread and butter, sandwiches and cake.

The coffee-stall keepers appear around four in the morning to be ready for the delivery drivers, for after all the carts and wagons have unloaded, the drivers are sharp set, and always make their way to their favourite stall for a drink and a ham sandwich, or a doorstep of bread and butter.

And here is the first customer of the day. Not a carter though. A good-looking young woman, neatly dressed and shawled. Her face is pale and tired, but does not bear the expression of habitual depravity that marks out the loose girls who patronise the night-stalls.

She approaches one of the stalls and asks in a low voice for a cup of coffee and a slice of bread. The stall-holder pours the steaming drink into a white china cup and invites her to choose her bread from the jagged slices arranged on a tin plate.

She makes her selection, hands over two pence and walks her cup and slice to one of the pillars where she sinks down, leaning her back against it. It is only when she stands up and stretches wearily, placing one hand flat against the small of her back, that her condition becomes clear.

The young woman brings back her empty cup. She thanks the man, then asks for directions to the nearest cheap lodging house. He tells her and she sets off once more, picking her way delicately over the shit-spattered cobbles.

The coffee-stall keeper watches her leave the square. Same thing the whole world over, he thinks. No wedding ring. Well, good luck to you my gal, and to the babby. Gawd knows you're going to need it.

****

A few hours later. A thousand chimneys have belched forth their smoke; hundreds of shops have opened, and river boats and omnibuses have landed their living freight in the heart of the city.

Now London is busy doing what it does best: buying and selling. Pavements are crowded with people and roads with vehicles of all descriptions. Oxford Street, long enough to take the population of a small town, fills with private carriages, fashionable loungers, women on horseback, men of business and curious strangers.

The shops provide a similar mix from elegant drapers shops to the lowest oyster-stall, and there are legions of costermongers and shoals of advertising vans.

By contrast, here in this pretty sitting room, overlooking the garden of a large town house in Belgravia, all is seclusion and exclusion. The town house has a grand porch with classical columns and a balustrade above.

Its palatial splendour befits its occupants: Margaret Marie Barnes Baker (formerly Hammond), and her husband Chatham MP Richard Barnes Baker (currently about his Parliamentary business). Margaret is the mother of Digby Barnes Baker. Here she is awaiting the arrival of her dear school friend Charlotte Lawton (formerly Lightowler), the mother of Daisy.

The house has been opened up for the Season. Normally Barnes Baker only uses it when the House is sitting late and the last train has departed from Victoria Station. The two ladies sip tea and exchange family news, for there is much to talk about. They have not seen each other since last Season, when Margaret successfully hooked a wealthy bachelor for her daughter Effie.

Indeed, so successful were Margaret's project management skills that she has now been entrusted with her sister's girl Africa (named after her father's colonial past). It is hoped by all concerned that Africa, a rather jerky young woman with unreliable hair, will also achieve engagedhood by the end of August.

A hard task, but none better to take it on than redoubtable Margaret with her thick ankles and strong features. Today Africa has been dispatched with one of the maids to buy a fan and some pairs of evening gloves, thus leaving the two ladies free to converse in peace.

They crumble their cake and exchange social niceties, for the matter in hand cannot be approached directly but must be sidled up to discreetly, as one might stalk a shy skittish gazelle.

"Daisy is so looking forward to the Mason-Freeman ball," Charlotte Lawton murmurs, "It will be her first ball. Ah, such a golden time." She pauses, studies her gloves thoughtfully, "I expect Africa is also looking forward to it."

"She is very excited. These girls - how young they are."

"We were their age ... once."

"Indeed we were, and what fun we had."

There is a pause while both ladies plumb the reticules of their memories for their days of wine and roses.

Charlotte sighs.

"I hope Daisy will not want for partners; I feel for her - we do not know any suitable young men in London."

"On that matter, I am happy to help, for Digby will be squiring his cousin and I am sure he will find a dance for her. Dear Daisy! What a little beauty she is. I will make it my business to *insist* he dances with her."

"Oh,\ you are *too too* kind, Margaret," Charlotte says, rolling her eyes to the ceiling while inwardly exulting.

"Perhaps Daisy might like to take Africa under her wing? It is lonely for her in London with no young people of her age," Margaret suggests, looking vaguely at nothing in particular.

Charlotte Lawton understands completely. There is always a price to be paid for these arrangements. Though in this case, it is a negligible one. A gawky thing like Africa (briefly glimpsed throwing herself into a cab) could only serve to highlight her own Daisy's loveliness.

It was a role that Margaret herself, with her stern and rather forbidding demeanour, fulfilled for her pretty friend Charlotte in those dear dimly remembered days of yore. Though one doubts if she would see it like that, if asked.

"Daisy is the dearest, brightest of girls with such a sunshiny disposition. I am sure she would like nothing better than to make a new friend," Charlotte says, brushing some invisible crumbs from her dress.

The two ladies smile warmly at each other, the light of complete mutual understanding glowing in each maternal eye. Tea is sipped. Cakes are nibbled. Futures are planned. Eventually Daisy's Mama rises and is shown out into the hallway by the parlour maid. Mission accomplished.

Now all she has to do is gently persuade Daisy to fall in love with young Digby Barnes Baker whom, she is sure, will be primed and ready to fall in love with her. This is how it is often done in the world these two ladies inhabit. And really, it is as easy as that.

****

Sadly, the only plans being made for Letitia Simpkins' future are punitive ones. Since losing her brothers (even though she didn't), and thus subjecting them to the perils and dangers of London (even though they weren't), she has not been allowed to leave the family home.

Mama has fallen even further into a decline as a direct consequence of her actions. The family physician visits every morning to comment on the state of Mama's heart, which is not good. The comments are then translated into bills, which have to be paid by her reluctant and increasingly irate father. Which is also not good.

And it is all Letitia's fault. All. Meanwhile the boys, having tasted the sweets of freedom, are becoming adept at running rings round the rather inadequate maid who now accompanies them to and from school as their sister is No Longer a Person To Be Trusted.

She hears their gleeful tales of flea circuses, Italian bands, street jugglers and stolen fruit as she continues to oversee their evening studies. It is one of the few things she is still allowed to do.

Of course, she has written to her friend Sarah Lunt and to other friends at the Regent Street Ladies' Literary & Philosophical Society, explaining the reason for her absence. Indeed, she has written several times, leaving her letters on the hall table for the inadequate maid to post. So far, she has received no reply. It seems they have forgotten her.

Letitia sits in her Mama's frowsty bedroom, reading aloud from a tale by Mr Charles Dickens. Mama seems calmer when she is read to, so this is how she spends a lot of her afternoons now.

Even though it is a sunny afternoon, the blinds are drawn down and there is a fire in the grate. In the shadowy blue light, Mama's face is ghostly, like a skull. The eye sockets are hollows of darkness. She looks like someone who hasn't slept for a lifetime.

Letitia lets her voice die to a whisper, then stops reading altogether. There is no response from the prone figure in the bed, so after waiting a few seconds for the feeble words of protest and hearing only silence, she rises and tiptoes out of the room.

In the time between absenting herself from the sickroom, and the discovery of Mama's dead body by the maid (who will drop the tea tray and scream the house down), Letitia will have darned three pairs of socks, turned her bothers' sheets sides to middle, and stared longingly out of the window.

Today is her seventeenth birthday. Nobody seems to have noticed.

****

Young Sergeant Ben Hacket is becoming quite an expert at noticing. Here he is standing in the doorway of a small and dingy house in a low and litter-strewn street. The sunshine, so lovely and genial at this time of year, only serves to light up the blight and mildew.

Hacket has been told that one of the pits dug for the dead in the time of the Great Plague lies hereabouts and its blighting influence seems to cast a malign shadow over the area. It smells shadowy and dark with rottenness and putrefaction. Ironically, just a few streets away, the bustling commercial life of the city goes on its merry way unregarding.

From his post of observation, Sergeant Hacket has his eyes fixed on a particular property, where, according to the latest information supplied to him by *Pastorelli fils*, the couple suspected of taking in and murdering small babies for money might have sought safety since their precipitous exile from Hind Street.

Hacket is wearing street clothes as he is working undercover once more, though he carries his identity card in a pocket, along with his truncheon and rattle just in case a member of the public should challenge him.

So far, nobody has come forward to do so. Nor does it look as if they will do so. The house seems abandoned. As it did when he took over from a fellow officer at eleven o'clock.

Now the shadows of the late afternoon are creeping into the alleyway, taking away what little light there is, but unexpectedly bringing with them a dog and a tall dark-skinned man of about thirty years.

The man has a full beard, wears a workman's cap and carries a basket of tools. A livid scar runs from his left eyelid to the centre of his cheek, puckering up the corner of his mouth.

The man stops in front of the house. He extracts a key from an inner pocket, and unlocks the front door. Hacket steps forward and hails him. The man pauses on the step, then turns and regards him with a face of mild inquiry. The dog bares its teeth in an unfriendly growl, which is silenced by a swift kick of the man's boot.

Hacket explains why he is here, and who he is looking for. The man shrugs.

"Ain't nobody living here but me and Bully," he says, indicating the dog. "Whoever told yer, got it wrong."

They eye each other for a minute.

"Railway business, you sed?" the man comments.

Hacket nods.

"Well, if I see anyone answering to the descriptions wot you have described, I'll let the *railway* people know."

The man enters the house, closing the door. Hacket hears the sound of the key turning. A short while later, the flickering light of a candle appears in one of the upstairs rooms. He waits for a couple more minutes, then turns to go.

The man watches him from behind the curtain of the upstairs window. As soon as Hacket reaches the corner, he goes downstairs, unlocks the front door and comes out again. He is wearing a bowler and a different jacket. The collar is pulled up. There is an absence of dog.

He sets off briskly after Hacket, always keeping his distance but equally always maintaining his vantage point. Hacket does not notice him. Only when the young sergeant enters Bow Street police office does the man turn away, disappearing swiftly down a by-street.

****

London in Springtime means the hectic whirl of balls and parties and dances. Paradise for daughters, and Purgatory for bill-paying Papas. It is the morning of Daisy's first ball and even at breakfast, the feeling of excitement at the prospect of the forthcoming event is almost palpable.

Indeed, Daisy is so excited that she is crumbling her buttered toast rather than eating it and she has left her plate of scrambled egg and bacon untouched. Her father glances across the table at her, his face mirroring concern.

"I'm sorry to see you so off colour, Daisy-duck. May I suggest a dose of nasty-tasting medicine and a week in bed?" he suggests.

Daisy twinkles at him.

"Oh Fa - you are such a tease! You know very well it is my first ball tonight."

"Is it?" Daisy's father looks innocently nonplussed. "But I'm sure you agreed to stay home and read the City business news to me."

Daisy rolls her eyes.

"I shall be quite happy to read you that dull boring newspaper tomorrow. Tonight, I am going to the Mason-Freeman ball with Mama."

"Ah. So that explains all the little brown envelopes that have been arriving on my desk recently. I knew I hadn't ordered new gloves, a fan, an opera cloak, two pairs of satin shoes, and a gold necklace. A ball eh. Do I approve of balls? ... let me think about it ..."

Daisy tosses her pretty curls.

"Oh Fa! You know it was at a ball that you first met Mama."

"So it was. Now, let me guess. This is how it will go: Tonight, you will meet a handsome young blade. At the second ball, he will flirt with you. At the third ball, he will court you and at the fourth ball he will offer. Is that what you have planned?"

Daisy blushes furiously.

"Mama," she appeals.

"Daisy-duck I am, as you point out, just teasing. I have already arranged for the carriage to be at the door at eight to whisk you away - or wait, was it a pumpkin I ordered? I can't quite remember."

Daisy rises from her seat and bestows a kiss on the top of his head,

"Funny old Fa! I wish you could come with us and see me dancing."

"I shall have to wait another day for that pleasure, I fear."

"When that day comes, you will have the very first dance," Daisy promises. "Now I must go up to my room and look over my clothes."

She hurries out of the breakfast-room.

"Were we that young once?" Lawton muses.

"Indeed, we were, and I remember being introduced to a certain young medical student who tried to get his name on my dance card far more times than was proper."

Daisy's mother rises and straightens the edge of a perfectly straight tablecloth.

"I shall go and see what our dear daughter is up to," she says. "We cannot have her spoiling her new dress by *romping*."

Mr Lawton finishes his coffee and collects his top hat and his surgeon's bag from the hall. He does not remember the last time Daisy romped. She seems to have slipped from adored child into poised young woman without him noticing.

He leaves the house, feeling a pang of regret for all the years that have passed so quickly by. He wishes he could turn back the clock. He'd give anything to see his Daisy romping again.

****

Letitia Simpkins wishes she too, could turn back the clock. She sits in the parlour in a creased black bombazine gown that doesn't fit, awaiting the return of her father and the boys. They are at Mama's funeral service and after it is over, they will bury Mama in Kensal Green cemetery.

Letitia has spent the past few days torturing herself with the thought that she left Mama to die on her own, even though the doctor has assured her father that Mama died in her sleep and would have felt no pain.

But how can he know? What if Mama woke up and realised she was alone but was too weak to call out? What if her very last breath was taken in agony of body and mind? She tries to push the thought aside, but it comes back. Some thoughts have glue on them.

The dull black gown is uncomfortable, and the colour has already stained under her arms. She also has a new black silk bonnet with crape trimming and ribbons. It will be a whole year before she can visit the Mitigated Affliction Department of the store where her clothes were bought to purchase a lighter coloured one.

Letitia has supervised the cook in the preparation of a cold collation for when father and the boys return, for the funeral is a very private affair and no members of either family nor any friends - not that Mama had any friends thanks to her long confinement in bed, have been invited to attend.

However, this has not stopped various people from sending condolence cards, which now lie in a heap on father's desk. It will be her job to answer them, just as it will be her job to take over the responsibility of looking after the boys, and running the household. Just as it is already her responsibility to shoulder the entire burden of guilt for her mother's death.

Letitia hears the sound of a carriage drawing up outside, then a key in the front door. She rises, taking a deep breath to steady her nerves. She has a little speech all rehearsed. She walks into the hallway. But the words die away. For her father and the boys, all wearing new white shirts and black armbands, are not entering the house alone.

To her surprise, they are accompanied by a stout middle-aged woman in a very well-tailored black costume and a fashionable black straw hat trimmed with black ostrich plumes. Letitia is sure that she has never seen her in the house before.

Stunned into silence, she watches as the woman pulls out a couple of hatpins with flashing jewelled stones, removes the hat, then stabs the pins back into it a couple of times before handing hat, cloak and veil to her father to hang up.

The unexpected visitor has deep set currant-dark eyes surrounded by little rolls of fat; her high coloured face is framed by a great deal of bright reddish hair, which is coiled about her head like a snake.

"This is Mrs Briscoe, an old family friend," her father says by way of explanation. "She was at the church service and has accompanied us back in the carriage."

The woman makes Letitia a very slight bow of acknowledgement. Then her father offers the 'old family friend' his right arm and leads her into the dining room.

Letitia follows with the two boys, who are very subdued and a bit tearful.

"Have you ever seen that lady before?" she whispers.

They shake their heads.

But her father is all smiles and affability, almost as if he has not just buried his wife. He offers Mrs Briscoe the plate of sandwiches. She helps herself lavishly, then bites into one.

Her teeth are large and gleaming. She glances around the room, appraising the furniture and ornaments as if she is making an inventory of everything, her gaze finally coming to rest upon Letitia.

There is something almost predatory about her manner. Perhaps you might be a pet. Perhaps you might be a quarry, the gaze says. Either way, the choice is not yours.

Letitia feels her face reddening under the scrutiny.

"How long have you known my Mama?" She asks, her voice coming out several octaves higher than normal.

"Oh - for a very long time, my dear."

"I do not recall her ever mentioning your name."

"Well, she was a very ill woman: I expect that is why. And you have been away at boarding school, haven't you?"

Letitia's father and the stranger exchange a look that Letitia doesn't understand.

"Go and mind the boys, Letty," he orders her. "They are pulling the cakes about - do you not see?"

Letitia does as she is bid. Time passes. As soon as they have eaten, the boys disperse to their room to play. Mrs Briscoe and her father sit either end of the sofa and talk. They appear to have a lot to talk about.

None of the talk involves Letitia, who hovers awkwardly by the refreshment table watching them. At length, the maid returns from the day off she was given to mark Mama's death and begins to clear the plates.

And still Mrs Briscoe stays. And stays.

Eventually when clouds fill the sky like old eiderdowns and the light is draining out of everything, she announces that she must be getting back and Letitia's father, who has barely noticed either his daughter or the ticking clock, offers to go and find her a cab.

Letitia accompanies Mrs Briscoe back out into the hallway and watches as she stands in front of the mirror, thrusting the flashing hatpins into her hat. Mrs Briscoe turns, and bares her teeth in a smile.

"There now. What a sad day," she says, "but it is over. It has been a pleasure to meet you. And I am sure in the future that you and I are going to be the best of friends."

Her father returns to escort the visitor out to the waiting cab. Letitia watches him hand her in, then lean forward to say something in her ear. She hears the tinkling laughter in response. Then the driver whips up the horse and the cab sets off.

Letitia goes up to her room, passing Mama's empty bedroom on the way. She pauses on the threshold, feeling bewildered and confused. Suddenly she wishes that Mama was still alive so that she could go in and talk to her about the events of the day, and ask her about the strange woman.

Letitia bites her lips tightly together, feeling the pain in that place where tears start. There is very little that she is sure of right now, but of one thing she is absolutely determined: she is not going to be 'best friends' with Mrs Briscoe.

****

Daisy, on the other hand, thinks she *could* become friends with Africa, but then she could become friends with the whole world, if the whole world consisted of music and champagne and a supper from Gunter's. Yes, indeed she could.

For who does not remember the thrill of their first ball? That moment when you step down from the carriage in all your new finery, and enter the lighted hall, its balustrades woven with evergreens and the odious entrance from the kitchen stairs concealed by a thick hedge of rhododendrons in pots.

Who has not stood entranced, gazing up at the crystal chandeliers, hearing the strains of delightful music come floating out of the ballroom with its oak beamed floor, polished to such perfection that you can see your face in it - and so you should, for it has taken the hired man with a brush under one foot and a slipper on the other four hours to achieve.

Daisy Lawton is dressed in white with a simple flower wreath in her hair and the gold necklace her only ornament. She sits on a red and gold chair next to her Mama, clutching her dance card with its little tasselled pencil, and surveys the brilliant assembly.

"Oh Mama, I am in Heaven!" she exclaims.

Next to her sits skittish Africa, wearing salmon pink tulle with jewelled combs in her hair and a necklace of diamonds around her throat. The girls have gone through the formal introductions and now all that remains is for some partners to emerge from the throng of young men.

Daisy's little white satin slippers beat time impatiently to the music, but she does not have long to wait, for here is young Digby Barnes Baker, tall and dark and handsome in black evening dress, his white cravat spotless, his gold cuff studs gleaming.

He bows low, requests to see her card, then respectfully asks,

"Will you do me the honour to dance the next quadrille with me?"

And because it is a quadrille and he is the handsomest man in the room (Daisy has already picked him out), she colours up prettily and replies,

"With pleasure, sir."

So, Digby Barnes Baker, who has been well drilled by his Mama, places his name on her card, then turns to Africa and engages her for the following dance before politely bowing and rejoining his companions. And both Mamas nod and smile at each other in satisfaction.

"Isn't this thrilling," Daisy whispers to her companion.

Africa nods her head vigorously, causing several combs to clatter to the floor.

"I have never seen so many beautiful dresses," she whispers, bending to retrieve them.

Daisy agrees.

"Your dress is particularly lovely," Africa says, sticking the combs haphazardly back into her hair.

Daisy dimples prettily, and returns the complement. Then the two girls stare out at the dance floor, where young, well-bred couples, the cream of London society, circle and waltz and laugh.

Later, after the fourteenth dance, Digby Barnes Baker will escort both young ladies to the supper room and make sure their plates are laden with good things and their glasses filled with just enough champagne.

Meanwhile outside in the street, people have gathered, as they always do whenever a ball is taking place in one of the grand London houses. They stare up at the bright balcony casements with their rich curtains unclosed and at the light streaming out of the open doors and down the shining steps to where carriages are parked in line waiting to retrieve their occupants at the end of the night.

Among them is the engineer, who finds he cannot settle without taking a turn about the city. Every night he walks for hours, just following his feet, never knowing where he might end up. It takes the place of sleeping.

On these nocturnal prowlings, he passes whole streets of ruined, deserted houses, lit by flickering street lamps that give texture to the darkness, dividing shadow from darker shadow.

Sometimes he follows the line of the great river that bisects the city as it creeps eastwards, glistening in the moonlight like something cut open. He walks like a man who no longer trusts his dreams, his head gnawing at itself.

Tonight, he has ended up here. He stands on the edge of the crowd, listening to the music and marvelling at the gay dissipations of the fashionable, whose lives are as far from him as from the ragged child beggar shrinking into the shadows of the area steps.

He is just about to push on when he is halted by a vision of such ethereal beauty that his heart almost stops beating. She stands by the open balcony window, her white dress shining like angels' wings.

The engineer fixes his hungry gaze upon her face, so sweet, and the rosebuds in her hair, so pure. He has never seen anybody as lovely. He feels tears coming to his eyes. That such beauty should exist in the world - it is almost too much to bear. She turns her head in response to someone in the room behind her. Next second she is gone.

The engineer waits, hoping that she might come back, willing her to return. But the curtain is drawn across the window by an invisible hand. He sighs and prepares to continue his peregrination. Reaching the corner of the street, he is suddenly bought to a halt by a man who steps out of a dark doorway. He stands in front of the engineer, arms folded, barring his way.

"Got a lucifer, mate?"

The engineer shakes his head.

The man comes closer. He is tall, with dark skin and a full beard. There is a livid scar running from the corner of one eyelid down his cheek. He smells of drink and bad teeth and cheap tobacco.

"So, what 'ave you got?" he asks.

"I do not understand," the engineer says, understanding only too well.

"I know you. I think you may 'ave something of mine - yes, I'm sure you 'ave. Turn out your pockets."

Wearily, the engineer digs in his jacket pockets, produces a wallet, a watch.

"This is all I carry."

The man snatches the wallet, then the watch - an eighteenth birthday present from his mother. It is precious both for its loving engraving and as the last thing she gave him before he left home.

"Thank you for giving back emy property," the man sneers. "And you never saw me, alright? But just in case you did, here's a little souvenir to remember me by ..."

The engineer glimpses the blade glinting in the man's palm, tries to fend it off, feels it enter his side sharp and clean. The last thing he sees before darkness claims him is the sweet face of the girl standing on the balcony.

****

It is two in the morning and Daisy Lawton and her Mama are being driven home from the ball. Daisy has danced every dance, flirted with numerous handsome young men and her bright eyes and pliant figure have been universally admired.

In the next few days, she will leave one of her cards with the hostess' maid, as good breeding dictates. The cards are new and she feels very grown up to have possession of them. She will also write to Letitia and arrange to call round. There is so much to tell her.

In the next few days Mama will meet her old school friend to discuss the next stage of the campaign. It is clear that Digby Barnes Baker admires her daughter (well, who wouldn't?), though as a perfect gentleman he did not ask her to dance more than was socially acceptable. Further meetings need to be set up. He is a catch and she knows there will be other women with their eye on him.

By the time they get home, the first people will have already set off for work. Amongst them will be Daisy's father, who has been summoned early to operate on a man with a serious stab wound who has been brought in earlier. In the absence of the carriage however, he will have to walk like everybody else.

****

London streets are lovely at this time of year. Shop owners put out tubs of geraniums to attract passing trade, ladies stroll in colourful dresses and parasols. In gardens all over the city, scented flowers release their perfume into the air.

It is the sort of day to gladden the heart of any man alive. Unless that man happens to be Inspector Lachlan Greig who has just had a report marked 'Urgent Report' placed on his desk.

It is much too early for urgent reports, but Greig begins to read it, silently tutting at the absence of paragraphing. As usual, the comma has looked in the face of the writer and decided not to disturb him.

As he reads on, however, his expression changes from exasperation to surprise. Reaching the end of the urgent report, Greig gets up and goes to the door. His shout brings the duty officer running down the corridor.

"Is young Hacket in the building? If so, tell him to report to me at once. We have urgent police business to attend to."

****

The engineer opens his eyes. He sees a white painted ceiling with a crack running horizontally across it. There is a lozenge-shaped damp patch by the cornice. Not Heaven then. He moves his head sideways, wincing as pain shoots up the side of his face.

He is in a bed in a small room. The door is open. He can hear footsteps going briskly to and fro beyond the door, the sound of wheels, a despairing groan fading into silence. His head throbs. His chest feels as if someone was trying to separate it from the rest of his body. He lies back on the pillow.

"He is in here, inspector," a voice says.

The word 'inspector' causes the engineer's eyes to fly open. He turns his head, again with difficulty. Inspector Greig, and the younger officer whose name he cannot remember and a man in a black frock coat and white apron enter the room and approach his bed.

"Well, well," Inspector Greig says. "We meet again, Mr Grizewood. You've had a narrow escape by the sound of it."

68

"He was brought in this morning," says the man in the frock coat. "Unconscious, stab wound in the side and cuts and lacerations to the head and face from falling. I've cleaned him up and stitched him back together. Lucky for him the knife just missed his vital organs."

The engineer remains silent, this interpretation of 'luck' being slightly beyond his comprehension.

The surgeon places a hand on Greig's shoulder and motions him aside.

"He does not seem to remember where he is currently lodging," he says in a low voice. "I have suggested writing to his father, but he has refused to contemplate it."

"I wouldn't even know how to begin tracing his father."

"His father is the Archbishop of York," the surgeon says. Then, seeing Greig's eyes widen in surprise, "I recognised the surname. We were at Oxford together. And young Fred has his father's features. Sadly, they have become estranged over the past few years. But I think he would like to know what has happened to his son, don't you?"

Greig glances over his shoulder at the engineer, who is regarding them with a puzzled expression.

"Is he in any danger?"

"The next few days will show whether the wound is healing. I have done what I can to prevent infection setting in, but knife wounds are always tricky."

"I understand. Will you keep him on here?"

"For a day or two. No more. We haven't the beds. I shall write to his father - he will need to go somewhere quiet to recuperate and regain his health and strength. And there is the matter of the bill to pay for his treatment."

Greig shrugs.

"As you think best. Can I speak to him now? We have reason to believe the man who stabbed him may also be involved in another case we are investigating."

The surgeon nods, then addresses his patient,

"I shall leave you, Fred. Rest, and hope. Those are the two best medicines in the world."

The engineer sighs. Greig pulls up a chair and motions Hacket to get out his notebook.

"Now then, Mr Grizewood," he says. "I'd like you to tell us exactly what happened to you in the small hours of this morning. Take your time and miss nothing out. We are in no hurry."

****

On their walk back to Bow Street, Greig issues his orders.

"I want you and two others to bring in our man with the scar. Take him straight to the station, but don't tell him why. 'Assisting the police' is all he needs to be told at this stage. Once I have him, we can use the attack to see what else and who else he knows," he says to Hacket.

"Do you still think he has something to do with Mr and Mrs Hall? I saw no signs of life when I was watching the house," Hacket says.

"That doesn't mean it was empty. People can lie low - in a basement or a back kitchen. Especially if they have something to hide. Never assume the obvious: chances are you'll always be proved wrong."

"I could get the men to persuade him to cooperate. Be a lot easier," Hacket suggests.

Greig turns on him in a flash.

"No! And don't let me ever hear you ask that again. We stick to the rules. You can do it the easy way or you can do it the hard way. The difference between the hard way and the easy way is that in the long run, the hard way works."

A few hours later Sergeant Hacket and two constables armed with handcuffs and truncheons arrive outside the door of the rundown property where the man and his dog were last seen. After knocking on the door for some time and receiving no reply, they station themselves at strategic points at either end of the street and wait.

When it becomes clear that the quarry is not going to return, Hacket gives the order and the two constables break down the door and enter the property, where they find signs of recent occupation in the form of a table, two chairs, and some cheap ornaments on the mantelpiece, but no sign of the previous occupants.

On Hacket's orders, the men descend to the basement kitchen, its walls so black and begrimed that it is hard to believe it has not been painted that colour deliberately. There they discover some still warm cinders in the grate and a pile of faeces in one corner.

But that is not all. Lying on a filthy cloth, curled up as if in slumber, they find the body of a new-born babe - a tiny premature thing, its darkly curling head nestled against a filthy glass feeding bottle half full of something that will, upon analysis, prove to be watered down milk mixed with lime.

****

It is rare for Daisy Lawton's father to arrive back home before dinner is served but *mirabile dictu*, here he is at the head of the table, carving the joint. Over dinner, he listens attentively to Daisy's girlish chatter of dances and dresses and partners and ices. After the dessert plates have been cleared, he rises.

"Daisy-duck, I am glad I was not there last night, for I fear your poor old father wouldn't have got a single dance with his favourite daughter."

"Oh Fa - I would have saved the supper dance specially for you."

"Well, so I should hope. But now I must leave you both - I have a letter to write and it will not wait."

Mr Lawton goes to his study and spends some time staring thoughtfully into the middle distance. Then he selects a clean sheet of writing paper and begins:

Dear William

I hope you are in the best of health. It has been some time since we corresponded, as we are both now such busy men, you in the Church and I in the medical profession.

It is in that latter category that I now take up my pen. Very early this morning a young man was admitted to my hospital. He had been set upon in the street, robbed and stabbed by his assailant. He was lucky to escape with his life, so brutal was the attack. But he has survived.

I have done my best to tend to his wounds - but there is one wound I cannot heal, and that is the breach that exists between you and him. For I am talking about your son Fred, who even now lies in a hospital bed fighting for his life.

I plead with you, for the sake of old times, for the love of God and family, for our past friendship at Oxford and beyond (as you recall, you officiated at our marriage, and christened our daughter), to be reconciled to your son.

He has suffered a severe blow to his head and now cannot recall where he is lodging. If he fails to remember, I do not know what will become of him, for he must leave the hospital shortly, and will require his wound to be dressed and other tasks performed for him as he recovers.

I shall continue to look after him both in my role as surgeon and as he is your son, for old times' sake, until I hear from you further.

Your friend,
Alexander Lawton

Having thus written, Lawton seals up the letter and goes to post it. Returning from the post-box he spends a few minutes in the street, looking up at his house. The symmetry always gave him great pleasure. The coloured brick-banding and round-headed windows reminded him of places he'd seen in Italy in his youth.

The sound of a piano comes drifting out on the balmy evening air - Daisy is practising one of her tunes. How warm and inviting the house looks, with its lighted windows and rose-coloured drapes.

How cold and miserable by comparison must life be for that poor young man lying helpless in his hospital bed. Lawton can only hope his words, inadequate as they are, will touch the father's heart. And that it will not be too late.

In the event, he does not have long to wait. The reply from the engineer's father arrives a day later. It is brief and brutal and to the point.

Dear Alexander, (the Archbishop writes)

I thank you for your letter and the information it conveys about Frederick. Since he has chosen, against my express wishes, to become a civil engineer, I have absolved myself of any further responsibility for his well-being. I informed him of my decision some time ago, he knows it, and I do not think he will expect me to change my mind.

Obviously, it is regrettable that he has sustained the attack you describe, but I am sure, with your expert help, he will recover. I enclose a bankers' draft for the cost of his treatment and take the opportunity to express my gratitude for your offer to look after him 'for old times' sake'.

I am about to embark upon a series of sermons on the Laws of the Prophets which I hope to publish, so I will be fully occupied for the next few months. Thus, even if I desired it, I should be unable to lodge the boy at Bishopthorpe.

Yours,
In His Name,
Wm Grizewood

Reading the letter over his evening glass of port, Daisy's father recalls the stern faced, aesthetic young man who once shared his rooms at College. He always wore fustian black, and spent many hours studying the bible or on his knees by his narrow bed.

He tries to recall Grizewood smiling, sharing a joke, getting drunk, flirting with the college skivvies. He cannot bring to mind a single instance.

He also remembers the tall black pillar of a newly ordained clergyman who officiated at his marriage. The wedding sermon was all about the sin of adultery and the fiery pit of torment awaiting anybody who strayed from the marriage bed.

Thinking back, he wonders why he is even remotely surprised at the man's response. Lawton crumples up the letter in disgust and goes to find his wife. A guest bedroom must be prepared and a private nurse engaged. He, at least, is not prepared to turn his back on a fellow human being.

****

Letitia Simpkins feels that the world has definitely turned its back upon her. She barely left the house after Mama's death, and she has barely left the house since Mama's funeral. Any thought that Mama's absence might lighten the domestic load for her has been brutally quelled.

The two servants who took turns to care for Mama, supplementing their duties with housework and waiting at table have been let go. Her father does not see it as a necessary expense to pay for services that can be performed (for free) by Letitia.

She is now expected to rise at dawn, light fires, fetch and carry water, supervise the cook, dust, sweep, sew and darn, aided by the remaining servant, for whom the words *lazy* and *skimps* might have been invented.

By the end of the day she is so weary that she has frequently fallen asleep over her supper. As a consequence, her clothes are beginning to feel loose, and her wrists protrude from her sleeves like two sticks. If she holds them to the light, she can see the delicate blue tracery of her veins.

Her unhappiness is compounded by the presence of Mrs Briscoe who, having buried two husbands, turns up regularly to instruct Letitia on the correct way to comport herself during the mourning period.

All, from clothes to table settings, comes under her basilisk gaze, and in all, Letitia is found wanting. Every morning Mrs Briscoe arrives on the doorstep bright and early to march the boys to school, returning a short while later to instruct and oversee Letitia in her domestic duties. She then leaves temporarily to march the boys back at the end of the day.

Most evenings Mrs Briscoe stays on to dinner, poking the food with her fork and tutting. After dinner, she and Papa adjourn to the parlour, where she reads aloud to him from the newspaper - a task she apparently always performed for husbands one and two.

The pleasant and instructive visits to the Regent Street Ladies' Literary & Philosophical Society seem a distant memory. The outside world seems a distant memory. There is nothing in Letitia's life now that she recognises. The joy of it has run out as quickly as it gathered.

Letitia pauses outside the parlour door which unusually, has been left ajar. She leans against the door jamb, bone weary and despondent. She sees her papa and Mrs Briscoe sitting side by side on the sofa. Mrs Briscoe is speaking. It takes Letitia few seconds to realise whom she is talking about.

"Really, it is a most unfortunate situation. The girl has barely learned sufficient to equip her for a useful life. I do so sympathise with you, my dear friend. That *mauvais quart d'heure* in between school and marriage is always difficult."

Her father snorts.

"It was Susan's whim to send her to the boarding school in the first place. She thought mixing with a better class of girl would help her find a husband. As if any self-respecting man will marry her. She hardly has the looks to attract a suitor. And I cannot offer a dowry - there is the boys' schooling to pay for, and then their university fees. They must have the best start in life."

"I do so understand. And of course, you are quite right. But as I wrote in my little pamphlet: *How to be Happy Though Unmarried*, there are many things a girl can do. The poor are always with us, so there is plenty of charity work.

"And there is no household task that any girl should deem beneath her position to perform, as I have frequently reminded Letitia. All these useful occupations will enable her to pass her days in dignified tranquillity."

Letitia's eyes brim with tears. She does not know what hurts more, to hear her own father admit her lack of beauty, or to understand that he does not care what happens to her in the future. Mrs Briscoe's next remark, however, causes her to breathe in sharply.

"Has she had any more letters from those vile Women's Rights creatures?"

"Not for a while."

"I am so glad you managed to intercept them, my dear. A parent must be vigilant at all times. One tiny slip, and a girl's reputation is gone, never to return."

"I have locked them away safely, never fear. And I have instructed Mary to make sure the post in and out of the house is always placed directly upon my desk."

Mrs Briscoe leans forward, placing her hand on his.

"It is no more than your duty as a loving caring father. And now that you are a widower - though hopefully not for too long, you must be even more vigilant on your daughter's behalf.

"A young girl's true sphere is in the home, and there she shines brightly. Skill with her needle is the only accomplishment she needs."

Letitia has heard enough. Setting her jaw firmly, she goes straight to her father's desk. The rolled top is locked, but she knows where he keeps the spare key. It is the work of a moment to unlock the desk and liberate her letters, which have been stuffed into a pigeonhole together with a lot of unpaid bills.

Tucking them into her apron pocket, she tiptoes past the parlour door and hurries up to her room. She has never forgotten Sarah, nor the other friends she made, and the hope they gave her for a better future.

Now it appears that Sarah and the others did not forget her either. Letitia lights a candle and takes up the first precious envelope. It has been opened, as have all of them, but she is beyond caring. She extracts the folded piece of writing paper and begins to read.

****

There is nothing like a bright May afternoon, with the sun darting its rays cheerfully down and all the enchantment of a beautiful day, to bring out the open carriages and the fashionable ladies. Let clerks go to their counting-houses, and queens to their parlours, the elegantly attired head for that exclusive shopping thoroughfare that is Regent Street.

Here the brilliantly ever-shifting scene is almost dizzying in its confusion. Tight-waistcoated flâneurs lounge languidly in front of gaily decorated plate-glass windows, watching and being watched, for there is always a dual purpose in everything that these society people do.

Not everybody is here for the shopping and the spectacle, though. Walk towards the top of Regent Street, crossing Oxford Street - if you are lucky, the road sweeper will go ahead of you to clear a path through the dust and filth.

Walk on until you are in sight of All Soul's church. There you will see a group of respectably dressed young women standing outside a building. They are handing out copies of a leaflet, entitled *Women: Education is your RIGHT!!*

Their actions are receiving mixed responses from people passing by. A tall, top-hatted city gent swats them away as if they were so many flies. A couple of boys snatch some leaflets, and then proceed to make paper boats out of them. Two young women stop, accept a leaflet, skim read it, giggle and hand it back.

Eventually the group is approached by a patrolling constable who folds his arms and regards them sternly.

"Ladies, I have received a complaint about you and I must ask you to desist from your current actions," he tells them.

"Really? Who has lodged this complaint?" demands one of the group (Carrie Bradstreet by name, writer of pamphlets by occupation).

"I am not at liberty to say," the constable replies. "I can only divulge that the complainant believes your behaviour is inflammatory and may lead to a breach of the peace."

"Do you have a daughter, officer?"

"Whether I have or not, is none of your business, miss."

Unabashed, Carrie hands him a pamphlet.

"Please give her this, with my best regards. I am sure you would like her to have a happy life, and without a proper education, that is almost impossible."

Taken back by her boldness, the policeman stuffs the pamphlet into his jacket pocket without thinking.

"Now then, I must ask you to cease pestering members of the public, or I shall have to take further action," he says.

Carrie makes an expansive gesture with one arm.

"Officer, do you see all the men with sandwich boards, the beggars, the street entertainers, the costers and coffee sellers .... is it your intention to take 'further action' against them also?"

The policeman rolls his eyes.

"They are engaged in legitimate selling enterprises, miss."

"And so are we."

"Oh really. And what, may I be so bold as to inquire, are you selling?"

"We are selling a vision for the future. A dream that must and will come true. A hope that one day all the young women and girls of this country can stand intellectually shoulder to shoulder with their brothers."

And having delivered her speech in a ringing voice, Carrie squares her own small but determined shoulders, and looks up at the policeman, as if daring him to contradict her.

"Now see here, miss ..." he begins, but he is suddenly interrupted by a cry of triumph that causes them both to turn towards the building behind them.

It is Sarah Lunt, and in her hand is a piece of paper which she waves aloft.

"A letter!" she cries.

Carrie immediately hurries towards her, to be joined seconds later by the rest of the group. They crowd round Sarah, who holds up a hand for silence.

"I have just received a letter from Letitia Simpkins. You remember how worried we all were when she suddenly disappeared and I had no reply to my letters to her home? Well, here is the reason. She writes that her mother has died."

A murmur of sympathy runs around the group.

"Ah, but even worse, her father has kept back our letters from her so she never knew of our concern for her situation. Indeed, she thought we had abandoned her completely, poor thing."

The sympathy is replaced by indignation.

"Why should he do such a thing?" one of the group asks.

"Apparently, ladies, we are dangerous radical feminists!"

"If wanting women to have access to the same education as men means being a dangerous radical, then so be it. I wear the badge with pride," Carrie says.

"But *even that* is nothing compared to what her life has become. Letitia says that since her mother's sad death, she can only go out for short periods, and is accompanied whenever she does by a female friend of her father who sounds, I have to say, like a most unpleasant person."

Sarah shakes her head.

"I do not understand it all clearly. But I simply cannot bear to think of her, or anybody wasting their life and potential in this way."

"This is grave news indeed. I had high hopes that she might be amongst the first to take the Cambridge Junior Locals - her mathematical and classical knowledge was formidable as I recall," Carrie says.

"We must put our heads together," Sarah says. "Slavery has been abolished in the colonies so there is no excuse whatsoever to practice it here in London."

"Amen to that. Let us talk about it over a cup of tea - I see our police officer has departed, so I presume we are not going to be arrested after all."

"We have much to talk about indeed," Sarah says. "I have rarely read anything that has made me crosser! I cannot believe that in any so-called civilised society, a young woman has to resort to guile and deception to live her life. It is not to be tolerated."

****

Meanwhile a short distance away in a pretty Belgravia parlour, Margaret Barnes Baker, wife of Richard Barnes Baker is also practising guile and deception - though as she is the wife of an MP, maybe guile and deception are rather too strong a description - let us call it social politics instead.

Seated next to her on the rose patterned sofa is handsome young Digby Barnes Baker, scion, possible future MP and dandy about town. He is being gently probed about the recent ball. The crashing about coming through the ceiling is from Africa, who is applying the same noisy enthusiasm to tidying her drawers as she does to everything else.

"I thought the supper was particularly delightful," Mrs Baker murmurs. "One really cannot go wrong with cold chicken and champagne. And the trifles looked quite delicious," she pauses. "Did Daisy Lawton enjoy them?" she asks innocently.

"Think so. Ate two platefuls," says young Digby, who is not a habitual pronoun user.

"Really? Well. I do like to see a young lady with a healthy appetite. So many modern girls just pick and poke at their food nowadays. Scared of losing their figures."

Digby says nothing. He remembers Daisy as a pretty, lively girl (or 'gal') but his priorities were more towards making sure his pocket flaps, coat revers and the colour of his gloves had been noticed by his sartorial rivals.

"I am so glad you like her, dear. As you know, her Mama and I went to school together when we were young and it gave us both great pleasure to see our children getting on."

Again, Digby says nothing. He cannot imagine either of his parents as young and is sure it is some myth put about to spoil his fun as in: *when your father and I were young we never...*

"Your father and I are anxious that you should start thinking about settling down - a young man about to enter Parliament ought to have a wife. It sits better with the electorate. Daisy Lawton comes from a good family and will bring with her, according to her Mama, a considerable dowry."

Ah. Now Digby sees where Ma is coming from, but he keeps his handsome face strictly neutral. He knows he can have the pick of the girls - indeed he has already plucked several, though not the sort his parents would approve of.

"We are thinking of holding a little dinner party - we owe invitations to several people. I shall invite sweet little Daisy. And can you run through your friends and invite somebody suitable to sit with Africa? I'm afraid her dance card was not very full at the ball and I promised her mother I would do my best for the poor girl?"

"See what I can do, Ma."

Mrs Barnes Baker gives him her most radiant smile.

"You are a good boy, Digby. I'm sure you will do very well when you enter the House. Now, what have you got planned today?"

"Oh, meeting some chaps at the Club, seeing my tailor and my barber, that sort of thing."

"Well, have a splendid time, dear - don't forget your father is expecting you at five, and you are to dine in the Members' Dining Room. He is going to introduce you to some of his more *influential* friends who can help you win your seat."

Digby Barnes Baker, fashionable man about town and (maybe) future MP rises, bows gracefully and saunters out. At his mother's summons, he has come hot foot from his rooms in town and there is a little something he needs to go and sort out - although he is hoping she will have sorted herself out and left by the time he returns.

On his way back, he thinks about Daisy Lawton. She seemed a nice gal. Lively manner. Pretty face. But would he like to come home to her every evening, to wake up with it on the pillow next to his? He noticed several men eyeing her up appreciatively at the ball. She is definitely a catch - as his mother would say.

Still ...

Digby reminds himself that even if he were to marry Daisy Lawton, he wouldn't have to be home when the House was sitting late. Indeed, most of his married friends who've moved out of town have kept on their bachelor quarters for when they need, or want to stay overnight. On the whole, it seems a satisfactory arrangement.

But ...

Does he want to be tied down right now, when the world of pleasure has just opened its arms and welcomed him in?

Digby is known among his pals to be a bit of a gambling man, never one to refuse a bet or a challenge. He takes a coin out of his jacket pocket and flips it into the air. Heads, he stays single. Tails, he goes after the Lawton girl.

The coin arcs, silver in the dim carriage light, then lands in his open palm. He glances down. So be it.

****

Totally unaware that her future is being decided upon the spin of a coin in a hansom, Daisy Lawton is on her way to visit her best friend Letitia. She is dying to tell her all about the ball, and she is sure Tishy is dying to hear all about it.

Reaching Tishy's street, she is surprised to see the blinds of the Simpkins house drawn down, and a black ribbon bow on the door knocker. There has been a death in the family. How did she not know? Her heart misgives her ... Tishy? Oh no, surely not! She hurries to the front door and beats out a most unladylike tattoo.

The door is opened by a most unpleasant looking woman in black. She doesn't smile or curtsey a greeting. Daisy is not used to rude servants, but she has had lessons on dealing with them from Mama, and there is a first time for everything.

"Is Miss Letitia Simpkins at home?" she asks in her best 'society' voice.

The woman is clearly taken aback. She glances over Daisy's shoulder, her cold pebbly eyes taking in the carriage and the groom. Her face changes subtly.

"If you would care to walk in Miss …, I shall go and find out if she is receiving visitors today. The family has recently suffered a bereavement, as you see."

Daisy proffers her card.

"I did not know. But we are old acquaintances from boarding school, so I am sure she would want to see me and I her. Please take my card to her at once."

A few minutes later, Daisy is shown into the small sitting room where Letitia, wearing full mourning, immediately rises from the sofa.

"Oh Daisy, how good of you to call," she says.

Daisy tries not to look shocked. This Letitia does not resemble the bright girl of their shared past. This Letitia is thin, and white-faced. Her hair looks unwashed and her black dress only accentuates her pallor.

She holds out both hands.

"Tishy - it is so good to see you too," she says warmly.

The woman hovers by the door.

Daisy unties her bonnet, and shrugs off her mantle.

"Thank you," she says, handing them over.

Clearly offended by being taken for a servant, the woman stares at her, but receives the bonnet and mantle and goes to hang them up in the hallway. As soon as she has left the room, Letitia darts over to the door and turns the key. Then she draws Daisy onto the sofa next to her.

"I must speak low: she will be listening to our conversation," she murmurs.

Daisy stares at her in astonishment.

"What is going on? Who is that woman?"

"Mama is dead. And Papa has invited Mrs Briscoe to be my companion and help me to look after the boys. That is who she is."

Daisy frowns.

"Invited? She is not a servant, then?"

Letitia bites her lip.

"She is a good friend of the family - at least that is what I have been told. But I never heard Mama mention her, nor has she ever left her card. And the boys say they have never seen her before.

"I do not dare name what I suspect she is. Oh Daisy - it is so disgraceful. I think she and Papa ... are ... I cannot utter it."

"*Mrs Archer's Downfall*?" Daisy says, naming a certain sensation novel that was passed clandestinely around the older girls at boarding school. The story was of a man who murdered his sickly wife and then moved his mistress into the family home.

Letitia nods, looking down at her clasped hands.

"In a way. Though Mama died in her own bed from weakness of the heart - which I may have contributed to," she sighs.

Seeing Daisy's shocked expression, she tells the story of the boys' escapade, and the events that followed on after. The words come spilling out, followed by hot tears.

"But you were not to know she was dying," Daisy says stoutly. "She had been ill for such a long time; how could it be your fault?"

"Papa says that had her heart not been weakened further by the shock, she might have lived longer. And had I not neglected my duty, she might not have died alone and unattended."

"And is your Papa a medical man?"

Letitia shakes her head.

"Well, my Papa is, so I shall ask him for his opinion tonight," Daisy says. She gestures towards the door. "But why all the secrecy?"

"Oh Daisy, you have no idea what my life has become. I have barely left the house since Mama died and if I go anywhere, that woman accompanies me because it is not suitable for a young woman, especially a young woman in mourning, to gad about on her own, she says."

"Well, I gad about frequently on my own and I have come to no harm. This is 1863, not the Dark Ages."

"How very modern you have become," Letitia says, the pale ghost of a smile hovering around the corners of her mouth.

"Oh Tishy, I am so sorry about your Mama. I wish you had written," Daisy says, pulling a face. "And now I feel bad, for I came to tell you all about my first ball."

"I should like nothing more than to hear about it. It would cheer me up immensely and I need cheering up."

Daisy looks at her, head on one side.

"Then I shall tell you. But first, let us devise a plan to get you out of the house."

"It cannot be done."

"It can be done and it will, and this is how we shall do it: I'll tell your gaoler that I am taking you for a carriage ride. She can hardly object to that, for you will be accompanied by me every minute. On the way, we'll stop and have something nice to eat and we will have a really good long chat. What do you say?"

"I say what a truly excellent plan."

"Then let us execute it at once."

Daisy rises, holding out her hand for the key. Putting a finger to her lips, she softly tiptoes to the door, unlocks it and flings it open. Red-faced, Mrs Briscoe starts back, her guilty expression revealing all too clearly what she has been up to.

"Please fetch my bonnet at once. Also, Miss Simpkins' bonnet if you wouldn't mind. I am taking her out in my carriage," Daisy says in a very lordly manner.

It is clear that Mrs Briscoe minds. Minds very much, but there is nothing she can do. Bonneted and shawled, Letitia sails out of the front door on Daisy's arm and is helped up into the phaeton. The groom whips up the horses and off they go.

Just as they reach the corner, Letitia glances briefly round. Mrs Briscoe is standing in the doorway, her face contorted into a mask of fury. She is shaking her fist at the departing carriage.

Faces, contorted or not, are also the hot topic of conversation at Bow Street police office. Two faces in particular - and they are currently staring out at Inspector Greig from the front page of the *The Inquirer* under a banner headline that reads:

Archbishop's Son in Brutal Attack! Scarface Man Hunted by Bow Street Police Officers!

Beneath these uncompromising words is an artist's impression of the scene, which seems to have taken place outside a cathedral. The engineer, in vaguely clerical garb, is lying on the ground *'weltering in his own gore'* (quote).

Above him looms a ferociously grimacing man with flowing hair, wildly staring eyes and a scar running the length of his face. He brandishes a knife and is snarling: *'Give me all your possessions at once!'* (quote).

When Greig arrived for work earlier in the day, both the outer office and waiting room were packed with the usual members of Crimestoppers Unanimous, all eager to claim that they recognised the scarfaced man, and knew where he lived.

There were also several men with scarred faces, equally eager to insist that *they* were not involved in the fracas in *any way whatsoever* and had alibis and witnesses aplenty to prove it.

It is turning out to be another frustrating day, most of which Greig is spending in his office gently fuming. The question foremost in his mind is how, exactly, did the penny-a-line hacks that call themselves journalists get hold of the story in the first place?

The only people who knew the identity of the engineer were the surgeon (unlikely to talk to the press), the engineer (not in any fit state to talk to the press), himself and young Hacket and he knows that he didn't speak to any member of the fourth estate.

Having eliminated three possible suspects, he has just sent a constable to find Sergeant Hacket, who is currently dealing with something somewhere else.

In the meantime, the list of people to be questioned and people not to be questioned ('coz they weren't there, were they?') is growing exponentially. All of which means endless paperwork, with his officers being tied up in pointless interviews and following up tenuous lines of inquiry when they should be out on the street tracking down the real scarfaced man and his baby-murdering friends.

By the time Sergeant Hacket returns to Bow Street the lunchtime edition of *The Inquirer* will appear, in which the story has become embellished by a lurid description of the actual injuries inflicted (with graphic diagrams) and the revelation that the victim is currently at death's door.

Eventually a rather sheepish Sergeant Hacket slides into Greig's room. Stern faced and unsmiling, Greig points him to a chair.

"Sit yourself down, Ben. Now then, can you throw any light on this?" he asks, handing the sergeant *The Inquirer's* front page.

"I didn't know he was a journalist, sir."

There is an ominous pause.

"Go on …"

"I was in the Bunch of Grapes with ... er ... a young lady."

Greig raises an eyebrow.

"Drinking on duty?"

"No sir. It was strictly out of work hours. Anyway, we were in a private booth and I was telling her about my work and then a man asked if he could join us. He bought a round of drinks and, well, one thing kind of led to another ... I'm so sorry," the young man tails off awkwardly.

"You had too much to drink and blabbed about the investigation, is that correct?"

Sergeant Hacket is turning his helmet round between his hands so fast it is a wonder it doesn't take off.

"Tell me, do you always drink in that public house?"

"Oh yes sir, a lot of the officers from local police stations do. It's a well-known place to meet up."

"And members of the gutter press would also know that?"

"I suppose they might."

"Clearly they do. Can you recall anything else you might have said in your cups? Did you name the Halls at any time, do you think?"

Ben Hacket shakes his head.

86

"Well, that's one mercy, I suppose."

"It won't happen again sir, I promise."

Greig allows the silence to continue slightly beyond the comfort zone.

"Right. Well I hope you've learned a very useful lesson. If not, then I'm afraid you are of very little use to me in this case, and to the force in general."

Hacket pulls a wry mouth.

"May I suggest that you choose your drinking place with a little more circumspection from now on. And never - I repeat, *never* speak of anything that happens between these four walls to anybody out there. Your girl, your brother officers, don't even tell the neighbourhood cat. Because you just don't know who might be listening."

"No sir."

"Get out."

Hacket goes.

Greig writes himself a note to call in on a few other police offices and have a word in private with their superintendents. He has sometimes wondered where members of the press picked up their information about police business. Now he knows of one source. It will need to be plugged quickly.

He acknowledges that the young sergeant never intended to do any harm. Nevertheless, his foolish actions might inadvertently be the cause of harm to others and he cannot allow that to happen.

Greig sighs and stares into the middle distance. Ever since he started investigating the child murders, he knows he is shouldering his way through the ghosts of the past. Though they do not follow him, he senses their eyes on his back.

****

Unaware that he is weltering in gore and at death's door, the engineer is being transported to his place of convalescence. Heavily sedated, he knows no more than that he is being jolted about, and there is a lot of street noise in the background.

He wakes to a cool breeze and soft sheets. A white capped and aproned figure is sitting by his bed. For a moment, he is totally confused. The figure speaks,

"Glad to see you have opened your eyes, sir. Mr Lawton says you are to take this tincture upon waking."

The tip of a spoon is placed against his lower lip. Obediently, he opens his mouth and swallows the reddish-brown liquid. The taste reminds him of incense and for a moment he wonders if he is back in his father's church. Then he feels his head growing heavy, the room filling with clouds ....

Downstairs, Mrs Lawton is reading the cook the diet sheet that has accompanied the patient. Beef tea and milk puddings seem to feature. She has had the patient's situation carefully explained to her and she has been shown his father's missive.

Even so, she hopes he will be back on his feet soon. Back on his feet and back in his own lodgings. It is the Season, after all. She and Daisy are hosting a five o'clock tea party tomorrow and as soon as that young lady reappears, they must start organising the food.

The presence of an injured young man - even though she has been reassured that he does not bring any contagion with him, is inconvenient to say the least.

Still, she reassures herself, as long as the nurse uses the back stairs, so that guests do not realise there is anything untoward happening, and Daisy herself stays well away from the sickroom, she supposes that no harm will accrue from the short time the young man is under their roof.

****

Mr Sprowle, landlord of number 18 Hind Street, which is now cartographically the last house standing, surveys the view from his doorstep. It has been raining and the gravel in the front garden has turned to clay, which has been steadily trod into the house by returning tenants.

The temporary way of planks, erected for his use and the use of passers-by over the yawning cavern underneath the pavement is wet and slippery. Nobody has begged his pardon for the weeks and weeks of disruption, and he strongly objects to the constant noise, dust, chaos of timber, shaft holes and earth mounds.

Muttering imprecations, Mr Sprowle fetches mop and bucket, fills the latter from the tap which by some mercy is still giving water, and prepares to do battle against the combined forces of man, machine and nature now the house is temporarily empty.

Eventually he reaches the first floor and the rented back room of the two young upstart bank clerks Edwin Persiflage and Danton Waxwing. He tries the door. Usually it is locked. Today it opens and Mr Sprowle and his mop and his bucket of greying scummy water enter.

Tutting to himself, he surveys the mess of plates, bottles, clothes, papers and fruit peelings. The room smells fusty. He goes to the window and opens it, pausing to peer down at the iron buckets, chains and pumps working below.

They may be clerks, but they live like ruddy pigs, he thinks sourly as he gets to work swishing water around the floor, pushing the piles of detritus into various corners.

As he swills and mops, the mop handle accidentally knocks against a small sealed can on the mantelpiece. The can tips, topples, and falls into the fireplace.

There is an almighty explosion.

And suddenly number 18 Hind Street is no longer the last house standing.

****

Nothing lasts forever, except forever itself. All too soon Letitia Simpkins and Daisy Lawton have scraped the last delightful morsel of food from their plates and drunk up the fragrant coffee. It is time for Letitia to return home. Her golden few hours of freedom have melted away like icing on one of the cakes.

Slowly, reluctantly, she trails after Daisy and climbs into the carriage. All the way back she feasts her eyes on the brightly dressed women passing by the carriage window, her spirits sinking with every mile that is bringing her nearer to home and closer to Mrs Briscoe.

"I have enjoyed our outing so much," she sighs.

"Then let it be the first of many."

"Ah, but that is easily said, less easily accomplished."

Daisy frowns.

"They cannot prevent you coming and going from your own house."

"It is not my own house and they can. Mrs Briscoe has asked me several times to give up my front door key. I have declined, but it is inevitable, after this afternoon, that she will make another foray."

"Then let her try!" Daisy declares. "We shall not give in, dear Tishy - just as we did not when that hateful Miss Porbelle tried to stop us having midnight dormitory feasts."

"Sadly, I do not think barricading myself inside my room is going to work," Letitia smiles wryly.

Daisy lapses into silence, her brow furrowed. The carriage halts outside the Simpkins house. The two girls fondly embrace.

"Write to me," Daisy says.

"If I can get to the post-box."

Letitia is helped down. She walks slowly up the path. She takes a final look round at her friend, and raises her hand in farewell.

Her heart heavy within her, Daisy flings herself back into the seat. She cannot allow her dear friend Tishy to wither away in that terrible house with that dreadful woman. She must - nay she WILL come up with a plan to save her.

Meanwhile Letitia hangs up her bonnet and heads for the stairs, ears strained to catch the heavy footsteps of Mrs Briscoe advancing towards the parlour door accompanied by the Disapproving Sniff that always preceded her.

Hearing nothing at all - in fact the house is strangely silent, she breathes a sigh of relief and mounts the stairs. She opens the door to her room. And freezes on the threshold.

Squatting on the end of her bed like a huge black toad, sits Mrs Briscoe. Strewn all about her are all the letters that Letitia retrieved from her father's desk.

Mrs Briscoe rises, her face mottled red with anger, eyes spitting venom.

"Yes, miss, yes!" she hisses, "Here I am, and here is the evidence of your wickedness and wilful behaviour. Your Papa shall know of this before the day is out, oh indeed he shall!"

And gathering up the precious letters, she stalks out, pushing Letitia roughly aside as she goes. There is the sound of a key turning in the lock, then heavy footsteps descend the stairs. The parlour door is slammed shut.

Letitia rushes to the door and turns the handle frantically. The door does not open. She is a prisoner. She has never been locked in her own room before. She bangs on the door, demanding to be let out. There is no response.

Eventually, after shouting herself hoarse and bruising her fists, Letitia sinks down and leans her head against the door. Her mind feels empty, like the volute of a shell.

She no longer thinks of herself, but of turning points. Of how quickly lives fall back on themselves. There is a tightness in her throat and she feels dizzy. On the other side of the door, the silence gathers, dark and ominous.

****

It is a chance comment from his sergeant that has brought Inspector Greig hurrying hot-foot from Bow Street to the railway construction site. Having read a report in one of the lunchtime papers of a 'gas leak' destroying the last remaining dwelling in Hind Street, Sergeant Hacket had observed that as far as he recalled from their previous visit, the gas had been cut off.

Most of the time Greig treats the opinions of the young officers with a degree of benign scepticism. But something about what Hacket said had resonated. So now here he is, pushing his way through the sightseers and the sellers of ginger beer, fruit, cakes and coffee who have all miraculously materialised once again and set up temporary stalls in the hope of picking up trade.

Greig surveys the wreckage of what was once number 18 Hind Street but is now a jumbled, smoking pile of timbers, lath and plaster being carefully picked over by a team of workmen.

Then he goes to find Albert Noble, the onsite chemist, who is packing up his bottles and equipment.

"You're the expert on big bangs Mr Noble, aren't you? Tell me this wasn't a gas explosion," Greig says.

The chemist shakes his head.

"It was certainly not. The gas was cut off to the whole street a long time ago, Inspector. But the house was on borrowed time - it would have been destroyed sooner or later. The tunnel was already undermining the foundations."

"Looks like someone did the job for you," Greig says drily. "So could ... say ... a can of nitro-glycerine be enough to bring down a house?"

"Oh yes, certainly. Particularly a house like that one. The contractor had already shored up the side with timber beams."

"I think we have discovered where your missing can went to, then. Though how it got there is still to be revealed. Do you have any ideas?"

"I am a mere chemist, Inspector. What would I know about such matters? I leave speculation to other heads," the chemist says primly. "Now if I can be of no further help, my services are urgently required at another construction site."

Greig goes to chat to the four Metropolitan police constables currently holding back the crowd who, having been drawn initially by the explosion, are now hanging on in the hope that something gruesome might be discovered in the clearing up process.

"Any sign of the previous occupants?"

"Body of a man found," one says with lugubrious relish. "Horribly burned it was. They found bits of flesh and pieces of bone as far as thirty yards away. All taken to the police morgue, if you want to have a look for yourself."

Greig does not. Given the time of day, he hazards a guess that the body is, or rather *was* Mr Sprowle the landlord, as the rest of the tenants are likely to have left for work earlier. He also doubts that the landlord would be the one who helped himself to a can of nitro-glycerine. Too old and not enough gumption.

Inspector Greig curses his own stupidity. Why did he not get a list of the tenants renting rooms at number 18? At the time, it seemed irrelevant. Not any more. Whoever stole the can of chemicals may now be guilty not only of theft of railway property, but also of murder.

Without giving away his true reasons, he orders the constables to mount a special watch over the site, and to apprehend anybody trying to access it, or making such inquiries indicative of their former tenancy, or interest in the property.

He gives them his card, telling them to send a man over, day or night, to Bow Street. Then he takes a last long look at the devastation. Babies murdered, lethal explosions - who would have thought that one poor dilapidated street could contain so much evil?

****

The life of a bank clerk is, on the whole, pretty monotonous. Ranged in long rows they sit high off the ground casting up accounts on sloping desks. All day long they weigh and pay, weigh and pay.

It is no wonder then, that at 5.30 pm Waxwing and Persiflage dismount thankfully from their stools, don their street coats and proceed to their usual alamode house, where they order a fourpenny plate of boiled beef with carrots and suet dumplings and bespeak a copy of the evening paper.

Hoping to read of some terrible disaster that may have befallen an MP or a member of the upper classes, they are instead struck dumb by an account on page two of a mysterious and very fatal gas explosion that has taken place earlier in a street next to the Metropolitan Railway workings.

It takes a couple of readings before the penny drops and they realise that the article refers to number 18 Hind Street, and their former dulce domum is now a non domum.

A further reading elicits the notion that the accompanying illustration of the body found at the scene is an artist's impression of what might be Mr Sprowle, or rather Mr Sprowle at the moment of impact when according to the artist, his arms and legs parted company with his body in rather dramatic fashion.

"Here's a to-do," Waxwing exclaims. "I say, do you suppose it was ..."

Persiflage gives his co-conspirator a stern look.

"Muller said the mantelpiece weren't a safe place to keep it," Waxwing continues, ignoring the look.

Persiflage says nothing.

"I had two guineas and a brand-new pair of trousers in there," Waxwing laments. "Do you think it'd be worth going back to see if they've turned up?"

Persiflage turns on him.

"Of course they haven't turned up, you stupid, bloody fool!" he hisses.

"Now now, no call for bad language. We've both had a shock. Thing like that ... it can ... unseat you a little."

Persiflage downs the last of his porter. Then rises.

"Since our friend Muller is such an expert on ballistics, I think we should pay him a call and see what else he is good at. Hopefully finding temp'ry room and board for two homeless men," he says.

"So you don't want to go and see if any of your stuff is left?"

Persiflage smiles bitterly.

"What 'stuff' would that be, Danton? Eh? My Hind Street Anarchist writings? Leftover bits of nitro-glycerine on the mantelpiece? A big sign saying: we caused it - we blew up the building, we killed the landlord: arrest us now?"

Waxwing, whose diet is somewhat deficient in irony, regards him bemusedly.

"Let them think it is just a gas leak. The moment anybody suspects different, we will be Marked Men," Persiflage says, striking a dramatic pose. "The best thing we can do now is to disappear completely. Just melt away into the background. Muller shall lend us some cash to tide us over until I can get funds released from the bank."

"I didn't know you had funds."

"I will have by close of business tomorrow."

"Ah. I see. *Those* sort of funds."

"Precisely. Now, get your hat and let us sally forth. The old is behind us, the new is before us. This time it wasn't to be, but there will be a next time. And when that next time comes, we shall be ready and waiting for it. Onward to the Big Boom, my friend."

****

A few hours later as dusk gently falls, Inspector Greig pays a visit to Marylebone police office, where a couple of former tenants of number 18 Hind Street are being held pending further questioning.

He is shown into one of the station's bleak whitewashed interview rooms where Miss Adelina Makepiece Chiappa, seamstress, and Miss Florina Sabini, bonnet trimmer, nervously await his arrival.

The women are young, shabbily dressed and white-faced with shock. They sit close together on the bare wooden plank bench that doubles as a bed when the holding cells are full. Someone has given them a mug of tea each. Other than that, they have nothing. Their entire worldly possessions lie in two small baskets at their feet.

They stare at Greig mutely.

"Ladies, I am sorry indeed that you have had to lose your home in such a way," he says. "Do not be afraid, I am sure you have done nothing wrong. I am just making sure all the tenants of number 18 are safe and alive and accounted for."

Miss Adelina Chiappa clutches her empty mug tightly as if she is drowning and it is a life-preserver. She swallows a couple of times, then says shakily,

"We were just coming back to get a bite of supper before our evening work started. We turned the corner and ... and ..." her voice falters, dies away. Tears streak her cheeks.

Miss Florina Sabini, though equally shocked, seems a bit more composed. She sets down her mug and puts a comforting arm round her companion's shoulders.

"Can you tell me who else lived in the house?" Greig asks.

"There was old Mr Sprowle the landlord: he had the ground floor. I gather he's gone. We had the first floor front and the two clerks had the first floor back. That was all, sir," she says.

"The clerks - what can you tell me about them?"

"Edwin and Danny, I think that's what they was called. Never knew their surnames. They moved in a bit before we did.

I b'lieve they worked for a private bank. Kept themselves to themselves. We'd occasionally meet one of them on the landing going out or coming back, but they never spoke to us. Snooty pair they was. Looked down their noses coz we're only working girls."

"Tell him about the man," the seamstress whispers.

"Really? You think he wants to hear about that?"

"Let me be the judge," Greig says.

Miss Florina Sabini shrugs.

"Well, one night some time ago, don't ask me exactly when coz I'm not good with time, we returned very late as the company we work for had a rush order on. Anyways, as we came in, one of them clerks was showing a man out.

"He had a beard and a foreign accent. I heard it when they bid each other goodnight. Which I thought at the time was a bit odd, them being British as far as we could tell."

"We heard the foreigner a couple of times after that," Miss Adelina Chiappa says. "The walls were quite thin, so you could hear people talking and moving around clearly. But that's all we know," she continues. "For the rest, you'll have to ask 'em yourself. And now we have nowhere to live and all our piecework has gone up in smoke."

Her lower lip quivers.

"Which no doubt we will have to pay for, knowing the boss," the bonnet maker adds tartly.

They stare at each other, the disaster of their position mirrored in each face.

"Ladies, I thank you. You are, of course, free to go."

Miss Florina Sabini helps her friend to her feet and adjusts her shawl.

"Thanks ain't going to put a roof over our head, nor food in our bellies," she mutters, pinching her lips together.

Greig reaches in his inner jacket pocket and produces some coins.

"Here, until you get back on your feet."

The bonnet maker snatches them eagerly.

"Well, ain't you a gent. I'd never have thought it, you being a policemen. See, Addy, here's enough for two hot suppers and a bit left over for a night's lodging. We won't be bedding down in the park after all."

The seamstress stares at Greig.

"It's very kind of you, sir. I don't know how we can ever repay you."

"My pleasure, ladies. If you can give me a description of the two clerks who lodged in number 18, we'll call it quits."

"Oh, we can do that an' it's our pleasure. Typical innit, that we're the ones suffering while they're probably living in the lap of luxury somewhere," the bonnet maker declares.

Greig seriously doubts this, but the picture that is emerging, coupled with the non-appearance of the two clerks and story of the foreign visitor, is confirming his worst suspicions. Wherever they are, there is clearly more to the two young men than meets the eye.

After the young women leave, Greig sits on for a while to gather his thoughts. Hind Street, one of those places that exist merely so that people can have come from it, looks like becoming the focus of two criminal investigations.

Even though the street has gone, the houses demolished, and the inhabitants scattered to the four winds, Hind Street still casts its evil shadow, he thinks. And at the centre of it squats the old enemy who can never be defeated: Death.

****

Letitia Simpkins watches the shadows lengthen on her bedroom wall. She has been locked in for hours. Occasionally she hears noises outside on the landing, but nobody comes.

At length, there is the sound of scuffling feet, then someone taps on the door.

"Letty?"

"William, is that you?"

"Yes. Art is here too. Have you done something bad?"

"No, of course not."

"Then who locked you in?"

"Mrs Briscoe."

"Are you going to have any supper? We have had ours ages ago. Now Father and Mrs Briscoe have gone into the study

97

and shut the door," William tells her. "Do you want us to let you out?"

Despite the gravity of her situation, Letitia cannot help smiling. The twins are such dears.

"I'm sure I shall probably be allowed out for some supper soon," she reassures them.

"I wouldn't bother. It was only boiled mutton and rice pudding," William says disgustedly.

"We hate boiled mutton. And rice pudding," Arthur adds.

"Oh-oh … Father is coming out of his study. We had better go to our room and pretend we weren't speaking to you," William whispers.

The scuffling dies away, to be replaced by the sound of footsteps coming up the stairs. Next moment the key is turned in the lock and Mr Simpkins stands in the doorway, his face hard and cold.

"What is this I hear, Letitia? Stealing from my desk?"

"I only took what was my own, Father. The letters were addressed to me. I should have been allowed to read them, surely?"

Mr Simpkins advances into the room, allowing Letitia to catch sight of the black clad figure of Mrs Briscoe hovering on the landing. She is listening intently to the conversation.

"May I remind you Letitia, that nothing in this house is 'your own' as you choose to call it. Your clothes, your food, the roof over your head are all paid for by me. You live here at my expense and are likely to do so for the foreseeable future. Therefore, you will obey me and abide by my decisions in every particular. In my absence, you will obey Mrs Briscoe. Is that clearly understood?"

"Am I not allowed to receive letters from my friends, or call on them?"

"If we decide that such friends are suitable for an unmarried girl, such visits may take place - on a limited basis and only when all your household duties are satisfactorily completed.

"You have been out today I gather, and left many household tasks neglected. Mrs Briscoe has had to organise supper for the boys, a task that you decided was less important than gallivanting around in a carriage with some hoyden of a young woman."

"Daisy Lawton and I were at school together, as you know" Letitia says quietly. "Her family are respectable people - her father is a surgeon. They live in a respectable neighbourhood. She came to offer her condolences on the death of Mama. Was that not a proper thing to do?"

Out on the landing Mrs Briscoe clears her throat. Meaningfully.

"Yes, that reminds me," Letitia's father says. "I should like you to give me your front door key. In future, Mrs Briscoe will take care of it and she will accompany you on all outings. It is not acceptable for a young woman to go about London unchaperoned, as I have told you in the past, though you do not seem to heed my advice as is clear from your correspondents. I will not permit you to mix with such unsuitable people, and there's an end to it. The key."

He holds out his hand.

Letitia stares at him without replying.

"The key, if you please."

The silence deepens.

"I cannot give it to you, Father. Mama gave me the key on the day I came back from boarding school - it was her own key. She told me to keep it safe and never to lose it. I must do as she asked. Besides, it is the only thing I have left to remind me of her. I will accede to the rest of your wishes if I have to, but not this."

She looks down, twisting her hands together, digging her nails into her palm, riding the pain, because right at this moment, the physical pain is not as bad as the pain around her heart.

"I have had nothing to eat since I returned," she says, into the silence. "Am I permitted to go down to the kitchen and find something?"

Her father motions her roughly toward the door. Letitia gets up and walks out with as much dignity as she can muster in the circumstances. As she passes Mrs Briscoe, she pauses, deliberately making eye contact. She holds the hateful woman's gaze for as long as she can bear, then descends the stairs.

The key to the front door is still in her pocket. Letitia finds some string in a kitchen drawer, cuts off a length and hangs the key round her neck. Later, after she has eaten, she will add to it the key to her room. From now on she will make sure that she is never without either of them.

****

A week passes. The Hind Street Anarchists in the personas of Danton Waxwing and Edwin Persiflage have shifted to new quarters and now have rooms above the chemist shop of Bengt & Muller, where their friend Muller both lodges and works.

It is just far enough away from Hind Street for them to feel safe. A new notebook has been started, though still using the old name. Their quarters, though serviceable, do not yet feel permanent enough for a name change.

The principle advantage of the new accommodation is the access it allows them to the stock. After the shop has closed and the main chemist has departed, they come down and under Muller's guidance, they help themselves to various chemicals which can be combined into something potentially explosive. The lamentable loss of the nitro-glycerine is now a thing of the past. They are men with an eye to the future.

And here they both are in a back box of a cheap dining room, enjoying a meat supper together with their friend Muller and Millie girl, who is exhibiting a slight air of huff, having been ignored for several weeks.

The gift of a small bottle of cheap scent, a sample left in the chemist shop by a travelling salesman, has only slightly mollified her. For pretty Millie knows her worth, and if Eddy doesn't - well, there are gentlemen aplenty lining up to take her out and show her a good time.

Millie cuts her beef into tiny squares and covertly scans the other supper-room clientele. Meanwhile Persiflage, whose understanding of the female mind and its workings is as close to non-existent as it is possible to get, continues to act as if there is nothing the matter which, as anybody who has ever been in her situation knows, is Extremely Aggravating.

Eventually, Millie decided to move the huff out into the open by letting her knife and fork clatter onto her plate. Persiflage, who has been in deep discussion with the other two about the usual injustices and extravagances of the upper classes, turns to her.

"What's the bizz? Don't you like your dinner, Millie?" he asks carelessly.

"It ain't the dinner so much as the com'p'ny," the aggrieved one says, tossing her head.

"Well, I'm sorry for that. I thought a nice night out would do you good."

"Ho yes, maybe that woz what you thought, Edwin Persiflage, but my idea of a nice night out ain't sitting in some supper room being totally ignored."

The three men exchange a quick glance. Millie's role in any future operations has not yet reached job specification level, but it is tacitly acknowledged that she is going to be useful at some point.

"Aww Millie," Persiflage says, putting on his most *killing* air. "I wasn't ignoring you. How could I ignore such a *beeyootiful* young lady. It's these two fellows - they will monopolise a chap so. Now then, let me make it up to you - how about if we go for a nice little walk, just us on our own? And you can tell me all about your day. Would you like that?"

"I might."

Persiflage slips an arm round her waist and gives it a little squeeze.

"So should I," he whispers in her ear, blowing into it gently and Millie gives a little giggle and slaps him playfully.

Persiflage throws some coins on the table.

"My share of the supper," he says.

He steers the slightly less disgruntled Millie round the tables and out of the door. Several hours later he will return to the shared room with a satisfied smile on his face, and a mental map of the various entrances and exits to the Palace of Westminster.

****

Meanwhile the engineer sleeps and dreams and heals. Two floors below him, a tea party takes place, music is played, conversations are had, plans are discussed, meals are eaten and the members of the family come and go without him being aware of anything more than a cooling hand on his brow, someone turning his body over in bed and the metallic taste of a teaspoon.

After three days, he is pronounced well enough to be allowed to sit propped up in bed and hold his own spoon. He is just finishing off a bowl of beef broth when Daisy's father enters the sickroom.

"Good, you have eaten all your supper; that is a positive sign," he smiles.

"I might never have eaten again had you not taken me in."

"I think you exaggerate. It is your condition speaking. I am sure you would have been looked after one way or the other."

The engineer makes a wry mouth.

"By whom? I am a disgrace to my family - I should have gone into the church as my father wished. Instead I chose to find God in my own way, through structure and design. I see God's hand in the detail of a drawing, in the building of a bridge or a tunnel. He has disowned me, you know. My father, the archbishop. I am cast into outer darkness."

Mr Lawton glances at the pale intense young face and hot eyes, recognising the fanatic but also seeing the wounded animal beneath. *Mens sana in corpore sano*, he thinks. This young man's mind is as damaged as his body. Both must mend for wholeness to be achieved.

"Come now young man, this will not do. You are recovering well and soon you will be able to return to your work. So let us put all these gloomy reflections to one side and talk of more positive matters," he says, drawing up a chair to the bedside.

A short while later Lawton leaves, having first checked the wound and administered a mild sedative to ensure his patient has a good night's sleep. He has not mentioned his letter to the young man's father, nor the terse response. That is for another time. Sufficient unto the day.

He goes downstairs and enters the sitting room, where his wife is ticking off a list and Daisy is embroidering a fire screen.

Together they make a sweet picture of home and hearth. His wife glances up.

"How is your patient?"

"On the mend. I hope he will make a full recovery - at least physically."

"Why should he not?"

Mr Lawton sighs, running his hands through his hair.

"He is very down - that business with his father, it lowers his spirits."

"Perhaps I should play to him," Daisy suggests. "You always say how much my playing lifts your spirits, Fa."

He smiles indulgently at her.

"It does and I'm sure it would, Daisy-duck. But a sickroom is no place for my little girl. And I am hopeful that in a very short while, he will be fit enough to move back to his digs, now that he has recalled where they are. The railway company are anxious for him to resume work as soon as he is able."

"Poor young man. Can I see him before he goes?"

Mrs Lawton shakes his head.

"That wouldn't be at all suitable, Daisy! An unmarried lady visiting a young man in his bedroom! Now, really! What did they teach you at that school!"

Daisy bends her head over her embroidery. She thinks about the engineer, then she thinks about her friend Tishy. It makes her sad that not everybody is as happy as she is. When she is married, she will try to be a good wife and kind to people less fortunate than herself.

She stabs her needle into her work, rises, kisses her mother and father goodnight and goes upstairs to her room. She has a busy day tomorrow. A tea party at the Barnes Baker's residence. She wants to look her best for it.

Daisy's sleep is sweet and peaceful, unlike that of the engineer. He tosses and turns fitfully in his bed, finally waking with a start. The same old nightmare once again, catching something inside him and tearing it open. It is three in the morning, the house around him is silent and he is as alone as he has ever been.

****

What could be more pleasant than a tea party on a perfectly mown lawn, when the sun shines, the sky is cloudless blue and all the world seems in harmony? From inside the Belgravia town house of the Barnes Bakers, Mrs B would certainly be hard put to find anything to compare.

She stands at the open door of the conservatory, surveying the pleasant scene before her, while checking that all her guests are being served with delicious things to eat.

Daisy Lawton thinks she is in heaven. She sits on a white wicker chair in the shade of a plane tree, her rose sunshade becomingly tilted while two beaux stand by, ready to wait on her. Her plate and cup bear witness to the consumption of cakes and Indian tea. She is all smiles and dimples and white muslin.

Mrs Lawton is delighted with the way things are progressing. She remains in the conservatory with the other Mamas, all pretending to exchange polite chit-chat, while watching their daughters closely.

How nicely upright Daisy sits, she thinks to herself. Nothing worse than a lolling girl. How well she has positioned her parasol - the last thing she needs is to acquire any freckles at this crucial stage of the proceedings.

Digby Barnes Baker, eligible young man about town and prospective Parliamentary candidate is enjoying the tea party as well, even though it is a very feminine affair. He is one of the beaux favoured by Daisy, who is certainly the loveliest girl present.

The more he is in her company, the more Digby thinks she might indeed make him a suitable wife. She is lively, kittenish and very young. She has not been tainted by the wiles and wickednesses of the world. She is the exact opposite of his usual female companions.

Ma is quite right: Daisy Lawton would suit his future career. A man needs someone decorative and supportive. She'd certainly fit the bill better than his cousin Africa, who wouldn't do at all. Her loud laugh and forthright opinions have driven off all the chaps he invited and she is now happily romping with a couple of small children.

Servants glide discreetly to and fro, refilling cups and offering silver platters of sandwiches and tiny cakes. Gentle female voices rise into the air, girlish laughter trills, the fountain fsplashes and the family cat sits washing itself after finding and finishing off a discarded cream cake under one of the tables.

Outside the Belgravia townhouse a line of polished carriages and shiny horses await their owners' return. The grooms and coachmen lounge against them, smoking and flirting with a couple of pretty housemaids who have sneaked away from their duties to distribute some leftover food and mugs of tea.

Only one person seems not to be participating in the jollity of the occasion. Opposite the Belgravia townhouse, in the shadow of a doorway, a young woman waits. She cannot be one of the guests, for she isn't dressed finely enough.

She did not arrive in a glossy carriage, but on foot. Nobody has noticed her presence. She has not been offered anything to eat or drink. She leans her back against the house wall, her eyes fixed intently on the front door opposite, as if she is waiting for somebody to emerge.

Eventually as the sun dips, the guests begin to leave. Farewells are said. Carriages are loaded up and driven off. Daisy and her Mama are the last to leave, seen to their carriage by young Digby himself.

He hands Daisy into the carriage, his brown eyes smiling down into hers. He kisses her gloved hand in a dashing and romantic way. She dimples, blushing sweetly.

The carriage departs. Digby stands on the pavement smiling and waving it off. But just as he is about to re-enter the house, the young woman hurries across the road, calling his name. He turns at the sound of her voice, his mouth dropping open in shocked surprise.

"You?" he exclaims.

"Yes Digby, it's me," she says, laying hold of his sleeve with a shabbily gloved hand. "I have come to see whether you are going to fulfil the promise you made to me before it is too late."

And as she speaks, she lets her shawl drop from her shoulders so that her condition is clearly visible.

****

Up in his sickroom, the engineer wakes refreshed and coherent. His side still aches but the clouds in his head have dispersed and for the first time, he contemplates rising from his sickbed and trying a few steps unaided.

The nurse is not in attendance so he lifts the covers and slides his thin wasted legs to the floor. It takes a while for the giddiness to stop, but at length he is confident enough to let go of the bedpost.

The engineer advances a few wobbly steps, then a few more, heading for the window and the late afternoon sunshine streaming through the muslin curtains like melted butter. There is a chair by the window and he sinks into it, breathing hard, his face flushed with the effort but with an inner sense of triumph.

Beyond the window, he hears the sounds of children playing in adjacent streets, a metal hoop being bowled, the smack of the stick on its sides, and muffled voices from people passing below.

Carriages clip-clop by, their wheels ringing on the cobbles, the coachmen cracking their whips. He drinks in the sounds, letting his mind wonder back to happier times and places.

He is about to rise when a carriage pulls up outside the house. The engineer leans forward, resting his elbows on the sill, watching as the coachman dismounts and helps down an elegantly dressed older woman whom he guesses to be the surgeon's wife. She is followed by a beautiful young lady in a white muslin dress. She carries a rose parasol.

The engineer gasps, feeling the breath leave his body, his heart beating the blood into his face. It is she - the vision on the balcony. His Juliet, his adored Angel. He stares as she enters the house, never glancing up at the window to see his hungry eyes devouring her.

He gets to his feet. A feeling of wild joyous elation fills his body. Now he knows why he was attacked - so that he could be brought here, so that he could meet her. But as he lurches towards the door with no clear plan in mind, just desperate to see her sweet face again, his foot catches on the corner of the rug. The engineer flails his arms, cries out, then falls heavily.

He will be found a short while later by the nurse, lying full length on the floor. There will be blood and froth on his lips. When he regains consciousness, he will remember nothing of the fall, only that for some reason he was suddenly and deliriously happy.

****

Digby Barnes Baker may have been initially dumbstruck by the appearance of the young woman, but he recovers his equilibrium with a speed that bodes well for a future career at Westminster.

Taking her by the arm, he steers her quickly away from the house, marches her to the end of the street and whistles up a cab. He gives the driver instructions to "just drive" and bundles her inside.

"Now then Annie, what's this all about?" he says brusquely, once they are seated opposite each other and the cab is rattling towards the West End.

"You can see what it's about, can't you?" the woman says, her voice low but full of suppressed emotion. "I stayed at the house as long as I could, but in the end, I was showing too much, and Mrs Tabard sacked me. So I came up to London to find you and a pretty time I've had of it tracking you down."

"And what have I to do with your condition, my girl? As I recall, you had several suitors - wasn't there some curate on the scene who was sweet on you?"

She gives him a scornful look, her cheeks flushing.

"You think I'm *that* sort of girl?"

"I have no idea what sort of girl you are. You were a governess. A very pretty governess, and we had a bit of fun together, but that was the beginning and end of it, as far as I was concerned."

"You promised me marriage."

"I promised you nothing of the sort, I assure you. If you think I did, then you are deluding yourself."

"So you aren't going to do the honourable thing?"

"My dear girl, I am soon to become an MP. And I am shortly to be engaged to a young woman from a very well-connected family. The *honourable thing* doesn't come into it."

Her face darkens.

"Maybe I should speak to your father then. Or to your mother. Maybe I should show them what their precious MP son has done. Let us see what they have to say about it."

Now it is his turn to show anger.

"I highly recommend that you do not," he says icily. "For a start, they will not believe you. They may even have you arrested and put in an asylum. Is that what you want to happen?"

She gives a low cry, wringing her hands.

"Then what will become of me? I spent all my money getting here. I have been ill and only just got back on my feet."

Digby Barnes Baker watches her weep and does not try to comfort her.

"Now look Annie, pull yourself together. Let me think what's to be done. You are not a bad person, and I shouldn't like it noised abroad in the future that I turned my back on somebody in need."

He reaches in his coat pocket and produces a fistful of silver coins and a couple of notes.

"Take these ... they will buy you food and lodgings for a while."

She stuffs the money into an inner pocket.

"But what am I supposed to do with a child? Who will employ me as a governess now?"

Digby Barnes Baker stares straight ahead.

"I am sure there are ways to deal with this," he says. "After all, you are not the first young woman to find herself in this predicament, are you? Let me make some inquiries and see what I can find out for you."

He taps on the roof. The cab stops. He hands her his card and opens the door.

"I'll leave you now, Annie. Take care of yourself. Good bye and good luck. When you have found somewhere to stay, write to me. Do not attempt to call at my parents' house though. I warn you, if you do, I shall wash my hands of you altogether. Do you understand?"

Digby jumps down, and slams the door shut. Then he walks briskly away without looking back.

****

Another day in which much is attempted but little achieved is followed by a supper of indifferent quality at a local dining-room. Now Inspector Lachlan Greig sits at his desk writing his letter home.

Dearest Jeanie (he writes)

I hope this finds you and the bairns well. I was delighted to hear of Ishbel's birthday. I think a china dolly is exactly what I would have bought for her. I am delighted in your choice and her pleasure in the gift.

Many thanks for the tin of shortbread, which arrived safely. As usual, your baking is superb but it appears I am not the only one to think so - two pieces have already gone from the tin.

London is an amazing city, Jeannie. Everything is for sale, from goods to people. There are even nightmen here who make a living from human excrement. There is something wonderful in that, I think.

But still I feel lost in the vastness of it all. The streets are never quiet. Though it is nearly June, there is smoke and dust everywhere. I am told there are places where the birds sing all night because the street lighting keeps them awake.

As to my actual investigations, I will not write of them, for I would neither weary or worry you. Suffice it to say that they progress, although not as quickly as I should like. Please send my love and best wishes to the little ones and keep in good health and spirits yourself.

Your loving brother
Lachlan

Greig sits on awhile after finishing the letter, thinking about London, its stink, its sounds, the hoardings over waste ground, the alienation he experiences, as familial as the lines of his cheekbones.

His life has narrowed to such a point that the only thing left is his work: the need to know what is round the next corner.

The compulsion to reach the next junction. This is what gets him up every morning and propels him into the unwelcoming day. It is both a blessing and a curse.

Greig goes out to post his letter. Darkness is filling up the footstreets, leaving the main thoroughfares lit up with gaslight like yellow string. Somewhere in the white distance, there is the sound of church bells.

Above him, a silver peppering of stars. A city bright and cold as a diamond. Cobbles turning to asphalt turning to waste ground. He crosses from pool of light to pool of light, like someone connecting dots.

Everywhere he goes he hears the echo of construction sites. Carpenters and construction teams are still working under artificial illumination. London is one gigantic building site. Sewers, railways, rows of terraces, all are being built at topmost speed.

The city changes, mutates, is different from week to week. It is brittle but unforgiving. The constant spatial alteration means he has a sense of never quite knowing where he is, of people falling away, a line of eyes at a window, gone in a blink.

****

Letitia Simpkins wakes to a day that is already bright with sunshine. She watches the dust motes spiral in a shaft of sunlight like a fairy tornado. It is 6.30, time to start her morning chores.

Her hard-won victory has proved to be Pyrrhic. Yes, she has the key to the front door, but no time to use it. The one remaining housemaid has been sacked, leaving her to do all the cleaning and housework. Only the cook has been retained as both her father and Mrs Briscoe enjoy eating.

She rises, and goes down to the kitchen, where she stokes up the range and places a large kettle on top of it. Father must have hot water to shave, and the boys to wash.

Next, she lays the breakfast table, remembering how she used to lay Mama's tray ready to take up to the sickroom. How easy her life was then, and how little she appreciated it. The bad thing about death is not that it leaves one alone with one's memories, but that it changes the future.

Her future is a thing of the past. It stopped the moment she stepped over the threshold of the place she once thought of as home. Now books are rare treats, to be consumed at night, in the secrecy of her room. She wraps herself in a shawl and burns candles as she reads and makes notes.

Today Mrs Briscoe is going to go through the linen cupboard with her. It is a job that only requires one person, but her presence has been requested. Her presence is always requested. She pours hot water into jugs and begins the weary task of transporting them up to the first floor bedrooms.

By the time the cook has arrived and breakfast is underway, Letitia has already completed two hours of household chores. More await when Mrs Briscoe arrives. But unaccountably, she does not arrive. Father glances at his watch. The boys fidget and spill their tea.

Once breakfast is over, the boys put on their caps, locate their books and slates, and reconvene in the hallway, waiting to be frog-marched to school. But there is still no Mrs Briscoe to escort them.

"Do you wish me to walk the boys to school? They will be late if they don't leave soon," Letitia suggests after another five minutes has passed.

Her father harrumphs, frowns, fiddles with his watch chain, then says brusquely,

"On this occasion, you may do so. But make sure you come straight back afterwards. Mrs Briscoe will be here on your return. I do not know what has caused the delay, but I expect there will be a good reason."

Light of heart, Letitia ties her bonnet and sets out. How wonderful everything looks, fresh, newly minted and sparkling. The air is sweet with the smell of blossom. There are lilacs in neighbouring gardens and she can hear a blackbird singing its heart out.

The boys caper like small colts let out to pasture. They pass the pastrycook's shop and recklessly she treats them all to slabs of the yellow cake piled temptingly on a tray by the door. Happily munching, they progress.

Upon her return, Letitia finds no Mrs Briscoe *in situ*. Instead a note on the hall table from her father informs her that the hated one has a slight indisposition and will not be presencing herself today after all.

Letitia feels her spirits lift even further. She crumples the note and drops it into the parlour grate. Unexpected opportunities like this may never come her way again. They need to be seized with both hands.

She runs upstairs and changes from her shabby black dress into her slightly less shabby black dress. Then she slips out of the front door and sets off determinedly on foot for Regent Street. After all, she reasons to herself, what's the worst thing that could possibly happen to her?

Letitia's welcome, when she finally arrives at the Regent Street Ladies' Literary & Philosophical Society, is warm and effusive and all she could hope for. She is hugged and petted. She is led into the restaurant and bought coffee. It is in complete contrast to the way she is ignored and treated at home.

Carrie Bradstreet and Sarah Lunt sit with her, and gently coax her to tell them what has been happening to her since they last met. Their shocked faces confirm her own deep sense of injustice.

"We hoped you might be among the first group to take the Cambridge Junior Locals," Carrie says, then seeing Letitia's puzzled expression, "that's the exam sixteen-year old boys take. Your brothers will take it when they reach sixteen."

"It is the right of all girls to have the same chances as boys," Sarah says. "Several of our younger members are studying for the exam, in the hope that the authorities relent and let them attempt it. Sophie Jacques is petitioning for permission and we have high hopes she will succeed. Would you like to try for it too?"

"Do you think I am able enough?"

Both women smile at her.

"You are as able as any of us," Carrie says warmly. "Let me fetch you a copy of the syllabus to take away."

"The exam is in December," Sarah says. "It is quite a commitment and I am afraid all the students have had to turn down many invitations to balls and parties and afternoon teas to study for it."

"That will be no hardship - given that I do not receive any invitations. And even if I did, I could not attend."

Letitia gestures at her black frock.

"Of course you couldn't. Poor girl. Sophie is coaching the other candidates. I suggest you write to her and arrange to send her your work to mark. In the circumstances."

Letitia nods. She cannot see Father allowing her to attend classes. Actually, she cannot see Father allowing her to do anything. If she wants to take this exam, she will have to study in secret.

"Thank you, Sarah, I shall do exactly that," she says.

"And here comes Carrie with the syllabus. Let's go through it carefully together before you leave to make sure you understand what is expected of you."

"Will she do it, do you think?" Carrie asks, after Letitia has gone.

Sarah shrugs, "I believe she will try her utmost, Carrie. Whether she'll succeed against the tyranny of her father? Only time will tell."

Letitia returns home shortly after lunch - in her case, a ham sandwich bought from a stall on the way back. There are letters on the mat. She picks them up. One is from Daisy. She takes it up to her room to enjoy at her leisure. Before reading it, she hides under her bed the syllabus, and the notebooks and pencils she has bought.

Daisy writes that she has important news. And a new special friend for Letitia to meet. The word 'special' is underlined three times. Letitia guesses that it refers to the dashing Dragoon officer - Daisy's handsome beau.

She searches her heart and can find no jealousy lurking there. For all her present predicament, she would rather be herself than Daisy Lawton.

Letitia has no illusions about what married life entails - she has heard enough through the bedroom wall, and seen enough at the dining table to convince her that her future lies elsewhere.

As soon as the boys leave for boarding school, she will get down to her studies, pass the exam and then ... but her mind cannot contemplate what 'then' awaits. All she knows is that she must somehow earn her own bread and live independently. Preferably under a different roof.

****

Inspector Lachlan Greig is on covert surveillance with Inspector William 'Ally' Atherton. Recently there have been written and oral complaints from members of the public that it is taking the beat constables far too long to respond to street crime and robberies.

As usual these complaints have been picked up by the press, inflated beyond all reason and put on the front pages, resulting in a week of headlines like:

London Police Asleep on The Job (*The Daily Sun*)
Crime Flourishes While Coppers Kip (*The Inquirer*)

The police force's nemesis Richard Dandy has even gone so far as to declare that the presence of the press is a greater deterrent to the London criminal fraternity than the forces of law and order.

Greig is tempted to call him out, given that he has conspicuously failed to supply evidence of crimes that haven't been committed.

Be that as it may, the Superintendent is taking the complaints and the bad press seriously. Thus, the senior officers have bowed to public displeasure and decided that an unexpected morning visit to their men on the street might be a strategic move.

The two men walk on at the steady pace known throughout the police as 'proceeding'. Goods carts clatter by as they progress. London. It doesn't seem beautiful to Greig. Only permanent. They proceed in silence. London is like that, he thinks, it renders you speechless.

They pass rows of new houses, hurriedly thrown up by speculative builders to meet the growing population of the city. The houses all have the same three storey design. The top storey, the servant floor, is narrower as if the builders had run out of room in the dull London sky.

Some of the houses still bear the name of the developer. Some are unoccupied. Small dusty children follow the two

114

detectives, keeping their distance. Their ragged clothes and pinched little faces remind Greig of the children that hang about Covent Garden, snatching bruised fruit and sleeping in baskets or under carts.

London. The greatest city in the world. A place where children are abandoned to fend for themselves on the streets, and babies are sold off to be neglected and deliberately starved to death. The city is shaped by the shadow that it cast.

While awaiting developments in his investigation into the eleven (now twelve) baby murders, Greig has been looking into the backstreet practice of child minding for profit. What he has uncovered appals him. So many tiny babies kept in a state of continued sedation so that they perished from severe malnutrition.

In the interest of research, he has ploughed through page after page of coroners' reports all giving 'debility from birth' as the cause of death, when the truth is far darker, and probably contained in a bottle of Godfrey's Cordial or some other paregoric.

And these reports are only the tip of the iceberg. The ones whose deaths are recorded. Many other infants are probably just dropped into the river, left in a back alley, or dumped on the steps of a city church.

Greig has seen advertisements in newspapers for childcare and confinement services. A euphemism if ever there was one. Wherever there is money to be made, there are people eager to make it, even at the expense of innocent babes.

He regards it as deeply ironic that there are laws against mistreating animals, strict licensing laws for the numerous cow-keepers who supply the city with fresh milk, but not a single law to safeguard the lives of children.

It is the utter waste of potential that gets to Inspector Greig. Each dead child might have grown up to be a person, to live and laugh and enjoy life. That is why he is grimly determined to catch the Halls and make a public example of them.

As if reading his thoughts, Atherton breaks the silence and asks,

"How's your little matter coming along?"

"It moves forward, albeit slowly."

"I was mentioning your business to some of my pals in Scotland Yard," Atherton says. "They were of the opinion that you are wasting your time."

"They are entitled to their opinion."

"Ah, face it man, you haven't a chance of finding two people in a city of this size. There's millions of people and a billion places to hide. City's *built* of bolt-holes. Now, I am on the brink of bringing a couple of notorious villains to justice and I could do with an extra pair of hands. What do you say?"

"I say good luck to you. You go your way and I'll go mine."

Atherton gives him a sideways glance, raising his eyebrows. Greig pretends he hasn't seen it. He is not overfond of the fair haired, moustached, cigar smoking inspector, who has a reputation as a ladies' man - ladies being a polite way of putting it.

They turn a corner and spy two young constables leaning against a wall doing nothing much. Seeing their senior officers approach, both suddenly straighten up and look terrible alert.

"All right men?" Atherton inquires.

"Nothing to report sir," one says.

"Quiet as the grave," adds the other.

"Stay alert," Atherton nods. "The morning is yet young."

"Oh, we are ready," the first constable says. "Nothing will get past *us*!"

Privately Greig doubts this. In his experience, most beat constables had an uncanny ability to develop selective deafness and temporary blindness, unless a crime was taking place directly under their noses.

"See that it doesn't," he says crisply. "We do not want any more unfortunate stories in the newspapers."

"Ah, that was D division, sir. Not us," the first constable says virtuously.

"Well, as nothing criminal seems to be occurring in this doorway, maybe you should be on your way?" Greig suggests drily.

The two stroll off at a slouching pace. Greig imagines their conversation as soon as they are out of earshot.

Atherton touches his elbow.

"Shall we move on? I have to meet one of my contacts."

That was the other thing about Atherton, Greig thought. He had numerous 'contacts'. Most of them were female. Atherton swore that his interest was purely professional and that they, the 'contacts', were a useful conduit to the criminal underclass. What Mrs Atherton thought about it, nobody knew.

He follows Atherton through an archway, down a cobbled passageway and out into the bright sunshine once more. A few more paces, another footstreet, and his companion stops at the door of a shabby public house.

The painted sign proclaims that this is the Queen's Head, though from the peeling paint, it is hard to make out which queen and from what country.

"You are welcome to join us, if you wish," Atherton says.

Greig hesitates, then shrugs.

"Maybe just for a short while, then".

Atherton pushes open the door. The two men are greeted by a nasal kaleidoscope of smells broken down into: tobacco, stale beer, and cheap perfume overlaid with animal dung: the pub has a piggery to the rear.

Atherton glances round, then heads towards a round table where sits an attractive young lady in a low-cut dress. Greig follows him. On closer inspection, the attractive young lady is maybe not so attractive as she appeared from a distance. Nor as young. She has reddish dyed hair, a battered brown bonnet and the pale ashen complexion of a consumptive.

"Morning Freda," Atherton greets her. "Another gin?"

"Oh, go on then, h'if you insists," the not-so young lady agrees.

She hitches her salmon satin top back up onto her bony saltcellar shoulders. There is a grease stain on the front of it.

"Who's yer friend?"

"Fellow I work with. Lachlan - this is the lovely Freda Dowling."

Freda stares at Greig. Her blue eyes are heavily lidded and set slightly too close together, giving the impression of someone who might possibly be sixpence short of a half-crown.

"Nice to meet you," she says.

117

Greig perches temporarily on the edge of a bentwood chair.

"Any friend of Willyum's is a friend of mine."

"Indeed."

"Especially a good lookin' one like what you are."

"You are too kind, madam."

"Madam?" Atherton places three glasses on the table. "Hear that, Freda?"

"Very p'lite, I say," she says, giving Greig a slightly imbecilic smile. Her lips are wet and slack, her teeth stained and uneven. One bottom tooth is missing.

Atherton takes a long pull at his drink, then wipes his moustache with the back of his hand.

"So, Freda, how's tricks?"

"Not bad."

She pulls a man's gold watch out of her pocket.

"Look what one of my gentl'men friends give me."

Atherton takes the watch, turns it over, then hands it to Greig who reads the inscription on the back which says: *To Fred from your loving Mama.* Carefully keeping his facial expression tuned to neutral, he places the watch on the table.

"Nice watch."

"Another friend's gonna change Fred to Freda. Not that I had a lovin' Mama, but a gold watch's a gold watch, innit?"

"Indeed."

Finishing his drink, Greig signals to Atherton that he is leaving.

"I'll be seeing you later."

Atherton stands. They exchange a look over the top of the woman's head. Greig inclines his head significantly towards the watch, pats his pocket. Atherton nods his understanding. Without saying another word or giving him a backward glance, Greig walks out into the muddy shit-smelling street.

He had recognised the watch as soon as he saw it: it was identical to the one Fred Grizewood, the hapless young engineer, fiddled with each time they'd met. It needed only a look at the inscription to confirm his suspicions.

Atherton was wrong: it was possible to find people in a city the size of London. You just needed a chance meeting and a lucky break.

****

By no stretch of the imagination is the engineer a man who gets lucky breaks dropped into his lap. Yet here he is, in the very house inhabited by his beloved Angel. Since the revelation of her presence, he has taken to watching the coming and goings of the Lawton family from his window. He now knows that her name is Daisy, and that she laughs like a tinkling bell.

Sometimes when the nurse is off duty, the engineer walks stiff legged to the door. He opens it, and stands on the landing clutching the bannister rail giddily. From there he can hear the distant sounds of the family taking their meals, or the pretty rippling piano music, or the servants coming and going, and answering the door.

Recently he has noticed them opening the door with increasing regularity to an elegantly dressed young man, sometimes accompanied by a rather untidy young woman with a loud voice and a horsy laugh. He has seen his beloved Angel walking down the road with the man, her hand laid lightly upon his arm.

Every time he thinks of this, the engineer feels a fear rise in him, physical as vomit. He sits in the chair, scoured out, empty. Of late, his dreams have become more vivid and even more terrifying.

He cries out, clawing the bedclothes until the nurse wakes him, gives him more of the soothing drugs. In one of these wakings, he is sure he has seen Lawton standing by his bedside, his expression grave.

The engineer hears the sound of horse and carriage. He heaves himself upright and hurries to the window. He sees the family carriage standing in the street below, the footman helping down a thin pale-faced young woman dressed in deep mourning.

It is not the young man. His relief is almost palpable. He walks to the desk that has been provided for him, and takes out a sheet of paper from the folder that has been brought over from his previous lodgings along with the rest of his possessions.

He is working secretly on a drawing of his Angel, constructing her features with the precision and accuracy that he brings to all his work. Today, he will draw her rippling hair. He lays out pencils, eraser, ink bottle and pen. When he has finished the drawing, he will return to work. But he will take her with him into the uncertain future.

Meanwhile downstairs in the parlour Daisy and Letitia sit side by side on the striped Regency sofa. Daisy leans forward and pats Letitia's arm affectionately.

"How pale you look, Tishy dear. Are things still as bad for you?"

"They are certainly not improving."

"And that horrid woman?"

"Is still as horrid. But I have my own front door key, so she cannot stop me from leaving the house. And it is my intention to leave for good, one day."

Daisy's eyes widen.

"You have a secret admirer? Oh, do tell."

Letitia laughs.

"No, nothing as grand. But I hope to take an important exam at the end of the year which will allow me eventually to earn my own living."

Daisy's alabaster brow furrows gently.

"I ... am glad for you. If it is what you want."

"It is, Daisy. I can think of nothing better than earning my own bread and paying my own rent and being dependent upon nobody but myself."

"But what on earth would you do?" Daisy asks, puzzled.

Letitia smiles at her.

"Anything I wanted to. I could become a teacher in one of the new ladies' colleges. I should like that, I think. The main thing is to gain some qualifications. The more I get, the more I can earn."

"But don't you want to get married and have children?"

Letitia takes a deep breath, reminding herself before she opens her mouth, that Daisy's experience of what marriage is like is very different to hers. Here is no bullying, no fear and that other thing that she can barely name, but knows went on in the privacy of her parents' bedroom.

"Oh Daisy," she laughs lightly. "Who would have me? I am plain and I am poor and I have opinions. No man in his right senses would take me on."

Daisy pouts, sighs, stares at her friend in perplexity, then signals to the maid to pour the tea. The conversation steers itself into safer waters, much to Letitia's relief. A discussion about clothes and bonnets and fans might be as incomprehensible to her as her preoccupations are to Daisy, but at least she can join in, albeit at a fairly primary level.

Eventually the tea is drunk, and every aspect of Daisy's wardrobe has been brought under scrutiny. Letitia is just thinking about going, when Daisy suddenly takes her hand.

"Well now Tishy, I still haven't told you my news. You will never guess, so I shall come straight out with it: I am about to receive a proposal of marriage!"

"Aha! your handsome Dragoon officer has declared his undying love?"

"Oh no, it is not him," Daisy shakes her head dismissively. "It is from a young man called Mr Digby Barnes Baker - we met at a ball. His Mama and mine are old friends. He is very handsome too, and has quite the most impeccable manners. And his linen is beautiful. He is going to be a Member of Parliament and do all sorts of good things for the poor people he represents. That is what he says and I believe him. See - under his influence, I am becoming quite *political*."

She glances at the little carriage clock on the mantelpiece.

"He will be here very soon - I hope you do not have to hurry away for I so want you to meet him."

Letitia sets her teacup carefully down in its saucer.

"I am delighted for you, Daisy," she says, choosing her words with care. "If you love him dearly, then that is all."

"Oh, I haven't received the proposal yet. But I think I may accept him when he proposes and I'd hardly do that if I didn't love him, would I?"

"I expect not. But it is very sudden. A few weeks ago, you were in love with someone else."

"Oh, that wasn't love, not at all. You are so droll!" Daisy laughs.

She pauses, her head on one side.

"Listen, I hear a carriage drawing up. It is him. Now Tishy, you must like him, I insist upon it."

"I shall adore him on sight, I promise you."

"It may be quite a long engagement - Mama says she does not want me to marry until I am eighteen and he is yet to secure a seat in Parliament."

"I shall come to the church whenever it is, and wish you a long and happy marriage," Letitia says, as the door opens, and the parlour maid announces the visitor.

Later, as the Lawton carriage carries her back home, Letitia thinks about Mr Digby Barnes Baker. Obviously, nobody could ever be good enough for her dear friend Daisy, that is a given. Equally obviously, the young man she has just met possesses good looks and charm in abundance and she can quite see why Daisy is smitten with him.

And yet. Letitia is not entirely convinced by Mr Digby Barnes Baker and his impeccable linen. She noticed that he seemed excessively fond of his own voice and his own opinions, and when she ventured one of hers - on the subject of female education, a bemused expression crossed his handsome features, and he ignored her.

She is going to have to be careful and diplomatic when she and Daisy meet next. The young man is Daisy's choice, and she has no reason nor business to speak against him. Maybe it was just a case of first impressions and she will warm to Mr Barnes Baker upon further acquaintance.

The carriage drops Letitia outside the house. She has an essay to finish and hurries up the path, eager to get back to her studies. Unlocking the door, she manages to make it to the top of the stairs before the parlour door is flung open and Mrs Briscoe, arms folded, appears on the threshold.

"Ah, there you are," she exclaims angrily. "I have been waiting to go through the linen cupboard."

Letitia pauses, turns and regards her coolly.

"I was not aware that my presence was required. Surely, if you believe it is your business to sort through our family linens, you could perform the task yourself."

Mrs Briscoe advances a few steps closer, planting her feet firmly on the linoleum floor covering.

"Where have you been?"

Letitia pinches her lips.

"I insist upon knowing your whereabouts at all times, miss! I am here at your father's request to safeguard his family name and reputation. Answer at once. I will not tolerate any more of this wayward behaviour nor any further insolence from you."

"My father's *reputation* - as you call it - is hardly going to be enhanced by your constant presence here," Letitia says, stung (unwisely) into responding.

"Meaning what, exactly?" Mrs Briscoe says quietly, advancing to the bottom of the stairs.

"I think you know very well what I mean. My Mama has barely been buried a month."

"And who was responsible for her death, I wonder? Who left her unattended? Who was gadding out and about while she suffered and died alone?"

It is too much. White-faced with fury Letitia descends the stairs. The words pour forth, hot and angry,

"How dare you speak of my mother? You are not fit to mention her name! You are a vile vile woman and I hate you! And for your information, my Mama died from a weak heart - not from anything I did or did not do. And that has been confirmed by a qualified surgeon."

Without pausing for breath, Letitia lifts the lid that has only barely been holding down an entire young womanfull of anger and slaps Mrs Briscoe hard around the face. Then she rushes upstairs and unlocks her bedroom door.

Only when she is on the other side does she finally give way to tears of rage and mortification. She hears the hated enemy mount the stairs, then rattle the door handle.

"Your father shall hear of this," Mrs Briscoe shouts through the keyhole. "Oh yes indeed he will. And I wouldn't like to be in your shoes when he does!"

****

Inspector Greig awaits the return to Bow Street of his colleague Atherton. As soon as he arrives, smelling richly of brandy and cigar smoke, Greig beckons him into his office.

"Well?" he queries.

In response, Atherton brings out the gold watch from an inner pocket and drops it onto the desk. Greig picks it up, turns it over.

"How did you get her to part with it?"

Atherton laughs.

"By the time she'd drunk her fill, I could have taken whatever I wanted from the silly bitch. I left her asleep and snoring on the pub table. When she wakes, she'll presume one of the regular customers robbed her. That's if she even remembers she once owned a gold watch. What's your interest in it?"

"I'm pretty sure it belongs to the young engineer Fred Grizewood, the man who was stabbed and robbed. If he identifies it, then your Freda could be the link to his attacker. I'd value knowing the name of the man who gave it to her ... and where he says he got it."

"Ah. I see. I'll ask her then. Hopefully she'll remember his name. Mind you, the stupid cow doesn't know if she's on her arse or her elbow most of the time. Brain totally rotted by gin. Well, the fact that she talks to me is proof, isn't it?"

Once Atherton has left, Greig pockets the watch and sits for a while thinking through his next move. Suddenly it looks as if he might be about to catch both Grizewood's attacker and the baby killers in one fell swoop.

Greig has no illusions. He knows that the best laid schemes can go awry in an instant. But this is as close as he's come to success, so close he can almost touch it. It feels as if a door has unlocked itself and blown wide open. All he has to do, is walk through.

A short while later Greig arrives at the Lawton house, where a maid takes his card into the drawing room. A few seconds later, Mrs Lawton appears in the hallway.

"I am afraid my husband is not back from the hospital, inspector," she says.

Greig explains the reason for his visit.

"Ah, that poor young man," she says. "Yes, he is still here. My husband was hoping he'd be well enough to return to his lodgings and to his work long before now, but ..." she hesitates.

"He is still unwell?"

"It is worse than that," she lowers her voice, "the blow to his head is causing him to have seizures .... fits. They are quite severe, I gather and have left him somewhat confused as a result. It is impossible for him to leave at the moment, my husband tells me. I shall ask the nurse to take you up to him - perhaps the return of his watch may lift his spirits."

Greig follows the grey-uniformed nurse up two flights of stairs and then into a bright attic room. The engineer sits at a desk, bent over a drawing. He hurriedly covers it over as they enter.

"Mr Grizewood, I hope I find you well," Greig says.

He tries not to let his expression belie his words. The engineer seems to have declined physically since they last met in the hospital. His face has an unhealthy waxen hue, with two hectic spots of colour on each cheek. His dark eyes dart about the room, settling momentarily here, then there.

"I am well - though I do not enjoy the same health that I did," the engineer says. "I am awaiting an important letter from Mr Bazalgette - once it arrives, all will be as before. Yes. And it will come, the letter, I know it."

"Ah," Greig nods.

Behind his back, out of the engineer's sight, the nurse shakes her head.

"Now Mr Grizewood, we mustn't excite ourselves. See - your visitor has brought you something."

Greig produces the watch and hands it to the engineer, who stares at it wonderingly, turning it over in his hand to read the inscription. He glances up at Greig, his face suddenly elated.

"I believe this is yours, is it not?" Greig says.

"It is mine. My mother gave it to me. She is dead, you know."

Greig acknowledges the remark without speaking.

"My father has rejected me, did you know that also?" the engineer's voice is high, wild.

The nurse steps up to him, makes soothing noises, measures some drops from a bottle onto a spoon, offers it to him.

"But you have your watch back - and soon we hope to catch the man who attacked you and bring him before the courts," Greig says.

The engineer mutters something, then sighs and closes his eyes. His shoulders slump.

"It would be best if you left him now, sir," the nurse whispers. "He will sleep soon."

Greig takes a final look at the young man, now sitting sideways in his chair, his mouth slightly ajar, the watch dangling from his fingers by its chain. Increments of light and shadow cross the floor from the casement window, gilding his cheekbones with gold. There is something both pitiful and monstrous about him: a presence and an absence at the same time.

He follows the nurse downstairs.

****

It feels late. Not quite night, as there is some kind of daylight outside the window shutters. Letitia Simpkins crouches in a corner on the floor of her room. If she doesn't move, if she breathes very quietly, then this thing she cannot acknowledge has happened will go away, and all will be as before.

It was a strategy she adopted at boarding school, when the misery of being overlooked, of not being taken home for the holidays, overwhelmed her. She clasps her knees in her hands, wincing as the bruise to her left wrist sends stars of pain shooting up her arm.

She rocks to and fro gently. A sound escapes between her teeth. She is crying but there is nothing to be done. She swallows, her throat clicking on the tears. She feels like one who has turned around in a dream, knowing that something terrible awaits.

For a while after the shouting and the beating had stopped, and the door had been slammed shut, she'd heard the twins scuttering about on the landing, calling her name softly. She had not been able to answer.

Her life has fallen away into itself without plot or premonition. Everything is external, the details withdrawn. Her head is empty as the volute of a shell. Her world is reduced; it has become frightening, impossible in its thinness.

Now there is nothing. Just the darkness and the unravelling of everything and the silence, rising and rising around her.

****

Alone in his room, the engineer bends over his drawing, totally absorbed in conjuring up blonde curls with his set of pencils. Only when he is completely satisfied that he has every strand of Daisy's hair accurately down on paper does he open the bottle of ink and start to go over his outline. At some point the nurse comes in with his supper; he consumes it greedily. She seems pleased at the return of his appetite.

Later he will go to bed, tired out by his exertions, the watch placed on his bedside table like a talisman. The light above his bed will hiss and choke on its own gas. He will reach up into its glare and turn it out.

Tonight, he falls asleep quickly, moonlight twitching across his face, ghosting his pale features. He dreams of blonde hair, soft and glowing like molten gold.

****

Letitia wakes early, segueing from dream pain to actual pain. She rises with difficulty. Her left wrist and side are bruised. The left side of her face feels tender and swollen. She dare not look in the mirror. Instead, she hobbles to the door and descends sideways, step by difficult step down to the basement kitchen.

She drinks some water and splashes her face. For a moment, it hurts so badly she can hardly breathe. It is impossible to fill and lift the big black kettle, so she resorts to a couple of saucepans instead. While they slowly come to the boil on the hob, she leans against the scrubbed deal table and considers her position.

Last night she was given two choices: either she comply with her father's wishes to the letter, or she will be thrown out of the house and left to starve in a gutter. She has no doubt whatsoever that her father will fulfil his threat if she does not accede to his demands.

Letitia recalls the way her mother's face changed at the sound of her father's footsteps in the hallway, the way all life drained out of it as she tried to become small and insignificant, her eyes darting nervously from side to side in anticipation of his appearance, fingers plucking at her sheet.

She pours hot water into the twins' jug and carries it carefully upstairs, setting it down outside their room. She opens the door, to be greeted by the familiar fusty smell of sleeping boys. She goes to each bed, shakes them gently awake, pours their water into their bowls. The boys sit up, regarding her with horrified expressions.

"What's wrong with your face?" William asks, wide-eyed and staring.

"Toothache," Letitia lies.

"Does it hurt?"

She turns away from his gaze, unable to sustain the fiction without breaking down.

"Please get up now. Dress and come down for your breakfasts," Letitia says shakily, averting her face as she leaves their room.

She hauls the other jug of water upstairs and leaves it outside her father's room. Finally, she returns to the kitchen, where the cook has now arrived and is taking off her bonnet in preparation for work.

"Gawd miss, what happened to you? You look like you went two rounds in the boxing ring," she gasps.

Letitia tells her the same story. The cook, who is not as gullible as the twins, regards her sceptically with pursed lips.

"If you say so," she says. "Shall I make you some porridge - slip down nice and easy, and the hot would help the swelling go down a bit."

Letitia nods. "That would be very kind of you. And now I should like to discuss the day's meals," she says.

The cook waves her away.

"You leave it to me, miss. You go straight back upstairs. 'Toothache' like that needs all the rest you can give it. And so I shall tell Mr Simpkins when he comes down for breakfast. If he asks."

The tacit implication that he won't, for obvious reasons, which they both know, though neither is acknowledging it, hangs in the air between them.

Folding her arms, the cook nods towards the green baize door.

"Off you go. I shall be up with your hot water as soon as I've got my traps off and my apron on. It's going to be a warm day, so we won't need no fires and the dust can wait for a day or so."

Letitia tries to smile, wincing as pain stabs her jaw. She climbs the stairs and gets back into her bed. At least it wasn't her right wrist, she reminds herself. She can still compose letters; she can still produce essays. Her life has not come to a complete stop, just a brief temporary halt.

****

For Persiflage and Waxwing, anarchists *manqués*, life seems to be inching along unsatisfactorily in the metaphorical slow lane. Here they are at their favourite watering hole being waited on by the unattractive barmaid with the squint and downturned mouth.

They are drinking flat beer and bemoaning their lot. At least Persiflage is bemoaning. Waxwing is more concerned by the state of his shoes.

"I wanted them pointed - do you think these are pointed enough?" he asks, stretching out a foot for contemplation and comment.

Persiflage ignores him.

"I mean, I know I have somewhat broad feet, but these look more square-toed than pointed to me."

It is Friday evening. The weekend stretches ahead. The city awaits, brimful of more pleasures and delights than two young men could possibly imagine. And a lot more that they probably couldn't.

"Only I was looking at that messenger boy Willoughby's boots and they were considerably more pointed than mine were," Waxwing continues. "I wonder if I should return them - what do you think, Edwin?"

"I think it is time to lay down a marker," Persiflage says savagely, running a finger round the rim of his dusty glass. "I think it is time to let those who hold the reins know that we are primed and ready."

Waxwing frowns. His train of thought, which has been happily pottering along on a branch line, has suddenly been diverted.

"Ah. Umm. What reins are you talking about? I say, steady on, we aren't going to hurt any animals, are we? I shouldn't like to do that."

Persiflage rolls his eyes.

"I'm talking about people, not horses, you fool! The people who live in big houses and splash us with mud as they pass in their shiny carriages. The people who think they own us all, body and soul."

"Ah. Those people. Now I understand you. So, what are we going to do?"

Persiflage's face takes on a dreamy expression.

"We are going to send a little message," he says. "Boom," he adds nodding significantly.

Waxwing stares at him, open-mouthed.

"Yes, my friend. It will be the forerunner to the Big Boom."

"Didn't we do that when we were living in Hind Street?"

"No Danton, that was not the Big Boom, that was an unfortunate accident."

"It killed Mr Sprowle, though, didn't it? I'm not sure we should kill people."

Persiflage regards him askance. Truth to tell, he is becoming fed up with the oafish stupidity of his erstwhile roommate, who seems to lack the fire in his belly that he and Muller possess.

"Mr Sprowle was a dirty smelly old man who overcharged us on the rent and stuck his nose into our business whenever he could. The world is well rid of him," he says firmly.

"But did he deserve to die, is the question?" Waxwing muses, tracing patterns on the dusty table with a finger.

"Danton, we are *Anarchists*. You *do* understand what that means, don't you? Anarchists create anarchy. In a state of anarchy, people may just possibly die, yes - but that is their destiny. It is what happens. The old and rotten has to be cleared out to make way for the new."

"Like Hind Street, you mean," Waxwing says, brightening.

"Yes, Danton, yes. Exactly like Hind Street. Or rather, not like Hind Street in that this will be a deliberate act and I have already chosen our target."

"You have?" Waxwing is wide-eyed with admiration. "What is it?"

"Not what, my friend, who. We are going to blow up the statue at the top of Portland Place. The one of that fat German. Every time I pass his smirking face it makes my blood boil.

"They spend a fortune putting up a statue to some foreign fool with ugly legs when there are people dying in the streets and back courts for lack of food."

"Too right," Waxwing says. He pauses. "And when are we going to do it?"

Persiflage glances round, then lowers his voice.

"By Monday morning the world as these people know it will have changed, my friend. Changed forever."

He gulps down the last mouthful of beer and gets to his feet.

"Come Danton, there is much work to do in preparation. We have finally grasped the tiller of Fate and pushed the boat of Revolution away from the shore of Apathy. There is no turning back now."

****

Letitia Simpkins passes through the ornate gates of Kensal Green cemetery. In her hand is a tiny bunch of flowers picked from the garden, which she will shortly place on her mother's grave. It has been a while since she last visited. Indeed, it has been many days since she set foot outside the house.

Nor would she have today, but her father and Mrs Briscoe have left for the weekend to visit the latter's elderly mother in Harrogate. She is ailing. They have taken the reluctant twins with them. The whole party departed early in the morning to catch the first train north from Kings Cross and will not return until late Sunday night.

The bruises to Letitia's face and side are healing. The bruise upon her soul is not. It remains as raw as the day the blows to her body were struck. But her spirit remains unbroken, and much to her surprise, she is finding a certain satisfaction in realising that she cannot be 'made' to say or do anything against her will.

She has also discovered an unexpected ally in the cook, who dislikes Mrs Briscoe almost as much as she does. The good woman has been secretly supplementing her diet, strictly against the orders of her father, who has declared that until Letitia apologises to Mrs Briscoe, she is to have nothing but bread and water to eat, and that in very small quantities only.

More importantly, the cook has provided her with the spare key to the kitchen door. For some unaccountable reason neither her father nor Mrs Briscoe seem to have realised that there is a servant way in and out of the house. Or entertained the notion that Letitia might stoop so low as to use it.

So although she surrendered her front door key - in reality it was torn from her neck on that dreadful evening, Letitia has obtained the means to leave the house, subject to the absence of Mrs Briscoe. Who is not currently present. So here she is, face hidden under some black veiling which she has pinned to her bonnet.

On the way to the cemetery, she has posted her latest essay to her tutor, also a carefully worded letter to Daisy. Letitia has sometimes pondered, in the dark hours before dawn when hunger gnawed at her and sleep abandoned her, what it must be like to live in the sunny uplands of Daisy's world.

Daisy would certainly never be reduced to contemplating what she is planning to do later on, after her visit. But then Daisy has not had to walk for miles in shoes that are worn out and stockings that are more holes held together by darns than anything else.

Letitia reaches the plain white marble headstone that marks the final resting place of her mother. The simple inscription reads: *Here lies Mary Eliza Simpkins, wife of Reginald Simpkins. "Taken too soon and much missed."*

Kneeling down, she pulls out the weeds that have already started to encroach, and places her flowers gently against the headstone. Tears prick her eyelids and for a brief moment, she surrenders to the sense of abandonment that is never far from the surface of her life. If she lay down on her mother's grave and died right now, who would care? Who would mourn her?

"I am sorry, Mama," she whispers. "I should have been a better daughter. Please forgive me."

Wiping her eyes, Letitia scrambles to her feet and straightens her shoulders. This will not do. She cannot afford to weaken. She takes a final long look at her mother's grave, imprinting the image of it on her subconscious. She does not know when she will be allowed to visit it again.

Then she turns and walks away. It is time to do what has to be done.

A short while later, Letitia Simpkins stands outside a pawnbroker's shop in a fashionable district of the city (for even Fashion cannot dispense with its pawnbrokers). She stares at the unredeemed items in the window: enamels and miniatures, cashmere shawls, diamond rings, mathematical instruments, buhl clocks, watches, gold chains, and bracelets, while she mentally screws her courage to the sticking point. When she reaches it, she enters the shop.

The door opens into the common shop where a number of shabby looking individuals are engaged in earnest discussions with the gentleman behind the counter. From their casual attitude, it is clear that long usage has rendered them indifferent to public scrutiny of their poverty.

Glancing up, the gentleman sees Letitia's bewildered look, and directs her to a side passage from which some half-dozen doors lead to small closets facing the counter. Here the more timid or discreet customers can wait, shrouded from their fellows, until the pawnbroker behind the counter is disposed to attend to them.

Letitia waits patiently until the pawnbroker, who has curly black hair, a flashy diamond ring and a double silver watch-guard, arrives on the other side of the closet. She fumbles in her bag and brings out some jewellery boxes.

"I should like to pawn these things, please," she says hesitantly, placing the boxes on the counter and not making eye contact.

He nods, produces a jeweller's loupe on a chain and begins to examine the contents of the boxes: a gold eternity ring, a pair of ruby and diamond earrings and a silver cross on a long chain. All belonged to Letitia's mother and should, by rights, have been passed down to her as the eldest (and only) daughter.

They have not been though. Instead Letitia has removed the boxes from a drawer in her mother's dressing table. Initially she wanted to have the pieces as keepsakes. Now she needs money for such essentials as writing paper, ink and shoes.

The pawnbroker does some calculations in a notebook, then names his price. It is sufficient for her immediate needs and more. She knows she could probably get a better price if she haggled, but she has never haggled in her life and isn't sure how to begin.

So she hands over the boxes, gives the gentleman her name and address and a promise that these items are indeed her property, and receives in return a roll of bank notes and a pawn ticket.

Unexpectedly richer than she has been for a very long time, Letitia leaves the pawnshop, stashing the money safely at the bottom of her bag. Her first port of call is a stationer's, where she replenishes her diminished stock of writing materials.

Then passing a tea-room, she decides to throw financial caution to the wind and treat herself to afternoon tea. She has not eaten properly for a long time and the sight and the smell of all the freshly baked bread and cakes on display almost overpowers her.

A waitress shows her to a table in the window and hands her the menu. Letitia orders sandwiches, scones, a plate of cakes and a pot of tea. While she waits for her order to arrive, she watches the people on the other side of the glass.

The tea-room is very close to a park. Families and couples pass by in an endless stream all going in that direction. The women wear bright coloured dresses, and carry pretty parasols. The children smile and hop and skip. She envies them their happiness.

After a while, she starts to notice the others - the ill clad and barefoot children in the gutter. The pinch-faced women with ragged shawls. The faces at the edge of the banquet. The lookers-on in the doorways. The unwelcome reminder that life is not all sunshine and roses for everybody in the great city.

The waitress brings her tea to the table. Letitia consumes it with unladylike rapacity, making short work of the dainty sandwiches and the warm scones with their pats of sweet yellow butter. The richness of it leaves her dizzy and she has to close her eyes for a few minutes.

When the last crumbs have been consumed, she pays for her tea with a few of her precious coins and walks out into the afternoon sunshine, her spirits buoyed by her full stomach.

She is just passing the British Museum and wondering whether she might go in to look at the objects on display, when her attention is drawn to a couple walking just ahead of her.

The elegantly dressed man is Daisy's future fiancé Digby Barnes Baker - she is sure it is him and on his arm, a slender woman with blonde curls and a pretty straw bonnet.

It must be Daisy. Letitia's heart leaps. What a lucky coincidence. She quickens her pace and draws alongside. Reaching out her hand, she touches the woman lightly on the elbow.

"Daisy?" she murmurs in a low voice.

The young woman looks round. Letitia's mouth opens in an O of surprise. It is not Daisy; it is another young woman altogether - very pretty, but older than she looked from behind.

She has quick and greedy eyes and a small pointed chin and her expression bespeaks an experience of life that is worlds away from anything Letitia or Daisy might know about.

Red-faced with embarrassment Letitia stammers an apology.

The woman looks her up and down, the look taking in Letitia's shabby black dress, veiled face and worn out shoes.

Then she clicks her teeth, and tosses her head dismissively as she takes her companion's arm in a closer embrace.

The pair walk off quickly. But not before Letitia has confirmed that at least she was right in one respect: the man is indeed Digby Barnes Baker. He regarded her with the same expression of complete indifference as he did on the first and only occasion of their meeting.

So what is he doing here now, strolling in the summer sunshine in the company of another woman? And does Daisy know of her existence? Somehow Letitia doubts it.

She begins to follow them, but the crowd on the pavement is too thickly packed and she loses sight of them after a few minutes. Nevertheless, Letitia reminds herself, she had her suspicions about Daisy's admirer from the moment she met him.

At the time, she'd put it down to first impressions. Now it seems she was correct. Mr Barnes Baker is not what he appears on the surface. But how to tell Daisy? And *what* to tell her? That is the problem that occupies her thoughts all the way home. By the time she gets back, she still hasn't come up with a satisfactory answer.

****

London at night. The magic of millions of gas-lamps; brightly-lit stores resplendent with every masterpiece that human ingenuity can devise. Houses lit like shops, shops lit like theatres.

Like moths to a flame, people are attracted to the lighted streets, to the world of enchantment and illusion. They have a hectic appearance, their clothes appear strange and fantastical, like stage costumes in some vast drama.

Take a night-time promenade along Regent Street, past the troops of elegantly-dressed courtesans, their silks and satins rustling as they mingle with others of every order and pursuit, from the ragged crossing-sweeper to the highbred gentleman of fashion and the scion of nobility.

Satiety reached, step away from this gay scene. Almost at once you enter the shadowy world of danger and disorder, the world of introducing houses and gin-palaces, where space is reinterpreted into seeing illumination and blind shadow, where the familiar becomes unfamiliar, a confusion of dream and reality.

Here, behind the architectural splendour of the aristocratic street with its shops, cafes and concert rooms, sounds become distorted, so that the screams and shouts of night people course up and down the streets in strange shuddering echoes.

Listen. Saint Giles's Church clock strikes the hour. Inside the neighbouring gin palace all is light and brilliancy. The long bar is of carved mahogany. There are stucco rosettes surrounding the plate-glass windows and a dazzling profusion of gaslights in richly-gilt burners.

Leaning nonchalantly against the bar are two professional looking men in their mid-twenties. They look well fed and have a gentleman-like appearance, their clothes and demeanour being slightly at odds with the loud drinkers who sit at tables or booths, attempting to get as much cheap alcohol down their throats as possible before chucking out time.

The two at the bar smoke their cigars and sip their gin and water, the glasses discreetly topped up at intervals by the barmaid. No money is demanded or offered. Every now and then somebody comes in, eyes the two men, nods, and goes out again.

These two are professional cracksmen, the highest-ranking villains amongst the vast tide of criminal underworld that swirls around the great city. These men give time and skill to the meticulous planning of crimes. They are masters of their craft.

As evidence of their success, they rent an expensively furnished house in Russell Square. They have servants - fellow accomplices whose job is to dispose of the stolen property. Their mistresses have an abundance of fine jewels, and cash to spend on clothes and treats. Few passing them in the street would guess, from their superior manner and dress, what line of work their men pursue.

For the past week, the two men have been staking out a furrier on the corner of Regent Street and Oxford Street. They intend to make their move tonight, having ascertained that there is an easily accessible fire escape round the back leading to some garrets, whose panes of glass can easily be removed (fifteen seconds being the usual time to accomplish such an operation).

At length, the door to the bar opens to admit a very pretty young woman wrapped in a travelling cloak. She carries a carpet bag which she sets carefully down under a vacant table. She then approaches the bar, studiously ignoring the two men standing there and orders a pennyworth of gin.

Taking her drink to her table, the young woman busies herself with a copy of the railway timetable. So engrossed is she in the contents, that she does not notice the two men as they walk by her table, nor the removal of her travelling bag by one of them.

Even if she did, it wouldn't bother her. The bag does not contain her clothes and personal belongings, but the tools needed for the enterprise. The young woman's name is Lucy and as soon as she finishes her drink, she will start walking up and down the street in front of the furrier's shop, pretending to be a prostitute.

The men know that the beat constable is scheduled to pass by every twenty minutes. Lucy is there to engage his attention, flirting and pretending to offer her services. If necessary she will fake a fit and drop to the ground so that he will have to go and find her a cab.

Three weeks ago, these men successfully robbed a silk warehouse in Cheapside, removing goods valued at £3,000. They carried off their haul in a hansom cab, loading it up during the intervals of the beat constable's appearance.

The robbery took place on a Saturday night and the loss was not discovered until Monday morning. The beat constable saw nothing and heard nothing. All the fastenings and padlocks were intact. It was a complete mystery how the men got in and out of the warehouse.

However, as the various members of the group make their way to their destination, others also have the furrier's shop in their sights on this particular Saturday night.

Shadowy figures lurk in various dark doorways, unseen by the cracksmen and luscious Lucy, their canary. Thanks to his tip-off, Inspector Atherton and his team of hand-picked officers are ready and waiting to pounce.

As the two men make their way down the unlit alley that leads to the rear of the furrier's shop, Atherton nudges his companion.

"Off you go then, Constable Hill. Do your bit for Queen and country," he sniggers.

The young police constable looks distinctly embarrassed.

"I don't know - I'm a married man after all, sir."

"Aren't we all, constable," Atherton grins. "Look upon it as enjoying a bit of variety. Adds to the spice of life, they say."

Rolling his eyes, Constable Hill approaches Lucy, who eyes him speculatively.

"Now then miss," he says severely. "What are you doing loitering out here at this time of night?"

"I was waitin' for a good-looking gent like yourself to pass by," Lucy replies, dimpling and stepping daintily closer. "Are you the officer in charge of these streets? You are? Ow how lucky you come along then. I need some nice man to walk me home. Would you like to do that, big boy?" she asks, now standing so close that her mouth is level with his top button.

"Err ... is it far?" Constable Hill inquires, taking a few steps backwards and almost tripping over the kerb in his effort not to look down the front of her dress.

"Oh, not far. Just a short way," Lucy takes him by the reluctant elbow. "Follow me, handsome, and stay close."

As soon as Lucy and the very reluctant constable quit the scene, Atherton rounds up his men and they begin to creep down the alleyway after the burglars. Reaching the end of it, Atherton signals to the men to stand still.

Then, taking a dark lantern in one hand, he moves stealthily towards the fire escape. At the top of it, the two crackmen have already gained entry to the attic rooms, made their way down stairs to the show room and are folding and packing furs ready to pass through the shop door to an accomplice, who has just arrived with a hand barrow.

As Atherton reaches the top of the fire escape, there is a shout from the street. The officers left to watch the front of the shop have leapt out of hiding. What follows happens so fast that nobody, looking back, can recall the exact sequence of events. Only the outcome.

The two cracksmen have opened the shop door and are hurriedly passing furs out to the accomplice. Upon sight of the police, they run back into the shop and up to their original entry point, where Atherton is hurriedly descending, lantern in hand. The cracksmen jump him, pushing him off the ladder and sending him crashing into the alley below.

While his officers gather round Atherton, the two tie one end of a rope to the fire escape, throw the other end over the wall, drop into the next court and are off.

The cries of "Man down, man down!" echo out into the street where Sergeant Hacket and another constable are attempting to lay hold of the accomplice with the barrow who is hellbent on escaping with as many of the furs as he can.

Upon his refusal to stop, the constable grabs the man by the collar. Dropping the barrow handles, the accomplice instantly produces a wicked looking blade from his sleeve and makes a couple of random stabs at him.

The constable utters a yell of surprise and steps back. Seizing his opportunity, the accomplice takes to his heels. Sergeant Hacket gives chase. Coming alongside, he pulls out his truncheon, and in a gesture that would do credit to the best Punch & Judy show in town, whacks the man hard across the back of the head. He utters a groan, and drops like a stone into the gutter.

As his officers help a limping, cursing Atherton out of the alleyway, Hacket and the constable turn the man over and examine him. He does not appear to be moving. More worryingly, he does not appear to be breathing either.

The principle reason for this possibly relates to the knife sticking out from his chest. Blood is already starting to seep through his coat, staining the ground under him with crimson. Hacket checks for a pulse, a heartbeat. Nothing.

He wipes some filth off the man's face and takes a closer look at him. The man is dark complexioned and has a full beard. There is a livid scar running from his left eyelid to the centre of his cheek.

"Oh gawd!" he mutters.

"Trouble?" the constable inquires.

"I recognise him. Inspector Greig's been chasing him down for weeks."

"Looks like you've saved him the trouble then."

"Yeah. Looks that way. But I think he would've preferred him a bit more ... alive," Hacket says ruefully.

****

The night wears on. The last stragglers make their way back to their beds. The poor and houseless curl up in doorways, in parks or under bridges and pray that it doesn't rain. The labyrinths of tenements, huddled and crowded together, the stifling courts, yards and alleys welcome back their befuddled occupants.

Look more closely.

Three figures make their way stealthily through the quiet slumberous streets. They are wrapped and muffled and conspiratorial. Reaching their destination, they stand for a while in silent contemplation of their goal.

"It's a lot bigger than I thought," says Waxwing.

"All the better," Persiflage responds. "The greater the fall."

Muller says nothing. He is busy laying a very small trail of gunpowder round the base of the statue and then leading away from it.

"I will shortly put ze fuse in place," he says. "May I suggest you withdraw to a safe distance?"

The two clerks retreat to the far side of the park and thence to the far side of the street.

"I can't see what's happening," Waxwing complains.

Persiflage ignores him. A few minutes later, a rather breathless Muller joins them.

"When?" Persiflage asks the tall chemist.

Muller checks his watch.

"Any second ... now," he says.

The explosion sends ricochets of sound rocketing off the houses, the force of it shattering windows and causing every dog in the neighbourhood to start barking furiously. A line of light arcs across the square, a band of brilliance several feet across that lights up the night sky.

"Now we go quickly," Muller says.

Waxwing needs no urging. His hands over his ears, he scurries off as fast as his pointy new shoes will carry him. The other two follow him. At the corner of the square, Persiflage turns and looks back, his face alight with savage glee.

People are emerging from their houses, dressed in a variety of night attire. Some are screaming, some calling for the police. Others just stand in their doorways surveying the destruction in aghast silence.

"Boom!" Persiflage declares triumphantly. He jabs his index finger towards the scene of panic and devastation. "Long live Anarchy! Boom!"

****

A London Sunday. Cloud and light working off each other. A mass of circling pigeons. Train dust settling everywhere like grey sand. The sound of the river. Shops close their doors. Churches open theirs. For one day only Mammon is replaced by an older less materialistic deity.

Sadly, crime does not have a day off, and that is why Inspector Greig who was supposed to have one, is currently standing in the shop of Mr Joseph Ignatz Monteverdi, importer and purveyor of high quality furs and pelts. By rights, Atherton should be here, but Atherton is currently at home having his battered body and bruised ego tended by Mrs Atherton.

Outside the shop the usual crowd of devout onlookers have gathered to worship the bloodstained cobbles and allow the goddess of rumour free reign to run amok.

Amongst their number are a couple of toilers in the field of newspaper publication. Like the Deity currently being serenaded in a thousand churches across the city, they also do not sleep but are always awake and working their purposes out. Currently with notebook, pencil and an evil grin.

Inside the shop, Greig is receiving a lecture on the fur trade from Mr Monteverdi. He has checked his stock, ascertained that nothing is missing, and is now keen to aid the police by pointing out how very valuable the said stock is.

"You see this pelerine, officer?" Monteverdi says, unrolling it, "finest ermine. We import them all the way from

142

Russia, you know. Also the sables - I recently sold a pelisse lined with true sable for one thousand five hundred pounds. A wealthy gentleman - I will not divulge his name, bought it."

"Well well," Greig murmurs. "And so, as you have made sure all your goods are present and correct, I shall bid ..."

"This hat, now, is made of real beaver," Monteverdi continues.

He seems to have forgotten that Greig is not here to buy anything.

"Any man wearing a hat of this quality could pass for a true gentleman, do you not think? And look at these ladies' leather gloves - soft calf leather and fur lined. See the stitching on the finger seams? All done by hand."

"Unh-huh. Yes. Yes, I'm sure it ..."

"The cavalry officers buy their slinging-jackets here, did you know that?"

By now Greig has edged so far towards the door that he is actually half-through it.

"My men will take especial care to check your premises regularly from now on. Good day to you, sir," he says, slipping out into the street.

Avoiding the crowd and the shouted questions from the reporters, Greig sets off towards Bow Street, passing through the central avenue of Covent Garden Market. This is where the flower sellers sit, and normally Greig would enjoy the little world of flowers, some of them reminding him of the wild roses that twined up the fence of his boyhood home.

Today he barely pauses to admire the cut flowers, the sweet bridal posies, the ornate bouquets and flowery tributes destined to be placed beside the pale faces of the beloved dead, or planted upon a grave.

His mind is elsewhere. This morning he visited the police morgue and gazed upon the face of a man he badly needed to question.

The door that Greig thought was blown wide open has swung back and is now firmly shut. And the ghosts of the past, that are never far away, have edged a little closer.

****

Leaving Inspector Greig to his ghosts, let us instead follow that scion of the journalists' trade, Richard Dandy as he scurries back to the newspaper office, his notebook brimming with informative facts which it is his business to turn into fictitious opinion.

Dandy reaches Printing House Square, passes across a narrow court, pushes aside a heavy door, ascends a creaking staircase and finally reaches a green-baized door with a hand-written notice tacked to it which reads: *'Illustrated London News'*. On the other side of the door is the room where the journalists toil.

The news room is not a sight for the faint-hearted, nor the weak-stomached. Newspapers litter the floor, are piled on tables and drip off shelves. There are unopened and opened letters everywhere, wet proof-sheets and files of copy books sent by publishers for review.

Great splashes and dried up pools of soup and ink stain the floor, and the ceiling is darkened by the smoke of tallow candles. The floor has a crunchy texture caused by the amount of discarded food and even though there are notices from the management requesting that journalists do not smoke, the air reeks of stale tobacco.

This is where the news first arrives: reports of shipwrecks, embezzlements, fires, murders, fatal accidents, advertisements, showers of frogs, giant gooseberries, coroners' inquests, and the prices of shares are all delivered or written here, to be sifted and allocated and discarded according to the whim of the sub-editor, Erasmus McFluke, who snips, copies, revises, corrects, pastes and then dispatches the completed pages to the master printer.

McFluke is already at his desk, where he will work late into the night until the paper is put to bed. After which he will go and smoke a welcome cigar at the Crimson Hippopotamus in the Strand, before hailing a cab from the local stand, and rattling home over Westminster Bridge to his well-deserved bed.

Dandy greets his fellow toilers, throws himself into a cane-bottomed chair and places his boots on the table.

"Gents, I got a scoop," he says, taking a silver matchbox from his waistcoat pocket and lighting up a cigar.

There is a pause while all eyes swivel round to stare at him.

Dandy grins, taps the side of his nose with a nicotine stained forefinger.

"Ain't going to say. What I WILL say is that after I've written this, that sorry lot of so-called officers of the law are gonna regret telling their men not to drink with us or speak to us. Ho yes!"

He pulls a sheet of paper towards him and begins to write furiously.

"You heard somebody blew up that statue at the top of Portland Place?" remarks one of his lesser colleagues.

"Squinty-eyed cove with the curly wig and fat legs?"

"That's the one."

Dandy laughs.

"Well done. Good riddance. Never liked it."

"I was wondering whether to do a story on it?"

Dandy doesn't even look up.

"It'll be the railways. They're always blowing things up. Probably got to get rid of it to make way for a tunnel or something. That, or it's drains again."

"But it could be anarchists."

"Oh, for frig's sake," Dandy rolls his eyes. "You think everything's bleedin' anarchists don't you? Remember that last story you filed? We had the Whatsits and Howsyerfather Railway Company breathing smoke and fire coz their shares had gone down." He stabs his pen at the unfortunate conspiratorialist. "Repeat after me: There Are No Such Things As Anarchists. Leastways not here. Anyway, I've hooked the front page already. THIS is the story. Now stow your racket and let me write it - McFluke ain't got all day."

****

Sunday afternoon is a time for families to get together and enjoy the blessings of home. Certainly a bright sunny afternoon like this, when warm gentle zephyrs blow and all in the garden is green and fragrant and inviting.

The engineer sits in the cooling shade of a chestnut tree, a blanket over his knees, breathing in the sweet air. He is being allowed out more and more - soon, when the long-awaited letter from Mr Bazalgette arrives, he will be back at work doing the job he loves and has trained for.

In preparation, he has already filled several sketchbooks with illustrations of ingenious pumping engines and tunnelling devices. Now he watches from a distance as his kind hosts busy themselves with preparations for afternoon tea.

From the amount of food, they are clearly expecting some guests. A veritable feast is being laid out. His Angel, as he likes to think of her, flitters around in something cherry sprigged and gauzy, her divine face half-hidden under a red straw bonnet. Occasionally she pauses and glances in his direction and throws him a shy little smile.

The engineer tries not to react, mindful of the admonitions of the nurse that he must not excite or tire himself out, or it will be straight back to bed. He is determined to stay and observe the festivities (and Daisy) for as long as he can.

The guests arrive, are brought through to the conservatory and are announced by the parlour maid. The engineer feels a stab of jealousy as the good looking young man he has observed visiting the Angel before, strides confidently out of the French doors followed by an older couple - clearly his parents.

The two Mamas greet each other with affectionate cooes. The men shake hands rather formally. Everybody sits down. Cups and plates are handed round. The engineer receives his cup and a plate of cakes and assorted sandwiches. Nobody bothers about him. It is as if he has faded out and become part of the background.

He notices that although the two sets of parents chat, they are really focused on Daisy and the young man, who sit quite close together to one side of the tea table. The engineer cannot follow their conversation, but every now and then she looks down, and colours up prettily. He watches their every interaction, feeling his gorge rising, his tea suddenly tasting bitter.

Eventually, the young man rises, offers Daisy his arm, and they stroll off across the green lawn in the direction of a pretty shrubbery at the far end of the garden. The engineer sees the two Mamas exchange significant glances.

He tries to get himself out of the chair, meaning to follow them, but the nurse is suddenly at his side, gently pushing him back. Helpless the engineer sits on, his cup of cooling tea on his lap.

After what seems like a lifetime, but is in reality only ten minutes, the couple return. Daisy dances straight over to her papa and kisses him on the cheek. Then she dimples prettily and announces,

"Mama, Papa, guess what - oh, it is too delightful: I am engaged to be married!"

As the company stands, smiling, applauding their approval, the engineer feels his heart begin to beat far too fast. Something seems to burst in his head, red and terrible, filling his eyes with shadows.

He gets to his feet and opens his mouth, but the sounds spasm out, harsh and unrecognisable. Then he is toppling forward, the sun shimmering on his head and the smell of new mown grass invading his nostrils as he goes down into darkness.

****

Monday morning finds Inspector Greig in the small room that doubles as his office. He is staring in total amazement at the front page of the *Illustrated London News,* whose stark headline proclaims:

Police Brutality Outrage! Passer-by Struck Down & Killed in Cold Blood! Bungling Bobbies Fail to Catch Criminals!

Underneath this graphic headline is an equally graphic illustration of a toppling man being struck on the head by a policeman's truncheon. Slightly exaggerated in size. Underneath this is something that bears absolutely no resemblance whatsoever to events of the preceding Saturday night.

You could almost admire the way perfectly innocent words and expressions had been mugged and stripped of all true meaning, Greig thinks. Somehow, 'well-intentioned judgements' had become incompetent idiocy. It was garbage, but garbage cooked by an expert.

Also in his office is Sergeant Ben Hacket who is watching Greig read the article. As the perpetrator of the 'brutality', he is shifting nervously from one foot to the other. He winces every time the Inspector hits a particularly inflammatory bit.

Without looking up, Greig remarks:

"According to Mrs Aspasia Semmelhack, 24, proprietress of the Semmelhack School of Deportment, who just happened to be looking out of her first floor window, you and a fellow constable *'launched a ferocious and unprovoked attack upon a completely innocent man who happened to be strolling past pushing a wheel barrow and minding his own business.'* As you do at two-thirty in the morning."

"He wasn't minding his own business sir, he was helping himself to somebody else's. And he pulled a knife first," Hacket says. "Yes, I hit him but I swear it wasn't that hard."

"Oh, I am sure he died at his own hand - I have taken a look at the body. And I'm equally sure that the police surgeon will confirm it. But according to Mr Ibid Bateman, 53 (currently unemployed) who also happened to be looking out of his window, *'the two policemen went on beating and kicking the poor helpless man while he lay groaning and motionless on the ground.'*"

"We did not. We tried to revive him, but it was pretty clear from the start he wasn't breathing."

"So you deny *'causing him to utter great screams and cries of agony as his life ebbed away'*? That's according to the testimony of Mr Halbert Curvengen, 33, barber. I must say it is remarkable how many people were up and at their windows last Saturday night."

Hacket shakes his head.

"I don't remember seeing anybody at any window. And the gas lamps had gone out, so I don't understand how they saw us."

"Oh, I am sure they did not. People see whatever they want to see, particularly when the picture is put into their heads in the first place."

"I'm sorry sir."

"For what? Doing your duty - part of which is to protect a fellow officer in trouble, let me remind you. Had you not intervened as you did, young Sanders' wife could be looking at a dead husband and a future of abject poverty."

"It was him though, wasn't it? The scarface man you thought might know where those Halls are lodging."

Greig gives the window a thousand-yard stare.

"There will be others who'll know where they are," he says. "Meanwhile, we have the small matter of this rubbish to attend to - it won't be long before the usual crowd of malcontents starts gathering at our door shouting the odds."

"What are you going to do?"

"I am going to compose a stiff letter to the proprietor of the *Illustrated London News* telling him exactly what I think about his newspaper printing this meaningless and stupid rubbish, clearly written by someone without the intelligence or wisdom to see what harm they could do by clipping the currency of expression. When I have written the letter, you will take it round to Printing House Square and make sure it is put into his hands personally."

"I shall do that, sir."

"While I am writing it, you will prepare me a full report of exactly what happened on Saturday night and the part you played in it. Leave nothing out, and add nothing in. Is that clearly understood?"

"Yes sir."

"Now go."

Greig waves him away. It is only seven-thirty but he can tell already that it is going to be one of those days he hopes he won't remember. Wearily, he pulls a sheet of headed writing paper towards him and dips his pen into the inkwell and begins his letter of complaint.

****

Letitia Simpkins' day is going slightly better. To her surprise, her father has returned from Harrogate alone, and a changed man. Well, a slightly changed man. There has been no mention of the apology, her key has been returned, and he has indicated that she is free to come and go as she pleases, subject to certain limitations - these being the fulfilment of her household tasks.

The twins, on the other hand, seem subdued and quiet. They have told her about the sea bathing, and a strange black man with a tall hat and striped trousers who danced to a pipe organ. They have given her some pretty shells they collected on the beach, but all other inquiries have met with an evasive response.

Still. The relaxation of her twenty-four-hour curfew means that she can now call upon her dear friend Daisy, and with this in mind, Letitia has written her a little note asking whether she is free this afternoon and declaring her intention of calling round. There is a nettle to be grasped and the best way of doing so is firmly and unflinchingly.

But first she has another important engagement. After accompanying the twins to school, Letitia walks quickly across town until she reaches the building that houses the Regent Street Ladies' Literary & Philosophical Society.

Sarah Lunt is waiting for her. She embraces her warmly.

"Oh, my dear, dear Letitia, how wonderful to see you - but how pale and thin you look - and is that a bruise on your temple? What on earth has been happening since we last met?"

"I fell over," Letitia lies.

The truth is too shameful to be uttered, even to Sarah.

"You poor girl," Sarah lies back.

In her 'other' life, Sarah has a job at the London Women's Hospital. It is not the first time she has seen one of her sex badly beaten up by a family member.

"I believe father has now seen the error of his ways," Letitia says. "At least, I have been allowed out and Mrs Briscoe is not returning to London at the moment, as she has to nurse her mother."

"Well, if that is so, it is good news indeed. But seriously, we must not let any falls or suchlike happen to you in the future," Sarah says. "I'm sure accommodation could be found for you, should the necessity arise."

"That is kind of you, but I couldn't leave the twins - they are such dears. And at the end of the day, it is my home - everything I own is there. And it is where my Mama lived; all my memories of her are in that house. I am grateful, but I'm sure life will soon be back to normal."

She smiles so quickly that the expression is gone before Sarah can respond.

"And I am working hard for my exams - see, I have brought a couple of essays to be marked."

"You are indeed our top student. And certainly, the most diligent. We all have high hopes for your success," Sarah tells her. "That is why you must not let anything - or anybody," she adds darkly, "come between you and your studies."

"I shall not," Letitia promises.

They sit on awhile, discussing which groups of exams Letitia will go in for and the scholarships available for progressing her studies. Letitia visits the library and selects some books. Then it is time to part.

As she walks home, Letitia reflects how lucky she is to have the love and friendship of Sarah and Daisy. Even though they are poles apart in so many ways. She cannot help feeling a pang of guilt at the thought that she is about to cast down Daisy's lovely dream castles by her revelations about Mr Barnes Baker and his female companion.

Still, better the truth, however unpalatable, than a lifetime of marriage to the wrong man. She thinks of her mother, and the suffering and anguish that she went through. There is no hell on earth worse than that.

It is mid-afternoon by the time Letitia arrives outside Daisy's house and is let in by the beaming parlour maid who whispers, as she takes her card, "Innit luvverly, miss?"

Indeed, the whole house bears an air of festive celebration: bouquets of flowers adorn the hall stand and fill every vase in the sitting room, where Daisy and her mother are deep in conversation. Fashion magazines are spread all around them. Daisy, fresh and sparkling as a summer rose, jumps up from the sofa as Letitia is shown in. Her face is wreathed in smiles.

"Tishy! How wonderful! I received your letter - and you clearly received mine! Oh, let me give you a hug. Today is such a glorious day, isn't it?"

"Is it?' Letitia asks.

A feeling of slight unease, no bigger than a small grey cloud on the far horizon begins to hover at the back of her mind.

"Mama - here is Tishy come to congratulate me! My oldest and my best friend!"

Mrs Lawton inclines her head and smiles graciously. Letitia always feels whenever she meets Mrs Lawton, that she is in need of gratitude and better clothes.

"Can I take Tishy upstairs? We have so much to talk about?" Daisy asks.

"You may, my love. But remember: we have important guests coming to tea."

"Of course I haven't forgotten, Mama. How could I?" Daisy dimples as she beckons Letitia to follow her.

There are flowers in Daisy's room, and a thick striped Turkey carpet and a delightful rosewood writing desk and matching rosewood dressing table (full of little stoppered perfume bottles and silver backed brushes). There are no books however, nor any overt sign that reading or writing takes place here.

Letitia sits on the little striped sofa and begins nervously playing with the tassel on the end of a cushion. Daisy goes to the wardrobe, from which she extracts a cherry-sprigged dress, trimmed with red satin ribbon. She holds it up against her reflection.

"Do you like this dress, Tishy?"

"It is very pretty."

"I think it is the prettiest dress in the world. It is the one I wore yesterday when dear Digby did me the honour of asking me to be his wife."

The small cloud suddenly becomes a much bigger, darker cloud.

"You have accepted him then?"

"Oh Tishy, how could I refuse? He was so pleading and he looked so handsome kneeling there at my feet. He is coming to tea and bringing his parents and some of their close friends. And I am hoping he will also be bringing the ring - he has written that he has chosen it, but of course I am to have the final say in the matter."

Letitia folds her hands tightly in her lap. She sets her teeth firmly together.

"Why Tishy, you do not look at me nor congratulate me - what is it? Have I offended you in some way?"

Daisy places herself on the sofa, unlatches Letitia's hands and takes one in her own.

"You are my oldest friend. I want you to be happy for me."

The pause that follows this remark seems to fill the room and beyond.

"And if I cannot?"

"What do you mean?"

Letitia takes a deep breath, and retrieves her hand. Then without looking at Daisy, she begins to relate exactly what she saw on Saturday afternoon. As she speaks, tiny details seem to swim into focus: a shaft of sunlight on the petal of a rose, a cream curtain gently moving in the warm breeze, the sound of a bird singing in the garden.

I will remember these things, she thinks. They were here when I told this, when I destroyed my dear friend's happiness for ever. She reaches the end of what she has come to say and falls miserably silent, staring down at her clasped hands.

When she cannot bear the silence any longer, Letitia raises her head. Daisy's smile remains but the rest of her face is trying to slide away from it.

"I am so sorry," Letitia whispers.

"No - it is I who am sorry. Sorry I allowed you to tell me these lies - for lies they are! Digby would never stoop to be seen publicly in the company of such a low woman as you describe. He is going to be an MP - think how such a liaison would ruin his career? It must have been someone else you saw and now you have rushed round here with your tales. Oh Tishy, how could you be so jealous and spiteful? When have I ever deserved such meanness?"

"I am telling you the truth."

"You are telling me a pack of falsehoods. Just because you are not capable of securing the affections of a man, you cannot bear for anybody else to."

"Then ask him yourself," Letitia snaps, stung by the remark.

"I shall do no such thing. The very idea! I am going to be Digby's wife: what sort of a wife would I be if I didn't trust my husband? And now, I'd like you to leave. As you heard Mama say, we have important guests arriving and I have to get changed to meet them. My dear friend Africa is one of the guests. She is Digby's cousin, so if anything were amiss, she would be the first to tell me. Please go. I think you know your way out."

Daisy rises and goes to the window, turning her back upon her friend.

Letitia takes a couple of faltering steps towards her, stretching out her hand.

"Daisy ... please?" she urges in a low voice.

The back quivers but does not move.

"Just go. Please."

Letitia goes.

Upon her return home, she is greeted joyously by the twins, who have made their way back on their own. They inform her that father has been home, packed an overnight bag and left. Mrs Briscoe's mother died in the night and now he is gone to Harrogate to help with the funeral arrangements.

A sense of relief pervades the whole house. It is almost as if a weight has been lifted off it. The cook has made a nice dinner of veal cutlets, new potatoes and peas, with a blancmange and bottled fruit to follow. Letitia tries to tuck in with enthusiasm, but her heart is not in it.

Eventually she pushes back her plate, declaring that she has a headache, and goes up to her room. She has an essay on Alexander Pope to complete. She reads through the poem set for study, wincing when she reaches the plangent line *who breaks a butterfly upon a wheel?*

Is that what she has done?

The title of her essay, set by the exacting Miss Sophia Jacques is: *What can we learn today about satirical verse in the eighteenth century from reading Pope's Epistle to Dr Arbuthnot?*

Letitia chews the end of her pen. She is not sure what she has learned today about satirical verse, though she has certainly learned a considerable amount about human nature and its capacity for self-deception. But alas, she will not get any marks for writing about that.

****

There is (as the song says) a tavern in the town, and there a man may sit him down, and drink some wine while the laughter floweth free, and never notice that his every movement is being carefully watched by another man at a corner table.

It is Monday night, two days from the failed robbery. Two days from the body of the scar-face man, who had a connection to the baby-killing Halls, arriving in the police morgue, where he lies unnamed and, so far, unclaimed.

If he has nearest and dearest, they are clearly taking their time to notice his absence. If he has no nearest and dearest, he will shortly be given a pauper's funeral and that will be that.

But what has this to do with two men drinking in a pub? A great deal. Especially when the observer, who is so inconspicuously dressed that he wouldn't stand out in a crowd of two, is called Hunter and is, as the term goes, Barnes Baker's man.

It is Hunter's job to ensure his master has the finest starched cravats, the shiniest top hats and the best tailored suits in London. It is Hunter's job to discover the locations of cockfights, dog fights and to place the bets. It is also Hunter's job to extricate his master from various scrapes and peccadilloes such as might, if they ever came to light, count against his future career in Parliament.

It is in this latter capacity that he is here now.

Eventually the man he is watching finishes his glass of ale, at which point Hunter rises from his seat, saunters over to the bar and orders another drink for himself. Feigning surprise at the man's empty glass, he orders the barmaid to 'pour one for my good friend here.'

The good friend, who wouldn't know Hunter if he passed him in the street and may well have done so on numerous occasions, accepts the unexpected bounty and when his drink arrives, is only too happy to follow his benefactor back to the same quiet table in the corner.

155

"Thanks, and good 'ealth, sir," he says, raising his glass.

"Indeed," Hunter responds.

"An' who may I be addressing?"

"Someone who has just stood you a drink."

"Ah. I see. One of them no-names drinks."

"Indeed it is."

The two sit and sup awhile. Then the recipient of free beverages remarks, "And is there any little matter I could do for you in return for your kindness?"

"There may well be one."

The imbiber of gratis libations taps the side of his nose with a nicotined yellow-nailed forefinger.

"Thort so."

A further period of companionable silence follows, after which Hunter sets down his glass, jingles some coins in his pocket to let the other know that there are coins in his pocket, and leans his elbows on the table. The man imitates his gesture.

"So," Hunter says. "I am looking for a man named Jem Hall. Would you know where I can find him?"

The man sits back and assumes an expression of total innocence.

"Never heard of him. Never. Dunno who he is. Nah, come to the wrong man, you have. Sorry an' that."

Unmoved, Hunter reaches into his inner pocket and lets the man see a fatly stuffed wallet.

"That is a great shame. My master is in a bit of a fix, and I was given to understand that this Jem Hall might be able to get him out of it. Oh well, thank you for your advice and I shall not trouble you further," Hunter says, getting up and making as if he is leaving.

"Now wait a bit. Wait a bit," the man says quickly. "Not so hasty, eh? I only said wot I did coz I thort you might be from the ecipol. Not welcome around here, are they? So, sit you back down and tell me what it's about."

Hunter resumes his seat.

"My master suspects that a certain person he knew once is about to present him with an unwelcome little remembrance of that time. And as he is about to be married, he does not wish to be encumbered with it, or her. I was given to understand the Jem was the man for the job."

"And so he woz, so he woz."

"But not any more?"

The man leans in.

"Jem ain't around to the moment, as it were."

"Is he likely to return?"

"I'd say not."

Hunter sits back.

"Ah. That then leaves me with somewhat of a problem."

"Well it might. Only could be I know something about the business in hand."

"Really? That is very interesting to hear. But you are sure Jem won't be angry if he finds out you have, as it were, slipped into his shoes?"

The man grins.

"He ain't gonna say a word, trust me."

Another pause. The man stares significantly into his now empty glass and Hunter looks straight ahead.

"So how would you be able to help me?"

"I might know some people."

"The same people that Jem knows?"

"Could be, could be."

"And when may I get to meet these people?"

The man pulls up a battered brass timepiece from his greasy coat pocket. His lips move as he carefully counts round the cloudy clock face.

"Should be able to take you there later. For an agreed price."

"Of course," Hunter says. "There is always a price to be agreed."

"Happy to agree it over another drink, if you're still in the chair, squire."

Hunter is very much still in the chair, so he goes to the bar, buys the man another pint and himself a gin and water and when they have finished their drinks, they both leave the pub. The man goes first, Hunter following a couple of seconds later.

They come together once more at the corner of the street. Money changes hands. Then the man leads Hunter down alleys and walkthroughs and noisome courts until they arrive in front of a brick archway. Although the hour is late, the archway is choked with gasping loungers who eye Hunter askance, but relax and let them pass when the man indicates that they are together.

"This is Bessie's Rents," the man says, stopping at the door of a crumbling tenement, whose windows seem more to shut the light out than admit it.

He thumps on the door, which is opened by a sallow-complexioned man with a long nose, wet hair and a limp spotted neckerchief. He wears down at heel carpet slippers and a sly expression.

"Brought a bit of business round," says Hunter's companion.

The man looks Hunter up and down, his gaze taking in his well tailored clothes and clean appearance.

"Better come on in then," he says.

Hunter follows him along a noxious smelling corridor to the ground floor back. Here the only window looks out into a high dead wall. The air in the room is very close, and musty, smelling of damp and faeces and sour milk. Light comes from a small tallow dip, which throws flickering shadows onto the unpapered walls.

The room is furnished with an armchair and a low bedstead upon which two small semi-naked babies fret and stir in fitful sleep. Neither appear to have any proper covering.

"Only here temp'rary, you unnerstand. Had to get out of the last place in a bit of a hurry," the man shrugs apologetically. "I'll call the wife - she's the business end."

He shuffles off into a back room, reappearing a few seconds later with a sharp-faced woman carrying a comatose child. Its head lolls on her shoulder, its face glazed, its small legs dangling limply.

"Little dear wouldn't stop carrying on," she says, almost tossing the child onto the bed. She folds her hands under her apron. "So, you are looking for a wet nurse, I gather?"

Briefly Hunter outlines the situation. The woman nods her understanding.

"Yes, I can see how a little encumbrance might be a problem. And he's a rich man, your master? Even worse. There's no telling what some gels will do to get revenge.

"I've seen many a rich man brought low and ruined by the scheming of some hussy. Marriages broken up, sons disinherited - oh there's nothing I ain't seen with my own two eyes. You have no idea what can happen. Best to make sure it don't."

She takes another long, calculating look at Hunter.

"My charges are fifteen shillings a month, or can adopt outright for fifty pounds and clothing."

"I think the latter would be preferable," Hunter says.

"As you please sir. I am full at the moment - but I guarantee by the time the baby is born, I shall have vacancies."

Wisely Hunter does not inquire how she can predict this. Instead he asks:

"How shall I get in touch with you, when the day comes?"

"You leave a message at the pub where you met my friend saying you have agreed a bit of business with Mrs 'Melia Hall. They'll let me know. I'll leave a message at the bar saying when and where to meet me. You come with the money and the baby. And all your master's worries will be over."

She smiles, her ivory-yellow teeth glistening in the flickering candlelight.

"I have to take precautions, you understand. There are those who want to stop what I do."

"Dear madam, I understand completely," Hunter says. "I shall convey your instructions back to my master exactly as you have conveyed them to me. Thank you for your time. And now I bid you goodnight."

He touches his hat and walks out of the meanly appointed room into the darkness of the noisome noxious night. Later, he will report back to Barnes Baker, who will heave a sigh of relief, before setting out for a night's revels.

****

Dearest Jeanie (Inspector Greig writes)
Thank you for the seed cake, which arrived safely. It was kind of you, and I am enjoying the taste of your excellent home

baking. I have taken the precaution of locking the cake in one of my desk drawers, so the sweet-toothed thief cannot appropriate any of it.

I hope you are all enjoying good weather. Here, we have had a run of stifling hot days and nights, almost too much to bear. I do not think this city is made for heat - the buildings seem to droop and look even more decayed and fine dust chokes the thoroughfares.

In the midst of the 'heatwave', Tibby, the Bow Street cat has given birth to four fine kittens, which she is currently nursing under my desk. This is unlikely to be a permanent arrangement as she moves them every few days.

If you are agreeable, I thought I might bring a couple of the kittens back with me as a present for you all when I get my leave in August. If they take after their mother, they are likely to be good mousers.

Last week I went to the British Museum where I saw a fine display of stuffed animals - wild ox, monkeys and numerous birds with beautiful feathers all the colours of the rainbow. I saw a foot from a Dodo, a strange looking bird that is now extinct and an Albatross, which is the largest seabird in existence.

There was also a Pelican, that is supposed to feed her young on her own blood, although the notes accompanying the bird indicated that it was more likely the way the fish was discharged through the beak.

I have included some drawings of the birds I saw on my visit - I hope you like them, though I am no artist, as you have frequently told me!

As always, I remain
Your devoted brother,
Lachlan

The light is fading as Greig seals the letter. Once again, he wonders if the city is changing him and if so, what he is becoming. He still has that feeling of being in transit. He hears his watch tick on the pinewood table by the bed.

Also on the table is a copy of the *Morning Post*, sister paper in scurrility and inaccurate reportage to the *Illustrated London News*. The front-page banner headline reads:

Anarchy! Royal Statue Blown to Smithereens!

Underneath in smaller letters (because some wag simply couldn't resist it,) is the subheading:

Large hole in pavement! Detective Police looking into it.

Greig has read and pondered about the accompanying article and decided to go over to Scotland Yard and have a word. There may not be any link to the Hind Street explosion and the two missing bank clerks. On the other hand, there might. He would not like to be accused, in retrospect, of withholding important information.

He blows out the candle and gets into bed, his eyes dilating in the familiar darkness. The June nights are short, and he is on early duty again tomorrow.

****

Detective Inspector Leo Stride of Scotland Yard has a reputation. Nobody knows exactly what for, but it stands him in good stead both within and outwith the detective division. Nothing is more guaranteed to earn respect from the hierarchy and spread consternation amongst the lowerarchy than having a reputation for having a reputation.

He also has a 'file it on the first available flat surface' habit. Inspector Greig, no mean slouch in the ignore paperwork department himself, sits in Stride's office and feels he is in the presence of a master. There are strata here that, if labelled chronologically, could form the basis of another fine exhibit at the British Museum.

The detective inspector is a middle-aged man with greying hair, pouchy eyes and an unbrushed brown suit. Having heard Greig out in silence, he now sits back and regards the young inspector thoughtfully.

"I read about the Hind Street explosion. I have to say, I had my doubts at the time. We've had gas explosions ever since we've had gas. They don't usually bring down whole houses - unless they're in the vicinity of one of those gasometers. And usually someone in the house notices there's a smell of gas beforehand and complains about it."

"I have the report of the site chemist," Greig says. "I have not shown it to anybody yet as I have no proof it was caused by the two clerks."

"Very wise. You also don't want the press getting their paws on it."

Greig pulls a face.

"Where I come from, detective inspector, the press is only too keen to help the police stamp out crime."

"Indeed. It's a different story here. Met Mr Richard Dandy? Dandy Dick, as he's known. Writes for a rag called the *Illustrated London News*: 'The voice of the man in the street'. I wouldn't wipe my arse on it, if you'll pardon the expression."

"I have met the individual. And I have written to the paper to express my thoughts about his writing skills."

"Good for you. I often say to my sergeant we spend as much time fighting lies in the press as we do detecting crime on the street. And that's even before …"

Stride's words are interrupted by a polite knock at the door, which opens to reveal a younger detective, clean-shaven but for a pair of side-whiskers. His face has a gaunt, unslept look.

"There's a gentlemen from the London Fine Wine Importers in the outer office. He claims their warehouse has been raided overnight. He has his carriage waiting."

"River Police?"

"They say it isn't actual water crime."

Stride rolls his eyes.

"Bloody typical. Right, if we're done here, Inspector Greig, I'll let you be on your way."

"We're done. I've said my piece and I thank you for your time."

Greig rises, puts on his hat. The younger detective nods a friendly greeting.

"Inspector Greig isn't it? From Bow Street? I'm Detective Sergeant Jack Cully. I hear on the grapevine you're after some so-called baby minders."

"Indeed I am."

"Then I hope to God you catch them," Cully says vehemently.

Greig raises his eyebrows.

"Jack's wife has just given birth to a baby girl. That's why he feels so strongly," Stride says. "And why he looks as if he hasn't slept," he adds, gathering his things.

"It is my intention to bring them to court, detective sergeant. By hook or by crook ... for crooks they most certainly are. And murderers of the deepest and most dastardly hue. And now I'll bid you both good-bye."

He walks out, humming the Bluebells of Scotland under his breath.

Detective Sergeant Jack Cully stares after him.

"Rum," he murmurs.

"How so? Seemed a perfectly reasonable man to me. Good thief taker, I gather."

"He's a single man. No children. But the Bow Street sergeants say he's like a terrier after a rat. Absolutely determined to catch these people, whatever it takes."

"Well, I don't drink wine - can't abide the stuff, but that won't stop me trying to track down this gang - if there is a gang," Stride says. "Now then, let's see what Mr Fine Wine Importer has for us. As they say, time and tide wait for no man."

****

There is no tide proximitous to the Lawton residence, but the time is early evening and the table is laid for dinner. Snowy table linen, bright silver, clear sparkling glass, wine and a bowl of soft fruit on the sideboard for dessert.

Mr and Mrs Lawton are seated on either side of the drawing room hearth, waiting to be summoned to dine by the parlour maid. A short distance away, Daisy Lawton stands in the bow window, looking out on the garden.

Mrs Lawton casts a quick glance in her daughter's direction, then leans forward, lowering her voice.

"Have you noticed any change in Daisy over the last few days?"

This is exactly the sort of question that strikes fear into any husband, freighted as it always is with the possibility of misunderstanding, leading to error and culminating in uxorial wrath.

163

"Would this have to do with her appetite? I noticed she hasn't been finishing her food. I put it down to the general seesaw between appetite and love."

Mrs Lawton purses her lips in disapproval.

"Typical of a man. Only thinking of your stomach. Look at her: moping by the window - is that the behaviour of a happy young girl who has just secured one of the handsomest and most eligible bachelors in London?"

"Is that what he is? Ah."

Mr Lawton sighs. His Daisy-duck is seventeen and engaged to be married. Yet it seems like only the other day she was in long-clothes and scrambling up the apple tree.

"Perhaps it is too soon for an engagement," he ventures cautiously, to be instantly quelled by A Look.

"What nonsense! She is clearly in love with dear Digby. And he with her. Why, her face lights up whenever he enters the room. No, there is something troubling her and I mean to get to the bottom of it."

Alerted by his wife's words, Mr Lawton watches Daisy carefully during dinner. He notices that she is not particularly preoccupied by anything that is going on. She joins in no conversations. She picks at her food, and crumbles her bread on the tablecloth. Her long eyelashes are seen on the clear tint of her cheeks.

After blackcurrant dumplings, always a favourite in the past, have been tasted and left on her plate, he makes up his mind. As soon as the meal is over, he pushes back his chair.

"Now, who is going to come and read the evening paper to me in my den?"

Daisy looks up, her eyes troubled.

"Daisy-duck, your old papa needs your young eyes," Mr Lawton says, rising and holding out his hand.

Listlessly, Daisy gets up and follows him to the book-lined room always referred to as 'Fa's Den' where Mr Lawton sits down in his favourite armchair and pulls his daughter down onto his lap.

"Now than Daisy - tell your silly old Fa what is troubling you. No - don't turn your face away. I am a doctor and I diagnose that there something amiss with my favourite daughter."

"I am your only daughter, Fa."

"That is why it is even more important to make it better."

Daisy colours a little. Mr Lawton who has learned the value of silence over many years of marriage, waits for her to speak.

Daisy sighs, plays with the fringe on her shawl.

"I have had a quarrel with somebody."

"Digby?"

Daisy shakes her head.

"It is Tishy - Letitia Simpkins."

"Ah. The funny little girl from school. I like her."

Daisy frowns.

"Funny?"

"She has a funny little face - always makes me smile, especially when she looks at you with her head on one side in that amusing way of hers, as if she is laughing at you inside. And she knows all about science and geography and quotes Byron! Quite amazing."

Daisy bites her underlip. This is Tishy in a new light.

"What could little Tishy have done to make you cross?"

Daisy wriggles off his lap.

"It is nothing Fa. Just a girlish thing. I am sure it will be made right in time. Now I must go and practice my pieces. Digby is coming around tomorrow and I want to be note perfect for him."

Mr Lawton watches her glide out the room. He has said something wrong, but he does not know what it is. He shakes his head, and sits for a moment in silent contemplation. Then with a long sigh, he picks up the evening paper.

Meanwhile Daisy goes to the parlour and sits down on the piano stool. This should be a delicious time for her: she is engaged to be married. But ever since Tishy came with her story - for it *was* a story, it *was*, Daisy has felt as if she has a great weight on her heart.

She opens her music: a gay waltz tune, and begins to play. But after only a few bars, her fingers falter, a wrong key is sounded, then she comes to a stop. Tears well up in her eyes. Daisy stares at the notes on the stave as they blur and wobble in front of her.

The world is out of joint and she doesn't know how to set it right. All she knows is that she has cast off her best and most loyal friend, and she does not possess the power spoken of by the poet Goldsmith:

'He threw off his friends like a huntsman his pack,
For he knew when he liked he could whistle them back.'

If only she could return to the sweet girlhood days when she and Tishy shared confidences and cake. But the door is shut forever on that happy carefree time. Daisy Lawton glances down at her left hand. The diamond in her engagement ring winks back up at her, lucid and elemental and cold.

****

Meanwhile Richard Barnes Baker MP is meeting with his election agent Edward Foxton in the dark-panelled dining room of the Palace of Westminster. A late supper of saddle of mutton with caper sauce has gone down very well along with a lot of fine wine from the excellent wine cellar.

Now the two men sit back, cigars and brandy to hand.

"Rumour is that Cardwell's for the chop, an't that right Foxy?" Barnes Baker says.

Edward Foxton, as red headed and sharp-faced as his name suggests, takes up his glass and swirls the amber coloured contents thoughtfully between his cupped hands.

"Mr Adolphus Cardwell may indeed be on the point of resigning his seat and having his election declared null and void," he says.

The two men exchange a sly look.

"*Cherchez la femme*, eh. I heard that Mr Cardwell, while claiming to be a married man of impeccable standing, pillar of the local church an' all that, has been secretly carrying on with an Irish heiress and that she and their two daughters have just arrived in town," Barnes Baker says.

"I gather Lord Palmerston's not too pleased and it has been indicated to Mr Cardwell that he must do the honourable thing and fall upon his sword," Foxton adds.

"It will mean a by-election, won't it? Tatchester and Crawley - always been a safe Whig seat, but I wonder if we can persuade the electorate to vote for my boy as the new candidate," Barnes Baker muses. "Pam's keen to get more Liberals into the House, after all he founded the party, so I think he'll back us."

"I also think that is very likely."

"Then so be it. I'll take some soundings and see how the land lies, but my reading of it is that Cardwell will resign quietly over the summer to avoid a scandal. There'll be an announcement when the House resumes in September, then we'll declare Digby's prospective candidacy."

"I gather that he is an engaged man," Foxton remarks.

"Yes. Lovely young gel - wife's known the mother since they were at school together. Father's a surgeon. May have to delay the wedding though - got to get him elected first," Barnes Baker says, giving Foxton a wink.

"The electorate will like it. We should arrange some visits nearer the time. Let people see them together - riding round in an open-topped carriage, young couple in love and that sort of things. Always goes down well. And after Cardwell ..." Foxton lets the inference hang in the air like a bad smell.

"Oh, there'll be none of that with the boy. No dirty little secrets coming out, don't worry. Not to say that he hasn't sown a few wild oats, haven't we all in our time, but he's settled, I can vouch for it. Got him on a pretty tight rein since he came up to Town."

"Glad to hear it."

Foxton raises his glass.

"To Digby then, the next Barnes Baker MP."

"Amen to that, Foxy," Richard Barnes Baker echoes. "Amen to that."

****

By one of those random happenstances, even as Barnes Baker senior and Foxton are toasting his success, the putative Parliamentary candidate is also celebrating, though in his case the worship is at the shrine of Eros rather than Eunomia.

Resplendent in full evening dress, here he is at the Britannia Theatre, Hoxton. He and his party of three other young

London bucks, having paid their sixpence a head, are at a table in the pit.

The Britannia is an immense theatre, magnificently lighted by a firmament of sparkling chandeliers. Audiences are seated at tables. Food and drink (mainly sandwiches and ginger beer) are served throughout the performance.

Glance round the auditorium. You will see dock labourers, shop-workers of both sexes, tradesmen, clerks, stay-makers, shoe-binders, professional men, loiterers, idlers, ladies of much, some and absolutely no virtue whatsoever, plus a plethora of workers from a hundred highways and byways.

The evening programme consists of a couple of plays, with variety acts in between. Tonight, there are two melodramas: *The String of Pearls* and a performance of *Lady Audley's Secret*, an adaptation of the scandalous novel about bigamy and deception and a murderess.

The star of the drama, playing the dastardly Lady Audley herself is Miss Lottie Turner. You might recognise her as the young woman who wasn't Daisy Lawton. Letitia certainly would.

Here she is approaching Digby's table, joshing and flirting with other admirers at other tables as she undulates her way across the floor. For Miss Turner is well known on the Halls and has a very loyal male following, being both an accomplished artiste, and a fine cantatrice in favourite ballads, some of which she will sing later tonight.

Miss Turner slides herself onto Digby's lap and places one white dimpled arm round his neck. Leaning forward, she blows seductively into his ear.

"Now then my big boy, did you remember to bring my little present?"

The little present in question is currently adorning the left hand of Daisy Lawton, having been sized down from its original owner, who shifts her weight and smiles sweetly.

"It's still being reset at Rundells, Lottie," says the big boy.

Lottie pouts.

"Seems to be taking an awful long time. I want my little di'mond ring back on my hand, where all the world can see it.

Not every day a girl gets given a beeyootiful di'mond ring, is it?"

This is true. It is also not every day that two separate girls get given the same diamond ring either.

"You must be patient," says the lord of the ring, as he slaps her rump playfully, causing Miss Turner to utter a little scream of protest, which can only be silenced by the application of champagne.

All this while Professor Golding, billed as the Premier Ventriloquist of the World and Humorous Mimic, is delighting the audience with his Mirth-provoking Ventriloquial sketch.

"Gawd, don't he run on?" says Miss Turner, cocking her head to one side in a *killing* way. "Right, time to get ready for my show. Keep my seat nice and warm till I'm back, won't you? I'll make it up to you ... later."

She plants a moist kiss on Digby's mouth, gets off his lap and saunters towards the exit, her hips swinging provocatively from side to side. Every male eye follows her. Professor Golding's final remarks are drowned out by wolf whistles and air kissing noises.

"Whew!" one of Digby's friends remarks. "Very spicy!"

"Oh, Lottie's alright," Digby shrugs.

"Wonder what she'll think when she finds out about you-know-who," the young swell grins. "Have you thought about that?"

As Digby Barnes Baker is to risk analysis what oysters are to dentistry, he merely laughs and repeats that Lottie knows the score. At which point the stage curtain is pulled back to reveal the famous Lime Tree Walk with a rather crudely painted representation of Audley Court in the background.

Lady Audley's entrance, in a low-cut dress and picture hat, is greeted by whoops and cheers from the audience. She plays her part prettily, saucing the men who are trying to find out her true identity, and tossing her head defiantly at all accusations and innuendoes.

It is noticeable however, that when she utters the immortal line: *"Once I used to be a mere governess, now I am Mistress of Audley Court,"* she pauses, her eyes seeking out Digby in the semi-darkness.

Does he notice? Probably not. And even if he did, and understood the underlying implication, he wouldn't worry. That is why he pays a man like Hunter. To smooth out his path in life and remove all little inconveniences on the way. Thanks to Hunter, Digby Barnes Baker's life has bowled along very smoothly and conveniently indeed. So far.

****

Leaving the frolicsome gaiety of the Britannia, let us return to the crepuscular and fumacious streets, where dark figures hurry determinedly through the crowds of flâneurs, strollers and night-time revellers.

They are the working girls - not those who earn a living horizontally (though sometimes penury forces them to pursue that perilous path) but the millions of milliners, dozens of dressmakers and hundreds of hat-trimmers.

It is the height of the Season, when every outworker in London is literally working their fingers to the bone to supply the big stores and private customers with ballgowns, day dresses and all the trimmings and accoutrements that accompany them.

Look more closely.

Two shabbily dressed young women hurry along Tottenham Court Road in the direction of Regent Street. They have wicker baskets on their arms and the preoccupied expressions of those who need to get somewhere in a hurry.

They are Miss Adelina Makepiece Chiappa, seamstress, and Miss Florina Sabini, bonnet trimmer, on their way to deliver their latest orders to the big department store that employs them.

They have not eaten all day and their faces look white and pinched in the gloom. Occasionally Miss Chiappa stumbles, and is held up by her companion. They reach Oxford Circus and pause to catch their breath.

"My head hurts, Flo," Miss Chiappa complains.

"Not far to go now, Addy," her companion says, patting her arm encouragingly. "Then it'll be baked potatoes and a cup of coffee each."

Cheered by the thought, the two make their way to Peter Robinson's department store, where the lighted window displays are attracting the usual crowd of evening strollers and ladies of dubious provenance.

They turn down a dark unlit alleyway, knock at a wooden door and are admitted to the basement sewing room, where the stitchers and pattern cutters work well away from the shop floor. Even at this hour, a few girls linger at the long wooden table, their shoulders drooping with fatigue, eyes barely open.

Their arrival is observed by Mrs Scabrous, the wall-eyed superintendent, who greets them unsmilingly, taking their baskets and complaining that they are late. The girls are so used to this greeting that they barely respond.

Useless to explain that they have trudged for miles on empty stomachs because they couldn't afford the omnibus fare.

Mrs Scabrous looks over their work with an experienced eye, finally proclaiming with a sniff that, "It'll do." The next order, along with the money for this one, is placed in their baskets and they set off back to their lodgings.

At Kings Cross Station they stop and buy their supper from one of the street vendors. They sit on a bench to eat it, blowing on their fingers as they wolf down the hot potatoes. They are just about to set off once more when Florina suddenly nudges her companion and points.

"Hey, in't that one of them snobby clerks we used to lodge with?"

It is indeed. Edwin Persiflage emerges from one of the station arches carrying a small package. He looks all about him, then crosses the road.

"Well I never thought to see the likes of him again. Wonder where's he off to," Florina murmurs, rising from her seat.

"Who knows," her companion says wearily.

"Well, I don't, that's for sure. But I intend to find out."

"Oh Flo, you can't ..."

"No such word as *can't* my old mum used to say. You go home, Ada. You're all but done in. I'll be back in two shakes of a lamb's tail, don't worry."

And with that, Florina Sabini pulls her bonnet down over her face, wraps her shawl around her shoulders and starts off after Persiflage, her mouth set in a determined line.

Unaware that he is being followed, the founder of the Hind Street Anarchists walks briskly in the direction of Somers Town, with Florina in hot pursuit. They pass St Pancras churchyard, where all the tombstones have been placed against the trees in preparation for the new railway to cut its way through.

To the passer-by it looks as if the headstones have dropped from the trees like ripe fruit, waiting to be gathered. Florina shivers. She can hear the clanking of trains from the Railway Depot. An owl hoots. She pauses under the bloom of the gaslight to wrap her shawl more closely.

Meanwhile Persiflage hurries down Union Street, and crosses the Polygon. Florina follows him. He pauses in front of a darkened shop on the corner of Seymour Street. Then he gets out a key and lets himself in by the side door.

Florina creeps nearer. The sign over the shop reads: *Bengt & Muller, Chemist & Druggist*. She watches from the pavement. A light comes on above. She sees the outline of Persiflage against the blind.

So this must be where he is lodging. And the other one? Is he here too? Florina turns and heads for home. As she walks the near-deserted streets, she remembers the nice-looking police inspector who gave them money and spoke kindly to them as if they were human beings not just work-slaves.

He seemed interested in the two clerks, didn't he? Concerned for their welfare. Once she finds out if they are both lodging above the chemist, maybe she'll pay the nice police inspector a visit and let him know where they have ended up.

She remembers the way this snooty one brushed past her, nearly upsetting her basket. And the other one, with his silly clothes and pimply face refused to carry Addy's basket up the stairs one day when she was near to collapse with exhaustion.

You reap what you sow in this world, Florina thinks grimly. She is not stupid: she is sure there is a reason why the nice police inspector wants to find out where the two clerks have gone. So now he will know, and serve them both right.

****

Sadly, all good things must come to an end, and so it is with a heavy heart that Letitia Simpkins receives a curt letter from Harrogate informing her that her father is returning to London.

The week of his absence has been like manna in the wilderness. While he has been away, she has managed to meet with her tutor Miss Sophie Jacques, and been rewarded with that redoubtable young woman's unstinted praise for her essays. She has taken the twins to the zoo and to Madame Tussaud's Waxworks. She has even bought herself a new collar and some handkerchiefs from her diminishing funds. But now all this gallivanting is coming to an end.

Letitia sits in the parlour waiting for the cab to draw up at the door. The boys wait with her, fidgeting in their starched collars and brushed jackets. Letitia has made them take a bath and dressed them in their best clothes. Downstairs, the cook is preparing a tasty meal for dinner.

It is her fervent wish that once her father sees how competently she has managed in his absence and how well the house is running, it might be the beginning of a fresh start. One in which Mrs Briscoe plays a lesser, not to say non-existent part.

She hears the sound of carriage wheels in the street. Then her father's familiar voice arguing loudly with the cabman over the fare. She feels her heart sink. He is clearly in one of his 'moods'. Letitia's little rock pool of hope begins to trickle away.

The front door is wrenched open, then slammed shut. She hears her father throw his hat, coat and bag on the hall floor. The boys exchange a look. Without entering the parlour or greeting his offspring, he goes straight to his study. He slams that door shut as well.

After a suitable interval has elapsed, and it becomes clear that Mr Simpkins is not going to emerge to greet the welcoming party, Letitia indicates to the twins that they can go and play.

They need no urging, slinking furtively up to the first floor of the house. Letitia sits on. The house sinks into absolute silence. Usually silence is an ally. Now it is pressing lightly on her ears. What has happened? And where is her father's companion?

She checks the time. Two hours until dinner. Then maybe her father will reveal why exactly he has returned alone, and in such a foul temper. Letitia suspects the temper is probably connected with Mrs Briscoe in some way. All of a sudden, she isn't sure she wants to know.

At six, the family make their way to the dining room from the various parts of the house where they have taken refuge. Mr Simpkins is the last to enter the dining room.

He stands in the doorway, regarding the assembled members of his family with lowered brows and an expression of dislike before taking his customary place at the head of the table. The roast mutton is carried in and placed in front of him.

Without looking up, he gestures towards the empty place laid to his right.

"What is this, pray?"

"I laid a place for Mrs Briscoe," Letitia replies quietly. "I had assumed that she would be dining with us, as she usually does."

With a roar of rage and a sweeping gesture, her father knocks the cutlery, wine glass, water glass and plates onto the floor. The boys yelp with shock and cower in their seats. Tears fill William's eyes.

"Mrs Briscoe will NOT be dining here tonight! Or any other night!" their father shouts, a nerve starting to tic at the side of his forehead.

Letitia sits as absolutely still as she can. When her father is in this mood, it is best to make oneself as small and insignificant as possible. She exchanges a quick warning glance across the table with the twins.

"For future reference, Mrs Briscoe has decided to stay in Harrogate. In her mother's house. Which is now her house. And I NEVER want to hear her name mentioned again in my presence. Is that CLEARLY understood?" their father shouts.

He glares round the table. The boys look down. Only Letitia meets his gaze. If the nerve beating in his temple accelerates any more, it might burst through his skin, she observes detachedly.

"Clear up this mess," her father orders roughly, gesturing at the broken plates and shattered glassware.

174

He seizes the carving knife and starts slashing at the meat as if it is an enemy to be defeated. Letitia rises and collects up the pieces. Her heart sings for joy. Much later, in the solitude of her room, she will stand by the open window, breathing in the quiet night air and watch the moon sail across the night sky.

Her world has shifted back into balance. The hated intruder has gone. She will then close the window, and sit in front of the looking glass, staring at her reflection, her face broken open with a smile, until the candle-end sputters and goes out.

****

Digby Barnes Baker wakes to a splitting headache (the result of rather too much champagne) and a vague recollection of plump white thighs, round breasts and the naked writhing body of Miss Lottie Turner.

He glances to his left, but there is no blonde head on the pillow. Whew. Lottie always likes a little morning encore upon waking and he isn't sure in his current state that he could perform to her, let alone his, satisfaction.

As he lies on his back reassembling the night before, there is a discreet knock at the door and Hunter sticks his head round to announce that Digby's bath is ready and there is a communication from his mother awaiting his perusal.

Digby yawns, stretches, then throws off the covers and makes his way to the bathroom. While he immerses himself in a tub of hot water, removing the effluvia of the night before, he instructs Hunter what clothes to get ready.

Bathed, scented and facing a large and well-cooked breakfast (the bachelor quarters provides two meals a day, shipped in from various local hostelries) he finally opens the letter from his mother.

It is short and succinct. Digby has been seen in the company of a woman of low repute - from the description supplied, it is clear that the woman is the luscious Lottie. He is to desist forthwith from being seen in public with unsuitable consorts. He is an engaged man. A reminder is also added of how much time, money and influence is being expended to secure him a seat in the Palace of Westminster.

Digby Barnes Baker swears under his breath. Does the mater expect him to live like a bloody monk? It could be years before he is able to marry. And who on earth could have peached about Lottie? A second reading of the letter brings to mind the young woman in mourning who accosted Lottie in the street a while back.

Digby sets down his knife and fork and focuses his thoughts. Was the young woman the same one he met at the Lawton house - some family friend of Daisy's? Plain and rather too fond of the sound of her own voice as he recalls.

She wore full mourning, had one of those flat thin figures that he hates in a woman. Yes, the more he thinks about it, the more he is sure they are one and the same person. So, was she the one to tip off the mater?

He summons Hunter, who has been consuming a hasty breakfast in the back pantry, and orders him to go and whistle up a cab. They have calls to make. People to see, women to shed.

While Hunter is cab hunting, Digby finishes his own breakfast, composes a quick note to his mother, and a slightly longer one to Daisy. He is sure Daisy will be delighted to accompany him on an afternoon walk in the local park, blah blah. In the course of which he intends to quiz her closely about her friend.

He hooks his top hat from the hat stand and heads out of the front door.

Arriving on the street, Digby finds the cab and his manservant awaiting. He hands over the letters and gives Hunter other careful instructions. Whatever else he is, Digby is not a reckless fool. He has staked his future on becoming an MP. He is not going to allow anybody to stand in his way.

****

Meanwhile Inspector Greig's hopes that someone would come forward to identify the unnamed man's body lying in the police morgue, and thus link him to the Halls, have been dashed.

It seems no person is willing to claim kin, and so the man has finally been laid to rest in a communal unmarked grave very early on a morning with a mist so thick it looked as if the coffin was being lowered into cloud.

Greig decided to allow details of the prospective funeral to be put in the newspapers, and attended the event himself, carefully scrutinising the mourners. This did not take long, as there weren't any.

It confirms his suspicion that somehow, word has got round the criminal fraternity that the 'Men from the Railway Company' who turned up at *Pastorelli & Rifkin* were not what they seemed. He does not know how this has happened, and there is probably no way of finding out at this late stage.

Greig sits at his desk, studying the latest advertisements in the *Daily Telegraph* that solicit for the weekly, monthly or yearly care of infants. All the advertisers claim to be widows with a family of their own, who are prepared to offer a home to a young child. For a fee.

To the general public, they look like genuine and kindly offers. To the initiated, as Greig now is, every advertisement carries a coded message to unmarried or desperate mothers. Money down and you will never see your child again.

To add insult to injury, the paper actually carries a story on its front page of the discovery of a four-month old baby wrapped up in a newspaper (unspecified) lying beside a road in Kilburn.

The story has, however, given Greig an idea. When his officers broke into the house used by the Halls for their baby minding business, they found a recent copy of the *Telegraph* in the kitchen. It suggests that the couple are literate and indicates what their preferred literature might be.

Thus, Greig has formulated a plan. He is going to place a fictitious advert in the paper. It will be from a Mrs Harding, who is seeking to place a young child with a couple to bring up as their own. The remuneration offered is tempting. There will be a box number for the response.

He spends some time drafting the advert before summoning a constable and directing him where to take the letter. It is a chance in a million that the right people will read and respond, but while there is even a straws-worth of a chance, Greig is willing to grasp it.

****

By coincidence, as Digby's cab is making its way towards her house, Daisy and Africa are being driven through Hyde Park. Letitia's revelation, dismissed out of hand at first hearing, has gradually worked its way into Daisy's subconscious like some tropical worm.

Unwilling to face Digby with her thoughts, she has chosen the lesser path and decided to quiz his cousin instead. Thus, the two girls, straw-hatted and sun-shaded, sit in the open-topped carriage and are drawn through the lush green park by the Lawton's bay carriage horses.

"Oh, isn't this such fun," Africa exclaims for the third time, twirling her sunshade madly. "I love carriage rides! Look at all the people!"

Daisy smiles vaguely. She isn't really listening to Africa's chatter. She is preparing her run up to the matter in hand. Eventually, when she can remain silent no longer, she remarks casually,

"I expect you see quite a lot of your cousin, now you are in town."

"Diggy? I see him now and then. He is supposed to take me out, but a lot of the time he doesn't turn up. His Mama is not pleased."

"Oh? I wonder why," Daisy says with feigned innocence.

Africa chews one of her bonnet strings. Truth is, she has a pretty shrewd idea what her cousin is up to - she has heard her aunt and uncle arguing about it in the drawing room, but she also knows that loyalty to family, especially family that is hosting her in their London house, must come first at all costs.

"I think he has a lot of men friends he likes visiting. And then there is his club and his tailor ..." she shrugs.

"I see," Daisy nods. "Yes of course."

"And then he has to see a lot of people about getting into Parliament," Africa continues. "I know my uncle is very busy arranging things for him."

Daisy stares out at the passing trees. She wants to believe Africa, she really does. But if it came to a choice between her and Letitia, she knows who would win the truth stakes hands down. Miserable and conflicted, she clutches the handle of her pink parasol, reminding herself how lucky she is to be engaged to such a talented, if busy, man.

All at once Africa clutches her sleeve,

"Oh, I say, look at those handsome soldiers!"

A mounted phalanx of red-coated Dragoon Guards from the Knightsbridge barracks has just entered the park for a little morning exercise. Sitting upright on their immaculate horses, harness jingling, they ride two abreast straight towards the Lawton carriage.

Daisy's face colours as she recognises one of the lead officers. It is Arthur Gerrard, her former beau. Since her engagement, she has seen nothing of him. Indeed, as soon as her relationship with Digby became public property, the steady stream of party and ball invitations and callers have turned into a trickle. She is taken, and society Mamas are no longer interested in securing her for their sons.

As the Guards draw alongside the brougham, Daisy hastily lowers her eyes. Her hands tighten compulsively on the parasol handle. She bites her lower lip.

"Did you see that?" Africa exclaims, "One of the soldiers saluted me! Oh, I am so thrilled! He had lovely moustaches! And tonight, I am going to a Cotillion ball and aunt has promised that there will be plenty of officers attending. Perhaps *he* will be there?"

Perhaps he will, Daisy thinks gloomily. But I shall not. And soon I won't ever be able to flirt and have handsome young men salute me - for it was me he was saluting, I am sure. She sighs.

"Shall we turn back now?" she asks dully.

Africa is leaning out of the carriage in a most unladylike way and staring back at the horses.

"What lovely lovely uniforms," she enthuses, nodding her head and shedding pins everywhere. "My Mama always swears she fell in love with an entire regiment of Hussars when they were camped at Brighton."

"Did she?" Daisy replies dutifully.

"She says they used to call it 'going down with scarlet fever'. Isn't that droll? Of course, she ended up marrying Papa and going abroad instead. That's where I got my name from, you know."

"Yes," Daisy says. "You have told me."

She instructs the coachman to take them back, telling him to drop Africa at the Barnes Baker's house first. As the carriage makes its way back through the park, she suddenly wishes Tishy was sitting next to her.

What fun they would have quizzing the people leaning against the rails watching them pass by. How they would laugh and talk about the old days at school, the secrets they shared.

As Africa descends clumsily from the carriage, Daisy is almost tempted to tell the coachman to drive her round to the Simpkins' house. But that wouldn't do, she reminds herself sharply. She has cut Tishy out of her life. It was her choice to do so. And for good or ill, she will probably now never see her again.

****

From his window, the engineer has been studying birds in flight. Now he is designing a flying machine. He sees it as an essential mechanism for connecting the two sides of bridges built to span wide rivers.

His desk is full of tiny drawings and scraps of paper full of intricate calculations. Right now he is working on the weight : wing span ratio, based on a pair of blackbirds nesting in the chestnut tree in the garden.

It would be easier if he could actually catch, handle and weigh one of the birds, but as that is impossible, he is making a set of calculations based on observation and surmise.

The way the engineer sees it is that the ability to join the two abutments quickly and accurately would obviate the need to construct the wooden derrick poles that stand in the river bed and act as cranes.

It is highly complex and technical work, and he has been busy with it for some time. He is allowed to walk to the post box as long as he is accompanied by someone, so he has sent his initial designs and thoughts to Mr Bazalgette together with a polite reminder of his previous letter. As yet, he has received no reply.

At night, when sleep evades him, the engineer often slips out of the house and stands in the darkened garden. Lights here and there in adjoining houses give everything the appearance of an unfinished puzzle.

At such times, he debates whether it would be possible to build a flying machine powerful enough to get to the moon. It is after all only a matter of scale and proportion.

He wonders what one would discover there. People like himself? Strange cities with tunnels and bridges of marvellous construction? Or just cold, icy, uninhabited desert stretching away to infinity and beyond.

****

Meanwhile in a small dusty room above a small chemist's shop in Somers Town, Edwin Persiflage sits on his bed brooding darkly, his ravell'd sleeve of care (in his case it is more a frayed cuff) unknitted by sleep.

He thinks back to his lost and abandoned childhood, how so many opportunities were denied to him. So many doors slammed in his face. He could have made it big if he'd been given a chance. There are some who dine on peacocks stuffed with larks' tongues. And some like him, who dine on stale bread and stagnant water.

Now his belly is filled with bile and spite. He swims in a flood of venom and vindictiveness that is only waiting for a chink in the dam to let it roar out. Despite having spent a perfectly pleasant evening in the company of Millie, he cannot forget the carriages full of rich people that passed them by in the street, the well-dressed young man who almost knocked him off the pavement and didn't apologise.

Persiflage adds it all to the septic reservoir of jealousy and resentment that he has built up over the years. He has now decided that he has had enough. Enough of the slights and oversights. Enough of the mundane job, enough of the scrabbling around, enough of being pushed off life's pavements.

In Persiflage's opinion, there is no difference between the richest man in his mansion and the poorest beggar in the gutter, apart from the fact that the former has lots of money, food, nice clothes and good health. These don't make him *better* though - just better dressed, fed and healthier.

Persiflage opens his mind to possibilities. When they return from wherever they have got to, he will summon his fellow Anarchists to a meeting and lay before them his ultimate plan. It is time to enact the Big Boom.

****

There are certain songs that are sung in taverns the world over. They tend to be sung (though maybe 'roared' would be a better term) by young men who have imbibed a lot of alcoholic beverages. The songs are usually about young maidens, often of the dairying profession, and their encounter with the aforesaid young men on a May morning. Such a song is even now being roared out in a certain tavern on the outskirts of Kings Cross.

The tavern is called the Three Turks, and is known locally as a black hole of bred-in-the-brickwork lawlessness patronised by the sort of locals who can progress from amiable badinage to fisticuffs in an astonishingly short space of time.

Among the singers are the unlikely duo of Waxwing and Muller, though the bank clerk only knows the first three verses and Muller doesn't know all the words and the ones he does know he doesn't really understand.

They are celebrating Waxwing's birthday. That is why they have, after many drinks in many pubs, ended up here. They are not sure how it happened, except that this pub is on the way back from wherever they started out. They can't remember precisely where that was either.

The usual clientele, after eyeing them up prospectively, have decided to leave them alone on the basis that one of the duo is over six foot, heavily bearded and speaks in a funny accent.

The song ends.

"Ach, I *see*," Muller says, swaying in his seat, "it is a humorous play on words, yah?"

"Yah - playonwrods, zactly!" Waxwing burbles happily.

He is at the lexical blurring stage of intoxication that precedes the falling over one. Muller raises his glass in salutation.

"Happy birthday, my friend," he says solemnly.

Waxwing raises his glass unsteadily in acknowledgement.

"Least you remembered," he says bitterly. "Not like bloody Eddy."

"Ach, our good friend Edwin has many deep matters to attend to, no?"

"All that matters to him is planning the next explosion. Not sure I care anymore, t'be honest," Waxwing says staring moodily into his glass. "No fun being an..an..kissed."

"Never say zat, my friend. Never!"

"Well, 's true. Where is he tonight?"

"Out with the lovely Millie, I believe."

"Yeah - tha's another thing: How come he has a girl an' I don't? I got better clothes, and I don't go on and on about blowing things up. I'm fun and amusing," Waxwing says, with the deluded self-belief of the very drunk.

"Ah - I am reminded: a woman came into the shop yesterday asking for you. She was quite young - I think she used to rent a room in Hind Street. She wanted to know if you were living over the shop. I told her yes. Then she went away."

With some effort, Waxwing focusses on Muller's face.

"Don't remember any young women. Did she leave her name and address?"

"No. But she was clearly interested in you. She did not ask about Edwin. So, I zink she will come back. Maybe you will have a young woman of your own very soon."

A lone voice at the bar begins another song. Muller drags a cheap watch from his waistcoat pocket.

"I zink we should be making our way home now, my friend," he says. "Work tomorrow, isn't it?"

After a couple of unsuccessful attempts, Waxwing finally pushes himself to a stand. Muller takes his arm and together they lurch erratically towards the door. Outside, the night is drawing in. The two men stand on the pavement trying to work out which way is home. Once they have ascertained the right direction, they strike out in search of it.

Persiflage hears the downstairs door open, and muffled voices coming up the stairs. He hurries out onto the landing.

"So here you both are at last!"

Waxwing stares up at him.

"'S my birthday. Been celibating with my good friend Muller."

Persiflage's expression darkens.

"Are you drunk again, Danton?"

Waxwing smirks.

"None of your beeswax, izzit? Didn't wish me many happy returns. Didn't come out for the evening. Go ter hell!"

He fumbles for his key, drops it, finds it, opens his door and falls inside.

Muller watches his progress from the safety of the top step.

"I zink he will have a very sore head in the morning."

Persiflage directs a hate-filled stare at the half-closed door.

"Who cares? I've had enough of his antics. I wash my hands of him. He can go to the devil."

He beckons Muller to follow him into his room.

"While you were out carousing with that fool, I have been here making plans. I can now tell you where we are going to strike next. And when. And this time, none of those rich bastards with their fine carriages and fine houses will be in *any* doubt that we mean business."

****

Letitia Simpkins is in no doubt that her life has taken a turn for the better. And for that she owes a debt of gratitude to Mrs Briscoe's newly deceased mother. Never was a death so welcomed as hers has been. If she were laid to rest anywhere but Harrogate, Letitia would be adorning her grave with daily bouquets (had she the financial resources so to do).

Breakfast is finished and cleared away. Her father has left for work. The twins are home for the summer holidays and have projects of their own to occupy them.

The day and the house are all hers. She carries her half-drunk cup of coffee up to her room. Today she intends to get to grips with a tricky mathematical problem. Then after luncheon she will pay a visit to Regent Street.

Sarah Lunt has obtained a copy of *Ruth* for her. Letitia has not enjoyed immersing herself in a good novel since returning from school. There are few books in the house - Mama did not read for pleasure and her father only ever reads the newspaper.

She throws back the blinds, letting the warm summer sun stream into the room. It is an omen, she thinks. Light into darkness. Life into what has been up until now a half-life. She throws off her morning wrapper and puts on the black dress that seems to render her invisible wherever she goes.

Letitia does not mind. Nobody noticed her before she went into mourning. She doubts that they will notice her once she goes into half-mourning. And much as she enjoys seeing all the pretty summer clothes on women she passes in the street, she does not envy them nor anticipate herself ever donning such dainty dresses - they are for the Daisies of this world.

She rolls her stockings up her legs, ties them above the knee with black ribbon and gets ready to attack the maths problem with gusto. She is never happier than when she is learning something new.

Later, while Letitia is out and about enjoying her new-found freedom, two letters will be delivered. One will contain the prospectus from Queen's College outlining the new free evening lectures for ladies that are about to begin over a six-night period.

The other letter bears a Harrogate postmark and is not from any college. Though as far as Letitia is concerned, its contents will be a learning experience. Of a sort.

****

Inspector Greig sits at his desk in Bow Street police office and frowns. It shouldn't have worked. He knows that it shouldn't have worked. It never usually did. You drew a bow at a venture. Total gamble. Million to one chance. It failed. You knew it would fail. Then you got on with plodding, mundane, boots on the ground policing.

On his desk are piled the thirty-three responses to his advertisement for somebody willing to adopt Mrs Harding's baby. He stares down at them in disbelief. Then he stares even harder and with even more disbelief at the thirty-fourth.

Now all he needs is somebody willing to play the part of Mrs Harding. And a baby.

****

Across London, Daisy Lawton sits at her dressing table and ponders. It is another sunny day, very like yesterday. But it is not the same as yesterday. She is not the same either. Yesterday, Digby and she went for a pleasant walk in the park. At least, it was meant to be a pleasant walk.

Admittedly the first part was very pleasant indeed. Birds sang, flowers bloomed at their feet. A light summer breeze ruffled the green leaves overhead. She had on her pretty peach voile dress, trimmed with peach velvet ribbon, her straw bonnet had little cherries that bobbed and danced as she moved her head. Digby wore a light wool suit and a new top hat. He smelled deliciously of cologne.

People eyed them with admiration as they strolled by, her little gloved hand placed trustingly on his manly arm. Looking back, she wonders whether it was significant that she had left the engagement ring in a dish on her night table, so as not to stretch her gloves.

They talked about this and that - well, he talked, she listened. It was beginning to dawn on Daisy that she did an awful lot of listening when she was with Digby. As a result of the dawning, she had started to study Fa and Mama when they were together. She noted how often Fa asked Mama for her opinions, or listened attentively as she described her day.

After a while they reached the rotunda, newly painted for summer. Digby suggested they sit down to admire the landscape. They sat in companionable silence for a while. Then he cleared his throat, adjusted his immaculate cuffs and remarked casually,

"There's a seat coming up in the House shortly. I'm going to have a crack at it."

Daisy nodded. A while ago, this would have been a foreign language, but now she understood.

"I hope you win," she said.

"Oh, I expect I shall. My parents think it might be an idea to bring the wedding forward a bit ... people like their MPs to be married. What would you think of next Spring?"

Daisy remembers studying her hands, feeling sudden panic at the thought of leaving her lovely home and surrendering herself to this man. She reassured herself that he was the most wonderfully handsome man in the world. And that she had never wanted anything else but to be a happy wife and busy mother.

"Of course, once we are married, you will be moving in quite elevated circles. As the wife of an MP, you will be expected to keep company with people very different to some of your current friends," Digby had continued.

Puzzled, Daisy had looked at him.

"What friends do you mean, Digby? Surely your cousin Africa is acceptable?"

"Oh, Affy's alright. No, I was thinking of that girl I met a while back. One you went to school with. Wore black."

"Tishy? What's wrong with Tishy?"

"Well, not to beat about the bush, Daisy, she didn't seem quite the ticket."

"The ticket?"

"Right sort. Right class. Clothes were shabby. Boots too. Not someone the wife of an MP should be seen with."

"I see," Daisy had replied, colouring up.

"Been seeing much of her lately?" he'd asked casually.

"No, we haven't met each other for a while."

Digby had nodded approvingly.

"Good. Be grateful if you'd drop her then," he had said shortly, lighting up a cigar and puffing smoke into the landscape.

Daisy stared into the middle distance, feeling her heart constrict. The bright sunny day suddenly seemed to darken around her. She glanced sideways, but Digby was busy with his cigar.

How handsome his profile was. She reminded herself that she was a very lucky girl to have the love of such a good-looking and talented man. Once she was married to him, she'd have a beautiful house and servants. Her dream was being offered to her on a plate.

So why was she sitting here, next to the man she loved and to whom she was engaged, feeling as if she wanted to burst into tears any minute? Daisy had clasped her hands in her lap, remembering what Tishy had told her. Every detail.

After a few minutes had passed, Barnes Baker had got up, and offered her his arm. She had not uttered a word all the way back. She was pretty sure he had not noticed.

Now Daisy leans forward, studying her reflection in the glass. There are little creases under her eyes as if she hasn't slept well. Which she hasn't. Over and over again, she has tried putting together what Tishy told her with what Digby asked her to do.

Daisy was no fool. Why should he request that she drop Tishy, unless he had a particular reason? And there was only one particular reason that she could think of: Digby was afraid that Tishy might spill the truth about his relationship with that other woman.

And what, a little inner voice keeps murmuring, does that say about him? And your chances of happiness if you marry a man you cannot trust?

****

Emily Cully, wife of Sergeant Jack Cully, dressmaker, mother of baby Violet (named after her best friend Violet Manning who was brutally murdered a while ago) is a very busy woman. Here she is rocking the cradle in the kitchen of the little terraced house that the Cullys rent.

At the same time as her foot rocks her daughter to sleep, Emily is smocking a little dress. Her friend Caro, the sewing room overseer at Marshall & Snellgrove, is expecting a baby in August and Emily is making a first outfit for the little one.

As she sews, she is thinking how little material it takes to make a baby's dress and how many bags of offcuts she has stored in the cupboard under the stairs. It is impossible to take on any more dressmaking - the baby needs her and she could not commit to meeting the exacting requirements of the ladies she formerly worked for.

But it takes no time at all to run up a pretty baby frock and it gives her something to do while the little one sleeps. Emily likes to keep her hands busy. Sewing calms her and helps her to think.

What she is thinking now is that she might run up a few samples and show them to a couple of her clients. The ones who have married daughters. She might even show them to some of the department store buyers.

While she sews and plans and rocks her daughter, she is also, with that third eye that all women possess, keeping an eye on the supper. Emily likes to have a good hot meal ready for Jack when he comes in. And tonight, he is bringing a fellow officer back with him.

She has bought a nice piece of beef from Caro's husband. All she needs do now is add the vegetables and lay the table. The baby stirs, stretches her tiny pink starfish of a hand, gives a little sigh and falls asleep once more. Emily smiles down at her.

There are flowers on the table, the comforting smell of good food cooking and a contented milk-filled baby. Emily Cully puts down her sewing and opens the cutlery drawer. She hears the sound of Jack's key in the lock, footsteps entering the hallway, a whispered 'Shh'.

She has told Jack that the guest must take them as he finds them. Looking around her cosy kitchen, Emily does not think that will be too difficult.

****

Another house, another family dinner. But this one is not nearly so convivial as the previous one. Here, the participants sit very upright and very still, nervously watching the figure at the head of the table as he doles out portions of boiled mutton, potatoes and green peas.

Ever since Mr Simpkins returned from Harrogate sans the Dreaded One, his temper has veered from irritable to irrational.

Even the twins, normally the favoured and indulged ones of the family, have felt the edge of his tongue.

It is as if Mrs Briscoe's malign presence is being channelled through their father so that although she is not there in person, she still haunts the house in spirit. Mealtimes are the worst. The empty place at the table rarely fails to evoke his ire, which he then inflicts in some way upon his fellow diners.

Tonight however, he contents himself with dishing up main course. A token and unconvincing grace is said. After which Mr Simpkins sets down the carving implements, looks around, and clears his throat meaningfully.

Nobody moves. Knives and forks remain ungathered.

Letitia feels the familiar cold terror knocking at her heart's door. Something important is about to be announced. Going by every previous announcement her father has ever made, it cannot but be bad news.

"I have today received a long communication from my dear friend Mrs Briscoe," their father says. "As you all know, she decided to remain in the north alone after the death of her mother. She now writes that after much thought she has seen the error of her decision to remain in Harrogate."

She is coming back? Letitia thinks, feeling her shoulders tense. Oh god, please don't say she is coming back.

"Before we parted company, I spoke to Mrs Briscoe about my plans to start a new business, and invited her to contribute a small portion of her inheritance to support it. At the time, she refused point blank. Now, she writes that she thinks she may have made the wrong decision, as she was at the time in a state of deep shock and grief. She writes that she is pleased to change her mind."

He glances round, an expression of triumphant satisfaction on his face. The boys bend over their cooling dinners, refusing to meet his eye. The silence is so complete that Letitia can hear the ticking of the clock in the hallway.

"So, what business are you going to start, father?" she asks at length.

"That is not your concern, Letitia. What is your concern is that I shall expect you to help Mrs Briscoe and the servants pack up the house."

"We are moving? When? Where to?"

"I thought that was obvious - we shall be moving to Harrogate. Mrs Briscoe has ample room to accommodate us."

Letitia stares at him trying to keep the horror out of her face and her voice.

"But ... we ... I ..."

"There is no future for a man of my talents in London. The rents are far too high and my abilities seem to go unrecognised. A new start in a new part of the country is what is needed. And Mrs Briscoe writes that she is willing to support me."

"But the boys," Letitia protests feebly

"Places have been reserved for them at a local boarding school. They will start as soon as we arrive. It has all been arranged. They will soon settle in to their new surroundings and the school has an excellent reputation for turning out scholars."

Letitia glances across the table. Two more gloomy prospective scholars could hardly be imagined.

"But what about me, father? I cannot leave London."

Her father brushes her aside as if she were an annoying insect.

"Cannot? You certainly can. And you will. You are needed about the house. It is a large one, and Mrs Briscoe can't be expected to run it on her own. Now let us get on with our meal."

After dinner, during which only one diner actually dines, Mr Simpkins gets up and without a word or glance, retires to his study, presumably to reply to Mrs Briscoe. Meanwhile Letitia and the twins remain at table, along with their plates of congealing mutton and cold potatoes.

"We don't want to move," William says.

"We like living in this house," Arthur adds. "Can't we stay? You could look after us."

"You look after us now," William says.

"We like you looking after us," Arthur says.

Letitia shakes her head. Never has the desire to earn her own living burned so brightly as now, when everything is about to be so cruelly snatched away from her.

"I am so sorry, boys. There is nothing I can do. I have no money to pay our rent or buy our food," she says miserably.

Nor will you ever be able to support yourself if you don't get any qualifications, an inner voice reminds her. *Aut Caesar aut nihil.* The Junior Locals are a mere six months away, but for all the chance she has now of sitting them, they might as well be six centuries.

****

Dinner is progressing nicely at the Cullys' home. Emily's beef has gone down a treat, the guest, whom she has taken to on sight, expressing his enjoyment of her excellent cooking.

If she hadn't already made up her mind about him, he has just secured an everlasting place in her affections by taking the newly-awoken baby in his arms, and declaring that he has never seen such a pretty bairn.

Occasionally his Scottish accent makes him difficult to understand, but Emily Cully prides herself on being a good judge of character, and in her opinion Inspector Lachlan Greig is somebody she is glad to have met.

An apple pie, warmed over in the oven, is placed on the table. Emily notes with satisfaction that the good-looking Inspector's face lights up at its appearance. She cuts him a big slice, passing the plate over with her nicest smile, which causes Jack to remark teasingly,

"Now then Emily, save a piece of pie for your poor starving husband."

Emily's grey eyes twinkle in amusement.

"You won't go short, Jack, don't worry."

She retrieves the baby, placing her over her shoulder. Baby Violet utters a burp that bounces off the walls, then settles into Emily's neck and closes her eyes. Emily catches Greig's expression, reading the hunger in it.

"You have no family in London, Mr Greig?"

"I have no family in the sense you mean, Mrs Cully," he replies. "I have a sister in Scotland, and her two children are as beloved as if they were my own."

There's a story here, Emily thinks, and not a happy one. But she keeps her own council and watches as he makes short work of his pie.

"Mrs Cully," Greig says, catching Cully's eye and receiving a nod of encouragement, "I have come here not just to sample your wonderful cooking. I would dearly like to ask you a favour - but it is a very big favour, and I shall not be surprised if you decline."

Emily lowers the sleeping baby gently into her cot and settles the snowy blanket snugly round her. Then she resumes her seat at the table, resting her chin on her cupped hands.

"Please Mr Greig, tell me what it is you want from me. If it is in my power to help you, I am sure I shall try my best."

Greig outlines, as circumspectly as he can, the details of the case he is building against the Halls and the reason he has come to appeal to her for her help in catching them.

Emily listens attentively, her expression becoming more grave and troubled as he speaks. When he finishes, she says quietly,

"I have heard of this happening - we had girls where I used to work who became pregnant while not married. Of course, they were dismissed as soon as the sewing-room supervisor realised their state. After their babies were born, they sometimes returned, saying the children had been adopted or fostered. So, what is it exactly that you wish me to do?"

"I need you to be Mrs Harding, and pretend that you are selling your baby to this woman," Greig says. "We shall set up a meeting in which you will hand over the money and the child - please do not worry, Mrs Cully, I and my officers will be there in force to arrest Mrs Hall the moment she accepts the money. It is my hope that the bad publicity from the case may deter other women from carrying on the same wicked trade in human life."

Emily glances across the table at her husband.

"What do you have to say to all this, Jack?"

"I say you decide, Emily."

Emily Cully rises from the table and goes to the cradle. She bends down and places a kiss upon the sleeping baby's soft cheek.

"We are so lucky, Jack. Violet will never know the want of love or kindness or food. It breaks my heart in two to think of other babies dying from neglect, cold and hunger, with nobody to hold them or love them as she is loved."

She takes a deep shuddering breath, then turns to face Greig, her eyes wet with tears.

"I shall do it gladly and willingly, Mr Greig. Only I will never let my Violet leave my arms, is that understood?"

"She shall not do so, I promise you."

"Well done, Em," Cully says quietly. "I knew you wouldn't let him down. Don't worry though, I'll be there to make sure no harm comes to Violet."

Emily nods, and resumes her seat.

Greig pushes his chair back from the table.

"I thank you both for your hospitality and now I shall bid you both goodnight. I'll write to you, Mrs Cully, when all is arranged, and once more, you have my deep gratitude."

Cully goes to the front door and sees Greig out.

"You have a wonderful wife there, Mr Cully," Greig remarks.

"Don't I know it. She is one in a million," Cully agrees.

He returns to the kitchen to find Emily stacking the plates in the small butler sink.

"He is a good man," she remarks over her shoulder.

"Funnily enough, he's just said something similar about you."

Jack Cully comes up behind his wife and puts his arms around her.

"I wouldn't be without you Em. Nor baby Violet. It's a very brave thing you've agreed to do."

Emily Cully pours a kettle of boiling water into the sink.

"One day, when women rule the world, these terrible things won't happen anymore."

"Do you believe that?"

She sighs. "No, not really. But I do believe these pots won't wash themselves. So why don't you make a start on them while I finish smocking Caro's little dress?"

****

A few hours later Mr and Mrs Lawton lie side by side in the marital bed that they still share, listening. What they are listening to is the pacing of the engineer, whose room is directly overhead.

It is not the first night that their rest has been disturbed by his nocturnal activities. Sometimes they have been woken by a crash as he falls over in the dark, or by screams and cries as he struggles in the grip of some frightful nightmare.

Mrs Lawton, while not unsympathetic to the young man's plight, has had enough. She's been searching for the right opportunity to broach the subject of his ongoing presence for some time. Now, as his halting gait continues overhead, she decides this might be the opportunity she has been seeking.

"I wonder whether it is not time for our guest to move to more appropriate accommodation," she says. "It cannot be good for him to be cooped up in that room day after day."

Mr Lawton, who has pondered the same thing for some time, pulls a wry face in the darkness.

"The problem is where would he go? The seizures are not ameliorating. If anything, they are increasing in intensity. He could not work on a construction site any more - it'd be too risky. He might have a fit while on the edge of a trench, anything may happen while he is in his present state."

"And there is another problem," Mrs Lawton continues. "he seems to have formed some attachment to Daisy."

"Does he? I have not noticed."

"That is because you are at work all day. It is very obvious. He stands at the top of the stairs and watches her come and go. I have seen him staring at her in the garden - his window overlooks it, you know."

"And what does Daisy have to say?"

"Oh, she hasn't noticed. A young girl in love has no eyes for other men. But still ... it might be embarrassing if it were ever to become more ... public. You remember the funny turn he had when her engagement was announced? People noticed. Some friends *commented*."

"Does it matter what people think?"

Mrs Lawton sighs gently.

"No. Not under normal circumstances. But now Daisy is engaged to the son of an MP - a young man who is himself destined to take his seat in Parliament, things are a bit different."

"Are they?"

"Yes. They are. We cannot afford to have any untoward gossip that might ruin Daisy's chance of happiness."

There is a silence. The pacing continues overhead.

"Do you think she is happy?"

Mrs Lawton turns to look at him.

"Naturally she is - what a question."

"Only she does not seem to be as cheerful as she was wont to be. And she has had a falling out with little Tishy."

"That does not surprise me one bit."

"No? Does it not?"

"Oh, my dear, you know so little about young girls. Letitia is a dear girl no doubt, but such a plain little thing. It would be just like her to envy Daisy's success. After all, to be frank, she is hardly going to attract a beau like Digby Barnes Baker with her looks, is she?"

"You think Tishy is the jealous type? I had not put her down as such."

Mrs Lawton pats his arm in a 'men-what-do-they-know?' way.

"Of course, that is it. Why, when I got engaged to you, I remember falling out with Margaret. She said some very spiteful things, as I recall. It was only when Richard Barnes Baker proposed that we became reconciled."

"I see. So, when little Tishy acquires a beau, she and Daisy-duck will be best friends again?"

"Her name is Letitia, my dear. Tishy and Daisy-duck were names for the nursery. Besides, Letitia's family are not very affluent, are they? One could hardly see them moving in the same society circles that dear Daisy will be. I'm not even sure what her father does for a living."

"Does that matter? In my time, I have operated upon rich men, poor men, beggar men and probably a few thieves. Funnily enough they all contain the same bits and pieces when you open them up."

Mrs Lawton clicks her teeth disapprovingly.

"Tch! This is not a suitable topic for polite conversation. Let us return to the question of our guest."

"What would you like me to do, my dear?"

"I suggest another letter to his father explaining the situation clearly. Surely he cannot be so hard hearted as to refuse sanctuary to his own poor suffering child?"

Mr Lawton has grave doubts as to the willingness of the engineer's father to offer his child a home, suffering or not. Especially as his condition is worse now than it was when he refused first time round. But. He is a man under orders.

"I shall write in the next few days," he promises.

"I'm sure that is the right thing to do," Mrs Lawton nods.

She rolls onto her side and in a few minutes, her regular breathing tells him that she is asleep. But the surgeon cannot drop off so easily. He lies awake listening to the frantic pacing over his head, wondering what on earth causes such agitation of mind.

The footsteps pass to and fro, to and fro. Long after Mr Lawton has fallen asleep the engineer still walks the floor, his opium-fuelled mind fizzing with ideas for projects. Only when the first streaks of dawn gild the sky does he collapse into bed, and silence finally descends upon the Lawton house.

****

Letitia Simpkins opens her eyes in the small back bedroom that soon will no longer be hers. She slips from between the sheets and reaches for her wrapper. Her expression is not that of somebody who has woken up expecting sunshine.

She creeps downstairs and begins the morning routine. There is much to be said for burying oneself in mundane chores. Letitia heats water, arranges jugs and bowls and lays out the breakfast table, trying to keep her mind from thinking about the awful prospect ahead of her.

She decides that she must share the news of her imminent departure with her friends at the Regent Street Ladies' Literary & Philosophical Society, and must do so today, before Mrs Briscoe descends like an avenging angel upon the house.

Breakfast, when it arrives, is a sombre affair. Only Mr Simpkins is happy, partaking liberally of the eggs and bacon and toast on offer. He does not seem to notice the lack of appetite exhibited by his breakfasting companions, who crumble toast and poke egg yolks in a desultory fashion.

Announcing that he may return late tonight as he will be meeting Mrs Briscoe from the York train, he departs almost as soon as he has finished his last mouthful. He is actually humming as he gets his top hat and light overcoat from the hall stand - an unheard-of occurrence.

As soon as the door closes on him, the twins get up from the table and drift off. Letitia supervises clearing up the breakfast dishes, contemplates breaking the sad news of their departure to the cook, then decides to leave it to her father.

She has other places to be, other people to inform. She puts on her bonnet, finds some gloves that vaguely match and opens the front door.

****

As Letitia Simpkins sets off determinedly in the direction of Regent Street, Inspector Greig makes his way through the throng of sightseers and market traders hanging about Covent Garden Piazza. He enters Bow Street to the usual wag's cry of "Oi, you ain't running! Har Har."

Today Greig doesn't even hear him. His thoughts are miles away. He is remembering a warm welcoming hearth, good food, a sweet baby girl and above all, the calm, clear eyes of Emily Cully as she agreed to be part of the trap he was setting for Mrs Hall.

Nothing must go wrong, Greig thinks. He is so near succeeding that he can almost taste it. He enters the police office, and is about to call up Sergeant Hacket when a shabbily dressed young woman sitting on the bench rises and touches his sleeve.

Greig turns.

"Miss? Can I assist you?"

"Aksherly, Mr Police Inspector, I've come to assist you. You don't recognise me, do you? Never mind. You helped me and my friend when we lost our homes in the Hind Street explosion - ah - now you remember, I see it in your face."

"I do indeed. And how have you both fared since then?"

"Middling to bad," Miss Florina Sabini says, pulling a face. "We have new lodgings, which is good, but the work is wearing us out, which is bad. We are paid, which is good, but we have barely time nor energy to eat which is bad. But that is neither here nor there, as my old mum used to say.

"I should've come to see you sooner, but I went to t'other police office first, thinking you'd be there. You asked us about the two bank clerks who lodged at Hind Street. I know where they are now. They are living above a chemist's shop, corner of Seymour Street. It's called Bengt and Muller and the foreign man I told you about works in the shop."

Greig gets out his notebook, asks her to repeat what she has just told him, and writes it down.

"Thank you, Miss ..."

"Sabini. Miss Sabini. And you are welcome, Mr Inspector. Now you know that they are safe and sound, so that's alright then, isn't it?"

And giving him her most innocent and incredibly helpful smile, Miss Sabini collects her basket and heads for the door, leaving Greig to ponder yet again on the role played in police procedure by the laws of chance, which are frequently far greater than narrative causality would like to admit.

****

Letitia Simpkins has decided that there is no God. She has put Him to the test on numerous occasions and He has failed each time. At boarding school, left on her own for the holidays, she'd pray and pray that a carriage would pull up and her mother (dressed in furs and velvet) would rush out and embrace her.

It never happened.

When she returned home, she'd sat by her mother's sick bed and prayed that she'd reach out her arms and start caring about her only and much neglected daughter.

That never happened either.

Now her mother is dead. She has lost the love of her only friend. She is about to lose her home and with it her one chance to better herself and make something of her life.

Letitia passes All Souls Church. There is a big rock where her heart should be.

She decides she will give the God she does not believe in one last chance to prove Himself worthy of her attention. If He can manage to cause the train carrying Mrs Briscoe to crash before it gets to London, she may start taking Him seriously. (Only one fatality of course; she would not like to be regarded as a mass murderer.)

Letitia approaches the familiar building. Her heart aches to think that she will never walk down this street again. Never share a cup of coffee with Sarah Lunt and the other ladies. Never borrow books from the library or engage in stimulating discussion with intelligent women.

In a very short while she will be at the beck and call of Mrs Briscoe. She does not think she is going to be kind to her. She pauses by the entrance to adjust the heavy bag of books she is returning. She will not need them where she is going.

As she steadies herself, a woman passer by suddenly stops, moans, then stumbles against her, almost knocking her off her feet. Letitia puts out a hand to fend her off. The woman grasps it.

"Help me," she falters.

Next minute, she drops at Letitia's feet, clutching her stomach and crying out. Letitia stares down in horror. The woman's cloak has fallen back, revealing her huge belly.

"I will get someone," she stammers. "Do not move," she adds, stupidly.

She opens the door and rushes into the building. A couple of members are grouped round the notice board. Letitia runs towards them.

"Oh please, you must all come at once - there is a woman lying outside on the steps, and I think she is having a baby," she gasps.

***

Mr Lawton has decided to err on the side of discretion, and after a very early breakfast has taken himself off to the hospital.

He needs to think through the letter he has promised to write to the engineer's father.

Unlike his wife, Lawton knows what the consequences might be if there is no agreement to take the young man back. To consign a fellow human being to an institution for the remainder of his life is not a decision to be undertaken lightly, even though he reminds himself that ultimately it will not be his decision.

He is not rostered on until later in the day, but there are always patients to visit, operation reports to write up. Mid-morning sees him walking to the men's surgical ward, where a patient he operated on a week ago is about to be discharged.

He is a young man and has healed well. He thanks Lawton, shaking his hand, his wife and small children staring with wide eyes at the black frock coat and white surgeon's apron.

Lawton signs the relevant paperwork with a glad heart. It is always gratifying when a patient makes a sound recovery. He is just about to leave the ward when a nurse comes hurrying in, looking all about her anxiously. When she sees him, her face clears.

"Sir, can you come at once? We have an emergency admission."

Lawton follows her to the waiting room. He pushes open the doors, hearing, before he even enters, the familiar cries and screams of someone in late labour. A young woman is sitting on a bench, her arm round the hunched form of another. She glances up as Lawton hurries over.

"This is Jane Smith," she pauses, giving him a meaningful look, "she collapsed outside the Regent Street Ladies' Literary & Philosophical Society, where she was found by one of our members. She is in the final stages of labour. The baby is posterior presentation and has stuck. She has been in labour for some time and has no strength left to continue. She needs chloroform and the baby may have to have a forceps delivery."

Lawton raises his eyebrows.

"And you are?"

The young woman stands.

"My name is Sarah Lunt, sir. I am a surgical nurse trainee at the London Women's Hospital. Please can you help us?"

Lawton stares at her, then nods. He barks out a series of orders that send the staff running. A trolley is fetched. Two porters gently lift Jane Smith onto it.

"Don't leave me," she cries, reaching desperately for Sarah.

"She shall come with you, my dear woman, do not worry," Lawton says as the trolley is wheeled towards one of the consulting rooms. "Will someone get this nurse a gown?" he calls over his shoulder as the trolley crashes through the double doors.

A few hours later, Lawton and Sarah stand by the woman's bedside. She is deep asleep, a combination of drugs and exhaustion from the birth. Her tiny new-born son sleeps in a crib by her side, his fists clenched as if defying a world that does not want him.

"Well done, Miss Lunt," Lawton says quietly. "You were a great help in there. It was not an easy delivery and your calm presence aided my efforts." He glances down at the motionless figure in the bed. "Do you know anything about this woman? She is clearly unwed."

"All she told me was that she was a governess for a family in the country. When she fell pregnant, she was turned out and came up to London to throw herself upon the mercy of her child's father."

"Whom she has not named?"

Sarah shakes her head.

"She only says he is from an upper-class family and he doesn't want any scandal linked to their name."

"How unfortunate."

"Indeed. He has made arrangements for the child though, and she must write to him after it is born."

Lawton makes a wry mouth.

"I can guess what those arrangements will be."

Sarah nods.

"Sadly, sir, I agree with you. But if you or one of your nurses could get hold of the letter, it might be possible to persuade the young man to make other arrangements. At the London, we have a list of suitable orphanages and country places that will take unwanted babies and look after them. Properly," she adds darkly.

"I will give instructions to the ward staff," Lawton promises her.

"Then I shall leave her here now. If I may, I will come back tomorrow to see how she is getting on."

"You are welcome to visit at any time, Miss Lunt. If there is a problem, mention my name. And I wish you all success with your training. You have done well today."

Sarah Lunt walks out of the hospital with a light step, a broad smile on her face and Mr Lawton's parting words ringing in her ears. One in the eye for the male medical students who are trying to get her banned from attending operations, she thinks. Yes, indeed.

****

Letitia Simpkins is walking back home because there is nowhere else to go. The day is slipping away, and every minute brings closer Mrs Briscoe and all that she represents. It is the end of everything. Her heart aches with the pain of it.

In a few days, maybe less, she does not know, she will be gone from London for ever. She did not say good-bye to Sarah. She did not explain. In the rush to get the woman inside the building, and from thence to the hospital, she ceased to exist. As she will soon cease to exist for real.

She turns the corner into her street and sees William and Arthur hurrying along in the opposite direction. They are wearing their outdoor coats and best caps and carrying bags. She calls to them. The twins stop and turn to face her, guilt written all over their faces.

"Where are you both going?" she asks sternly.

"We're running away," William tells her.

"You said you couldn't look after us, so we're going to look after ourselves," Arthur says.

"We have some cake and we are going to sleep at the railway station. It will be nice and warm and we will be able to watch the trains come and go. We shall offer to carry people's

203

bags. They will pay us and then we will buy more food," William says.

Despite the seriousness of the situation, Letitia cannot help smiling. They are such dears.

"Won't you miss me?" she asks.

"We shall miss you. Very much. But you can always come and visit," Arthur says.

Letitia puts an arm round them.

"I promise you that I will come and visit you - wherever you are," she says. "But please don't run away. If father returns and finds you are gone, he will ..." she stops, suddenly unable to finish her sentence. Tears fill her eyes.

The twins search her face, reading and understanding the unsaid message. Silently they pick up their bags and follow her back home. If she had been even one minute later she would have missed them Letitia thinks, as she unlocks the front door. The thought makes her feel cold and shaky inside. Maybe Somebody was looking out for her after all.

****

It has been a long day for Mr Lawton too, but finally he is getting ready to leave the hospital and return to the bosom of his family. He hangs up his white apron and is just about to reach down his hat from the shelf where he always places it, when one of the night orderlies enters his room.

"You wrote a note that you wanted to see any letters written by the new patient Jane Brown?"

For a moment Lawton is confused. He has worked solidly since his arrival, with patients being trolleyed to the operating theatre in a steady stream. Then he remembers.

"The young woman who was brought in earlier. Yes, I requested all correspondence to be given straight to me."

The orderly hands over an envelope.

"She asked for writing material as soon as she woke. I've been waiting for the chance to slip out and bring it across."

Lawton does not hear the words. Nor is he aware that a few seconds later, the orderly has left his office. His whole attention is focused upon the envelope, or more specifically, upon the man's name at the top of the envelope.

For a long, long time he stands immobile, his face expressionless. Then he thrusts the letter into a pocket in his frock coat and goes to the porter's lodge where Mr Horace Featherstone is surveying what he always refers to as 'my little kingdom'.

"Tell Winters I shan't be in tomorrow. Urgent family business to attend to. He will have to split my list between whoever is on duty," Lawton says crisply.

Mr Featherstone, for whom the term *a right little jobsworth* could have been invented, raises his eyebrows in disapproval. Lawton ignores him and with determined stride, pushes through the main door and out into the street.

****

Next morning breakfast at the Lawtons is an unexpectedly sombre affair. Usually the master of the house likes to tease the female members of the family. This morning he merely contents himself with a brief greeting.

"You are not eating much, my dear," Mrs Lawton remarks. "And you are being remarkably quiet. I do hope you are not sickening for something."

Lawton stares grimly down into his cup of cooling black coffee. He spent a restless night trying to work out how to deal with the startling events of yesterday. Finally, in the small hours of the morning he rose, slipped silently down to his study and wrote a couple of letters.

"Daisy-duck," he says without looking up and meeting her innocent gaze because he cannot trust himself not to betray his emotions. "Are you busy spending all my money this morning?".

Daisy pouts prettily.

"Oh Fa! What a thing to say! No, I am spending the morning with Mama. We are going to plan a grand dinner party to celebrate my engagement."

"Then I wonder if you might spare your poor old father a couple of hours?"

"Of course, Fa - if Mama can spare me."

"I'm sure she can. Be ready straight after breakfast."

"How mysterious," Daisy smiles. "Are we going somewhere special?"

"I think so," Mr Lawton says.

He gets up, crumpling his napkin on the table, kisses his wife on the top of her head and leaves the room.

"What is it about, Mama?" Daisy asks, intrigued.

Mrs Lawton shakes her head.

"He has said nothing to me. But you know your father - always full of surprises. I expect he has bought you something and wishes to show it to you in private."

Daisy claps her hands delightedly.

"Oh, that is just like him! Dear Fa. I shall hurry and get my best bonnet. He deserves no less."

A short while later Daisy and her father enter University College Hospital by one of the side entrances used only by medical staff. Daisy, who has been quizzing Lawton excitedly about the 'surprise' ever since they left home, pauses on the threshold, wrinkling her nose.

"Oh Fa! I thought you weren't working today."

"I am not, Daisy. But there is somebody in here that I want you to meet - though it breaks my heart to introduce you to her."

He takes Daisy by the arm and walks her to the door of the maternity room.

****

This is another room, somewhere else. A small poky room with a frowsty bed, bare floorboards and thin curtains that barely cover the grimy window. This is the room of dispensing chemist and would-be anarchist Georg Muller, who is currently below dispensing pills and potions to the local populace, who have constant headaches, horrible rashes which they insist on showing him, and fretful babies. Many have all three.

By midmorning the rush has died down somewhat, allowing Muller to close the shop temporarily and venture out into the street to purchase a ham sandwich and a cup of coffee, which he consumes in the street while walking back.

He returns to find two police officers peering through the small squares of glass, trying to see past the tall carboys filled with amethyst and red liquids that occupy most of the window space.

Muller's first instinct is to take to his heels. His second is similar. His third is to casually stroll by and listen to the conversation taking place.

"Seems deserted," says one of the officers, banging on the door.

"Maybe just popped out for a minute."

"Middle of the morning?"

"Don't seem to be many people around."

"What do you think?"

"Greig's pretty keen on tracking down these bank clerks. Wonder why?"

"That's Inspector Greig to you, constable. And it's none of your business why."

"It is when I'm the one wasting my time hanging around outside an empty chemist and druggist shop, Sergeant Hacket."

The other officer glances up and down the street as Muller turns his back and pretends to be engrossed in the contents of a fan maker's window.

"I'll tell you what we'll do, we'll take a turn around the block. By the time we return, the shop will be open."

The two officers stroll off at proceeding speed. Muller waits until they round the corner. Then he darts over to the door, unlocks it and scoots inside. He is tempted to draw down the blinds, but realises that will alert them to his presence.

Instead, he locks the door again, then mounts the stairs and goes into his room. He drags a chair over to the window from whence he can command a good view of the street. He sees the two policemen return, rattle the shop doorknob, peer through the window and then station themselves in exactly the same doorway he previously occupied.

Muller watches them watching him.

Time wears on. Every now and then some customers turn up, stand about, then go away. The men are relieved by other men. Muller manages to drink some water from the jug on his washstand.

He thinks about Waxwing and Persiflage sitting at their desks, adding up columns of figures. He thinks about the overheard conversation, about the ongoing police presence outside the shop.

The other men are stood down and the first pair take over again.

Muller checks the time. Soon his two friends will finish work and come sauntering down the road. They will be expecting to see him in the shop. But he won't be in the shop. And then what will happen, will happen. And there is nothing he can do to prevent it.

****

Daisy Lawton sits on a bench. The sun is shining brightly and she is sobbing bitterly. Her father sits next to her, waiting patiently for her to regain her composure. It takes some time, but finally she arrives at the sniffing and eye-mopping stage.

"I am so sorry Daisy," Lawton says gently. "I would have given anything to spare you - but you needed to know from that woman's lips the sort of man you are engaged to."

"Oh Fa - that poor dear little baby - what's going to happen to it?"

"I have every hope that it will be taken somewhere safe, and not left to the mercies of some so-called baby-minder who will slowly starve it to death - for that is what Digby had arranged."

"Oh Fa, how could anybody be so cruel?"

Lawton does not answer. Cruelty is something he witnesses every day of his working life in some form or another. He is also currently awaiting the response of the engineer's father to his letter describing the young man's declining mental health. More cruelty, he is sure. He cannot trust himself to speak without adding to his daughter's heartache.

Daisy twists her handkerchief between her hands.

"Tishy was right all the time. Why didn't I trust her?"

"Oh? What did Little Tishy have to say?"

"She saw Digby in the street arm in arm with another woman. But I don't quite understand because the woman I just met doesn't fit the description. Tishy said that the woman she saw was blonde and very slight - she even mistook her for me from behind. It was only when the woman turned around that she realised her mistake."

Lawton's face darkens.

"I see. So he has another lady friend in tow as well, does he? Daisy, I hate to deny you anything you have set your heart upon, you know that. Your old father loves you very much, but if you do not break your engagement and throw off this worthless young man, I am afraid I shall have to refuse my consent. I shall not be able to attend your wedding. And I shall never welcome him into my house."

"I do not want to marry him, Fa. I never want to see him again. I have lost my best and truest friend on account of him - I actually accused Tishy of being jealous. Can you believe it? Why was I so stupid?"

"Love makes us blind, according to the sort of people who say such things. Now take off your ring, Daisy-duck; I shall return it to the giver with some thoughts on his treatment of my daughter."

Lawton opens his hand. Daisy gives a shuddering sigh, then drops the diamond ring into his palm.

"What shall I do, Fa? People will soon get to hear that I broke the engagement. I will be a laughing stock. They will shun me. Mama will -"

"Leave Mama to me," Lawton says firmly. "As for society - I doubt that it will care. I have arranged a meeting with the young man's father after luncheon. It is my intention to make sure that no blame will ever attach itself to you."

Daisy gives his arm a little squeeze.

"Thank you, Fa. What happens now?"

Lawton smiles.

"Now, I put you in the carriage and you go and make your peace with a certain best friend. Who has been a very brave best friend, even though you did not appreciate it at the time."

"Oh Fa - do you think she will ever forgive me?"

Lawton gets up and offers her his arm.

"There's only one way to find out. Your carriage awaits, m'lady. Go and make your peace with Tishy, and then come home. I will tell Mama what has happened. With a bit of luck, we may never have to undergo another grand dinner party in our lives."

****

The Right Honourable Richard Barnes Baker MP is enjoying a post-prandial brandy and cigar in the Members Dining Room of the House of Commons when one of the waiting staff approaches discreetly with a note on a silver salver. Barnes Baker reads it, then gives the man his instructions.

A few minutes later Lawton enters the dark wood panelled room, his face set and grave. Barnes Baker rises, smiling broadly, and holds out his hand.

"Lawton, my dear chap! This is a pleasant and unexpected surprise. Carruth - a brandy here."

Lawton places his own hands firmly in his pockets.

"I have not come to exchange pleasantries, Barnes Baker. And I do not want a brandy. Please read this letter - it is addressed to your son, but I have permission from the writer to show it to you."

He hands over the letter.

Frowning, Barnes Baker skims the contents. He looks up, anger in his eyes.

"Who is this person? Why is she accusing my son of such behaviour?"

"The writer of this letter is under my medical care. Her history with your son is written in the pages you have just read. Your son, sir, is a blackguard and a scoundrel of the first order. I am here to tell you that both you and he may consider his engagement to my daughter to be at an end."

Barnes Baker's face colours up angrily.

"How dare you, Lawton! You come barging in here accusing my boy of fathering a child on some lying lower class slut - who is probably only trying to make money out of her situation."

"She does not lie," Lawton replies. "And as for her class - she is, or rather was a governess before she was turned out of the house. I knew the address of her former employer and I am quite prepared to write to him to corroborate what she has told me."

"Rubbish!" Barnes Baker blusters. "The woman is clearly lying through her teeth. She has probably never met Digby in her life."

"She has given a very accurate description of him to my daughter then," Lawton says drily. "Including some details that only a person in intimate contact with him would know - of course if you say she is lying, there is an easy way to prove it: let your son come to the hospital and face her. What do you say?"

"I say this is a concocted plot to get out of the engagement for some reason. Perhaps your daughter has another beau in the background, eh? Yes - that'd be it. My son is to be thrown over for another man. Well, I tell you straight I won't stand for it, Lawton. If your girl breaks with Digby, I shall make sure everybody knows what sort of people you are."

Lawton's mind circles the comment and compares it to the earlier one about lying lower class sluts. He smiles brightly.

"You are, of course, free to take whatever course you wish. But before you do, let me make clear certain sentiments expressed in the letter. Apparently, your son has arranged via his man, whose name I believe is Hunter, for the baby to be quietly disposed of. Infanticide is a crime, Barnes Baker. Planning to kill somebody - however young, is a crime also.

"One word from you or your son and I will have no hesitation in going to the police and to the newspapers. I think your son's chances of being elected an MP may subsequently be rather less than you both hoped."

He folds his arms, staring Barnes Baker down, daring him to respond.

"I think we are done here," he says in a voice that could cut teak. "The ring has been returned to your son, with a letter explaining how things stand. I do not expect to hear any more on this matter. If I do, you both know what the consequences will be. Do not put me to the test, Barnes Baker. I am used to cutting out diseased limbs. It would give me no greater pleasure than to excise you and your rotten offspring from London society forever."

Having thus successfully delivered his parting shot, Lawton spins on his heel and marches out, his head held high.

****

Persiflage and Waxwing are not so much marching home as dawdling. This is partly because the press of other homeward people on the pavements prevents any speedy progress. It is also because Waxwing keeps stopping to look in the windows of various clothes shops, where the new summer attire is temptingly displayed.

"I do like that straw hat," he says, peering into a hatter's. "Look Edwin - it has a curly brim."

I'll curly brim you one of these days, Persiflage thinks darkly, rolling his eyes.

Since the incident of his birthday, Waxwing has ceased to offer his fellow clerk the deference and homage that Persiflage feels is his due as instigator and founder of the Hind Street Anarchists.

Even when Persiflage outlined his plan for the Big Boom, with accompanying escape map, courtesy of the guileless Millie-girl, Waxwing seemed less than overwhelmed with admiration.

Muller, now, Muller - Persiflage was pleased with his response. Muller is the coming man. Waxwing is rapidly becoming disposable. In fact, Persiflage's intention is to make the thought an act: Waxwing will be the one chosen to remain *in situ* to light the fuse and it is in Persiflge's mind to make it a very short one.

The man is becoming a liability - his drinking habits are an embarrassment. And when drunk, he is loud and boastful. It won't be long before he spills the beans on the Hind Street Anarchists. To have got so far and then to be stopped in his mission by a stupid drunken oaf is unthinkable.

The two clerks dart across the busy road and venture into the quieter streets that lead to their lodgings. They pause to buy a heel of cheese, a loaf of bread and some bruised apples for their supper.

"Are you coming out tonight? Eddy?" Waxwing asks.

Persiflage quells him with a look.

"I have no time for 'coming out' as you put it. I have plans to finalise, Danton. Fine tuning and such like. The Big Boom must run like clockwork. Not that I expect you to understand."

Waxwing studies his shiny boots as they walk abreast towards the chemist's.

"Um ... about this Saturday, Danton. I was wondering ..."

But Persiflage will never know what his co-conspirator is wondering, for barely are they in sight of the shop when a first-floor window is flung open and Muller's head appears in the gap.

"Run!" he shouts, "Ze police are here!"

Waxwing freezes, like a rabbit caught in the coach lights, as a couple of burly police officers suddenly detach themselves from a doorway and race towards them. A third man starts beating on the shop door, yelling to Muller to open up at once.

Persiflage takes to his heels. As he dodges round the corner, he hears the sound of boots on the pavement behind him and voices shouting at him to stop in the name of the law.

But Persiflage does not stop. He keeps on running. And the boots keep on sounding and the voices calling for him to stop keep on calling. And then it begins to rain.

****

Inspector Greig sits behind a desk in one of the Bow Street interview rooms. In front of him is Danton Waxwing and a long evening.

"So, let us begin at the beginning once more, Mr Waxwing. What do you know about the explosion that took place at number 18 Hind Street?" he says patiently, for the third time of asking.

"Nothing. I know nothing," Waxwing repeats woodenly.

"Are you going to deny living there?"

"I deny living there."

"And your friend Mr Persiflage? Did he live there?"

"Never heard of him."

"Do you also deny any knowledge of Mr Georg Muller?"

Waxwing blinks.

"Who is he?"

Greig sighs deeply.

"He is the man you rent from. The one who tipped you off that the police were waiting for you. So, let's try again: do you know Mr Georg Muller?"

Waxwing studies the ceiling for some time as if it contains the answer to this perplexing question.

"I don't know," he ventures at last.

It is like wading through treacle, blindfold, in the dark, Greig thinks disgustedly. And he is running out of patience. What he first put down to a stupidity habit is now looking progressively like low cunning. If the clerk admits nothing, there is nothing they can hold him for.

Greig has already sent a constable hotfoot to Scotland Yard with a note summoning Detective Inspector Stride. In the interim until Stride arrives, he must keep up the pressure on the suspect.

"So," he says, sitting back and folding his arms behind his head. "If I were to tell you that Mr Muller has confessed to knowing both you and your friend Mr Persiflage very well, what would you say in reply?"

Waxwing adopts an expression tantamount to imbecility and shakes his head.

"Why did your friend run away?" Greig persists.

Waxwing shrugs in an 'am-I-my-brother's-keeper' sort of way.

"So, you aren't denying that he is your friend?"

"Who?"

Greig reminds himself that he is a man of principle and beating up people who have not (yet) been accused of any crime is not only barbaric but morally unacceptable. Though tempting. He stares at Waxwing, who refuses to meet his eye.

There is a knock at the door.

Finally, he thinks.

He rises to his feet and hurries across to usher Stride into the room. But it is not Stride. Instead Sergeant Ben Hacket stands outside the door. In his hand is a small green covered notebook.

"Found at the premises," he says, handing it over to Greig.

Greig returns to his desk, holding the book. As he peruses it, there is a gasp from the suspect. He glances up. All the colour has suddenly drained from Waxwing's face and his expression has changed from village idiot to blind panic.

Greig lays the book down on the desk, open at the last entry.

"So, Mr Waxwing, what can you tell me about the Hind Street Anarchists? In particular I'd like to know about a meeting that took place on June the fourteenth, where the following people were present: Mr Danton Waxwing, Mr Edwin Persiflage and Mr Georg Muller. The topic under discussion was the placing of an explosive device in the cellars under the Palace of Westminster."

He leans forward slowly, cupping his chin in his hands, and waits for Waxwing to answer.

"Look, it was nothing. It is nothing," Waxwing blusters. "Just a joke, that's all. A bit of a lark. We were only mucking about. It doesn't mean we were actually going to do it."

He swallows, meets Greig's gaze and drops his eyes despairingly to his bunched fists.

****

Meanwhile Persiflage continues running, pushing people out of his way, ducking and diving between carriages and drays. He is an outlaw. A fugitive from the law. He is almost enjoying himself.

This is what he craves, the raw naked excitement of taking control, of making things happen. Finally, he is the centre of attention.

He dodges down a footstreet, the houses on either side reduced to piles of rubble hidden behind hoardings. At the end of the street he sees a tunnel. It is the entrance to one of the sewers. To Persiflage however, it presents an opportunity to evade his pursuers, albeit temporarily.

He enters the brick archway and leans against the wall, his breath ripping out in rags. He is standing at the head of one of the labyrinthine crumbling brick-lined tunnels that transport London's rivers and London's waste down to the Thames, where filthy beggar children comb the mud under its mouth.

The dreary passageways wonder for miles under the city. Persiflage hears the sound of shallow water lapping below him at the base of some brick steps. Then he hears men shouting his name. A dog barks. Footsteps are coming closer to his hiding place. Holding on to the wall, he descends the slimy steps.

The water is around his ankles. Far ahead the tide is coming in and it is a late Spring tide, unusually high for the time of year. Persiflage, however, does not know this. He is only aware of the shouts at his back and the need to evade capture at all costs. He walks on into the darkness.

Gradually he loses all sense of time. He could be anywhere. Every now and then he hears noises overhead from the concourse of London streets. He can even hear people talking. In his tortured imagination, they all seem to be calling his name. Occasionally he glimpses a glimmer of light from a grating above.

All the while the water is rapidly rising. It reaches his knees. Persiflage turns, but he is unable to work out how to return. The darkness is absolute. There are no distinguishing marks to help him find a way back. The water rises to his hips.

Persiflage has no sense of direction any more. He is utterly cut off from the world above, lost deep under the city. The water reaches his chest. He starts swimming, the foul air hurting his lungs. The water is at his throat; it covers his mouth. He closes his eyes.

****

Dinner is over at the Simpkins residence, but there is still no sign of the master of the house. Letitia has rechecked the note: it said he would be 'late'; it did not stipulate how late he would be. She asks the cook to put a plate in the warming oven for him. Then tells her to make that two plates, just in case.

The evening wears on. Rain falls, painting the pavements so that the street lights are in pieces on the ground. For something to do to pass the time until bed, Letitia decides to start studying the English history paper, even though she knows she is unlikely to sit it.

The syllabus focuses on the century from 1715 to 1815, ending at the Battle of Waterloo. It all seems such a very long time ago. But then, last week seemed a very long time ago, she reminds herself.

Last week, she lost her best friend for telling her the truth. Now that same truth has regained her friendship once more, but too late to make any difference to the future, as she'd explained to a tearful Daisy once the stammered apology had been warmly accepted.

Letitia listens to the rain stuttering against her window. Reconciliation with Daisy has been the one positive thing in her life. At least she will be able to write to her from Harrogate, if she is permitted. Maybe visit occasionally.

Evening turns into night, a dark and stormy one and still her father does not come. Finally, when she can keep her eyes open no longer, Letitia blows out her candle and retires to bed.

She is awoken some hours later by a loud crash. Heart racing, she sits bolt upright, groping for the candle and box of lucifers. Lightning flashes stitch the sky as she cautiously tiptoes her way across the room to the door.

Letitia hears noises on the stairs, stifled female laughter, her father's slurred voice, the sound of a loud smacking kiss. Shocked to the core of her being, she stands by the door, her mind picturing the scene just feet away.

Her father's bedroom door opens, then closes. After a few seconds, Letitia ventures out onto the landing. She can see light under the door, hear muffled sounds. Sick at heart she turns and scurries back to her own room.

She had always suspected there was a relationship of some sort between her father and Mrs Briscoe; she had even joked about it to Daisy, but to be suddenly faced with the brutal reality is like a body blow.

So soon after Mama's death, she thinks. So wrong on every level. And what will the twins make of it? It doesn't bear thinking about. Letitia lies awake listening to the summer storm raging outside and the clock ticking in the corner while the unrelenting awfulness of what is taking place slowly seeps into her soul.

The engineer wakes in the centre of a dream that is no dream, a nightmare that is no nightmare. The screams breaking from him are his own screams. He flails with the bedclothes, pushing them off his body as if they are burning embers.

Semi-awake, the engineer falls out of bed, crawls to the window, heaves himself upright and leans out. The rain has stopped and the moon is high in a sky as black as his thoughts. Street lights turn the surrounding city into a network of silver lines and shadows.

The engineer takes deep breaths of rain-laced air while his mind tries to reassemble the fractured jigsaw of his thoughts. There has been a letter from Mr Joseph Bazalgette. At least, he thinks it was from him. There has definitely been a letter.

The surgeon whose name escapes him has told him that he is to move to another place. It will be all right. He has spent the evening sorting through his many drawings in case Mr Bazalgette wants to see them when he arrives.

Tonight, after his supper, he went and sat on the top step of the landing, waiting for his beloved Angel to appear. When she finally came, she looked happier than he had seen her look for many days. She glanced up and smiled shyly at him.

He remembers her smile. He pictures it now as he sits down in his chair, pulling a piece of paper towards him. He does not need to turn on the light; he knows the contours of her face so well that he can draw her by the light of the moon.

The engineer experiences that old familiar feeling of rising energy bordering on madness. He knows it will be succeeded by a peculiar glass-clear sense of clarity. When he arrives at the new place, he will show Mr Bazalgette the drawing he has made. He will explain about his Angel. He is sure the great man will be interested. He draws on.

****

Morning is already establishing itself by the time Letitia Simpkins creeps down to the kitchen. She has woken up late. She has not woken up in any happier frame of mind either.

Pausing at the top of the steps, she hears raised female voices coming from below. It seems that a massive row is taking place between Mrs Briscoe and the cook.

"You can't give me orders," she hears the cook declare. "You ain't my employer."

"In the absence of your employer, you take your orders from me," Mrs Briscoe says coldly.

"I take my orders from Miss Letitia. Always have done ever since her Ma - God rest her soul - passed on. You ain't nobody round here."

There is a harsh indrawing of breath.

"You will do what I tell you or you will live to regret it, my good woman," Mrs Briscoe says, venom etching every syllable.

"No, I won't. Coz why? Coz I ain't going to stay here to be ordered about by the like of you - whoever you think you are. Soon as I've washed these pots, I'm off. You can find some other mug to cook your dinners and put up with your carping and criticising. And I'm not your 'good woman'. Never was, never will be, and that's you told!"

"If you go, you leave without a character. My fiancée will not write a word of recommendation, I shall make very sure of that."

Letitia claps her hands over her mouth to stifle a scream. Surely she has not heard aright? Her father and Mrs Briscoe cannot be engaged to be married?

She hears the cook laugh harshly.

"Fiancée? So that's the way of it, is it? Well, good luck to you. I wouldn't be married to the likes of him if he was the last man alive on earth."

"You. Leave. Now!" Mrs Briscoe hisses.

"I'm going. Believe me. Only person I feel sorry for is Miss Letitia. She's worth a hundred of you and him, nasty piece of work that he is. I could tell you things about him. But I ain't going to. You'll find out soon enough and serve you right."

There is the sound of someone moving around and throwing things into a basket. The area door opens, then slams shut. Letitia is just puzzling over the final part of the exchange when Mrs Briscoe's heavy tread is heard coming up the stairs.

219

"You? What are you doing skulking here?" she demands roughly, then when Letitia does not reply, "Go and bring your brothers their hot water. And then you can start on their breakfast."

"Where is father?" Letitia asks.

"He is arranging train tickets for Saturday, when we will be leaving London for good."

"Saturday - so soon?" Letitia cries in dismay.

Mrs Briscoe stares at her malevolently.

"Oh, YOU won't be coming with us," she says.

Letitia's heart leaps.

"I am to stay in London?"

"Hardly. You will be going as live-in companion to an elderly aunt of mine. She is bedridden and owns an isolated house by the Yorkshire moors, so she struggles to get servants. Finally, you will be of some use instead of idling your life away in frivolous pursuits. Now get on with what I told you - your brothers need to rise and begin sorting their things. There is little time to waste. Go!"

She thrusts out her arm, pushing Letitia towards the stairs.

Letitia grabs the handrail to stop herself falling head over heels straight into the kitchen. As she steadies herself, she catches the look of scorn and triumph in Mrs Briscoe's eyes.

Pinching her lips together, Letitia descends to the kitchen, where she sinks into one of the worn Windsor chairs. The revelation of what has been planned for her future has left her shaken to the core.

She simply cannot go as a companion to some ghastly relative of Mrs Briscoe, to be harried and bullied for years and years. She must find some way to get her father to change his mind. But how is that to be managed in three days?

****

Emily Cully bites off her thread, and sticks her needle back into the felt needle book. She picks up the little baby dress and holds it up for scrutiny. Satisfied, she folds it neatly and lays it to one side.

The kettle purrs on the stove. Emily warms the pot, then fills it with a spoonful of tea. Small ordinary domestic tasks, done to take her mind of the massive task that lies ahead of her.

Having drunk her tea, Emily begins her preparations. She places the envelope containing the money in an inner pocket of her dress. Then she puts on her outdoor things. Finally, she gently lifts the sleeping Violet from her crib, wraps a shawl round her tiny form, and cradles her in her arms.

Locking the front door, Emily Cully sets out on what will probably be the bravest and most dangerous adventure of her life. She knows that she will not spot any of the police officers; that would give the game away. Even so, she cannot help looking round nervously as she approaches the arranged meeting place: outside a tobacconist's shop in Great Russell Street.

Emily stations herself in front of the shop window and waits. People pass by, some carrying tourist maps or copies of Bradshaw. She checks the time. The baby-minder is late. Her heart leaps: maybe she isn't coming after all. Then somebody walks past, eyeing her narrowly, retraces her steps and asks,

"Are you Mrs Harding?"

Emily tries not to appear surprised. The woman addressing her looks perfectly ordinary. She wears a drab grey cotton dress, and a black shawl. Her dark hair, streaked with grey, is tucked under a nondescript bonnet. She has a face one might see passing in any street. Ordinary. Plain.

Trying to keep her composure, Emily nods.

"And is this the child?"

The woman has a harsh voice, and now she comes closer, Emily can smell alcohol on her breath, see thread veins in her cheeks and a half moon of dirt under the fingernails that protrude from her ragged gloves. She reminds herself she was promised that at no time would Violet leave her arms.

"This is my daughter."

"You have the money with you, I presume?"

Emily digs into her pocket and produces the envelope. The woman opens it, flicks through the notes, then nods in a satisfied manner.

"Good. Well then, let us finish the business. No point prolonging it, eh. Give me the child and that's an end to your worries."

Emily glances around. Where are they? In a minute, it will be too late. And then while she is staring distractedly up and down the street, the unthinkable happens.

The woman bends forward, scoops Violet out of her arms and carries her calmly across the road towards an omnibus that is just about to pull out. She clambers aboard as the driver flicks his whip across the horses' backs to start them up.

Emily's heart almost stops beating. She screams, starts to run to the moving vehicle. Just as she steps off the curb, strong arms grip her shoulders, holding her back.

"Wait, Em ... let the police do their job," Jack Cully says urgently.

Emily tries desperately to fight him off.

"She has taken Violet! My God - she has got my baby - let me go to her!"

But even as she beats her fists ineffectually against his restraining arms, a tall, broad-shouldered figure leaps off the pavement directly in front of the moving omnibus and grabs hold of the reins.

"Stop this vehicle in the name of the law!" Greig cries loudly.

The lead horse rears, kicking out with its forelegs. The edge of a hoof strikes Greig's head. He falls. The driver jams on the brakes. The omnibus judders to a halt with Greig underneath it and the passengers shouting and trying to climb down.

Suddenly there are police everywhere, surrounding the vehicle, climbing aboard, swarming on every side. Amelia Hall is manhandled roughly off the bus and bundled into a Black Maria which is driven away at top speed.

And then through the chaos and confusion, Emily sees Inspector Lachlan Greig walking towards her. Covered in filth and dust, he has blood running down his face. But he is smiling, and in his arms, he carries a sleeping baby.

****

It has taken Letitia all day to work out a plausible line of argument to present to her father as to why she should not be sent away as a companion. Meanwhile she has busied herself with the numerous household tasks imposed by Mrs Briscoe.

Dinner has been sent in from a local cookshop as the catering department is no more. Now, with the boys in bed and her father retired to his study, Letitia decides the time is right to approach him.

She knocks on the door and enters. Her father is sitting at his desk, writing. He glances up, an expression of mild displeasure on his face at the sight of her.

"Yes, Letitia - what is it? I have a lot of correspondence to sort through."

She advances into the room.

"I wish to ask you something, father."

Mr Simpkins sets down his pen.

"Can it not wait until tomorrow?"

"No, it cannot."

He stares at her coldly.

"Then out with it, Letitia, but make it brief. At this rate, I shall not get to bed until the small hours," he snaps.

Letitia clasps her hands, digging her nails into her palms as all the logical pathways she so carefully constructed begin to implode.

"I don't want to go as a companion to Mrs Briscoe's aunt," she bursts out. "Please do not send me away, father. I am sure I can be of more use to you living in the new house. I can clean, I can cook, I can take care of the place. Please, I beg you, let me stay near my brothers. For poor dear Mama's sake if for no other reason. I am your daughter. Surely that must count for something?"

There is a long pause. Her father eyes her narrowly. Finally, he says,

"But you are not my daughter, you see."

Letitia gapes at him.

"You might as well know the truth. It is time you did and now is as good a time as any. You were two years old when I married your mother. I was just starting out in the world and she came from a very good family. And she had a small legacy, left to her in her late husband's will. Money which was set aside for your future, though I did not know that when I married her.

"Now she is gone, and her money has all been spent on your education. I have given you my name and a home here, and that is all I will do. Anyway, Mrs Briscoe has made it a condition of our moving that you are not to live with us. She has had enough of your defiance and your insolent manners.

"So, either you go as a companion, or you go to the devil. You are not my responsibility any longer. And now if you would excuse me, I have more important business to attend to."

Letitia stands and stares at his bent shoulders, at his hand moving across the paper, at the curve of his cheek, at the familiar signet ring on his middle finger. Waves beat in her brain. She feels suddenly ice-hot. She is a stranger in her own life, insubstantial as a ghost. For a long time, she does not move. Then she turns and silently walks away.

Without knowing how she got there, Letitia finds herself in her room. It is almost night, the sky balanced between twilight and dusk. She sits in front of her dressing-table mirror trying to see herself in the eyes of the gaunt, white-faced girl who stares back.

Later, as dawn rises over the sleeping city and while everyone in the house is still abed, Letitia Simpkins will pack her few possessions into the small shabby trunk that accompanied her to and (occasionally) from school. She will take the trunk downstairs, open the front door and carry it out into the silent street. Before she walks away, she will remove the string of keys from around her neck and post them through the letterbox. She does not need them any longer.

****

It is the following evening and Mr and Mrs Lawton sit in two conservatory chairs, enjoying the fragrant peace of the garden, where the last rays of sun shimmer over the newly mown grass.

"I cannot believe how much better Daisy seems," Mrs Lawton observes. "She is almost back to her old self again."

"I cannot believe how much wealthier I feel," Lawton says and is quelled by a glance from the opposite armchair.

"I shall never speak to Margaret again. Never. I refuse to believe she did not know what was going on. I don't care what she says. A mother always knows."

"Well, well, that is all in the past and it does no good to dwell upon it. The young man has gone abroad for the summer."

"And I hope he stays abroad for the winter too," Mrs Lawton sniffs. "In fact, I shall not shed a tear if he never returns to these shores again. Imagine if Daisy had married him and all this had blown up subsequently! It doesn't bear thinking about!"

"I advise you, do not think about it. Our daughter is safe and sound - thanks in no mean respect to little Tishy."

Mrs Lawton inclines her head graciously.

"I agree. She was the one who first planted the seed of doubt in Daisy's mind - though you also were magnificent, my dear. I do hope Daisy appreciates what a wonderful father she has."

"You are free to remind her whenever you like."

The sound of a tinkling waltz (played upon the piano with joyous insouciance) ceases. A few seconds later, the musician herself appears in the doorway.

"Ah, there you are Daisy-duck," Lawton says, holding out an arm and drawing her to his side. "We were just remarking how pleasant it is to hear you playing your piano again. Your happiness makes us happy."

"I'm so glad you feel that way, Fa," Daisy says, kissing the top of his head. "Because I have a HUGE favour to ask. And it will make me very, very happy if you grant it. Though given what it is and who it is for, I don't *think* you will refuse."

****

The engineer sits at a desk by a French window that overlooks a lush green lawn with a spreading cypress tree. The lawn ripples away between arbutus and laurel, losing itself in a green path under an arch of roses. The room is large and airy.

He is surrounded by his books, his sketchbooks and his engineering equipment. They show him where he has come from. They remind him where he is going. Light blankets the room.

The engineer believes that he is staying at a hydropathic hospital, and once the doctors cure him of his seizures, he will be able to return to civil engineering. Today is not a good day: he has felt the old despair beginning to rise up in him again. He tries to force it away.

To take his mind off his thoughts, he is reading an article in the Institute of Civil Engineers Journal about the funds being raised to complete Mr Brunel's magnificent suspension bridge over the Clifton gorge. He studies the revised designs with intense interest. Hours pass in contemplation.

Once he has finished reading, the engineer begins to write a letter to Mr William Henry Barlow, one of the new designers. The quill stutters in the black ink. He writes on and on, filling page after page, accompanying his words with small sketches in the margins.

When he is too tired to write any more, he puts his head on the desk and falls asleep. He will give the pages to one of the hospital orderlies, but it will never reach its intended recipient.

Four months later, on a bitterly cold Wednesday in November, the engineer will walk out of the Lunatic Asylum unnoticed, and make his way on foot to the newly opened Clifton Suspension Bridge. He takes nothing with him other than his drawing of Daisy Lawton and the clothes he stands up in.

He will spend two days and nights just contemplating the amazing structure, marvelling at the feat of engineering that has brought it into being. The stone towers, the triple chains, the suspension rods. His experienced eye will take it all in.

He will observe the way the girders support the deck so that it looks as if it is actually horizontal. Such is the power of his imagination that he will see every stage of the work happening in his mind from start to finish, exactly as if he built it himself.

Two days to feast his eyes upon perfection. On the third, under cover of darkness the engineer will place the picture of Daisy Lawton next to his heart, walk to the centre of the bridge and throw himself off into the deep gorge below. His body will never be found.

****

But long before that happens, Inspector Lachlan Greig sits at his desk in Bow Street police office, penning a short letter to his sister.

Dearest Jeanie (he writes)

Just a quick note to say that all is well with me. It has been a very busy time and I have been too exhausted at the end of the day to do more than fall into my bed. Thankfully, events have come to a satisfactory conclusion now and so I look forward to writing to you at greater length in the coming days.

I enclose a cutting from last week's Telegraph that might interest you. Yes, that is your brother holding up an omnibus, though you may be hard put to recognise him! I am not sure that I do. Nor do I quite agree with the headline, as I do not consider myself the 'Hero of the Hour' in any sense of the word, as I was only performing my duty.

It was certainly a rather dramatic end to a case I have been working on. I suffered a cut to my head which is now getting better and a broken collarbone which still plagues me, though the police surgeon assures me I can expect complete healing in time.

My other main bit of news is that I am considering applying to join the detective division of the Metropolitan Police. They are based at Scotland Yard. I have got to know a couple of senior officers from the division in the course of my case work. It would be an increase in salary, though that would not be my primary reason for applying.

I shall let you know what I decide in my next letter. In the meantime, I thank you for the oatcakes and send my best love to the little ones.

My best and warmest regards,
Always your devoted brother,
Lachlan

Greig has just sealed the letter when there is a polite knock at the door and Sergeant Ben Hacket appears in the doorway.

"All well?" Greig asks, glancing up at him.

"The manager of the London and County Bank says that the clerk, Mr Persiflage, has still not showed up for work. The men watching the chemist and druggist report no unusual activity."

"Ah well. I think in that case we may now presume that he has left town. Stand the men down, Ben. We have better things for them to do than watch an empty property. Besides I need you to accompany me to court tomorrow. The Halls are up before the judge and I have every hope that they will be found guilty of murder and suffer the due penalty of the law."

Greig stands, flexing his shoulders.

"So. It has been another long and wearying day and I'm away to my bed. Early start in the morning."

Hacket lingers.

"May I ask you something before you go?"

"Ask away."

"These dead babies - why was it so important to you to catch the couple? I've seen you work on plenty of other cases, but none seemed to affect you like this one did. It was almost as if you had a personal interest in the investigation. If you don't mind me mentioning it."

Greig nods, half-smiles.

"I don't mind you mentioning it, sergeant. But to answer that question, I have to tell you a story. Once upon a time on a dreich winter's night, an Edinburgh cloth merchant was riding home when his mare suddenly shied at something in the gutter, nearly unseating him.

The horse stopped and however much the man urged her, she refused to pass by. In the end the man dismounted, and went to investigate what was the bother. What he found was a tiny child, wrapped in a filthy threadbare cloth.

The child was thin, blue with cold and close to the point of death. It had clearly been starved, then abandoned on the street and left to perish. The merchant picked the child up, meaning to move it elsewhere and be about his business, which was to return to his own warm hearth and to his wife and young daughter.

But as he did so, the child suddenly opened its eyes and looked straight into his face, as if challenging him: *"Yes, you can let me die, or you can let me live. What is it to be?"*

The man looked down at the child. The child looked back up at the man. For a long while neither moved, nor averted their gaze. Then the man tucked the child into his greatcoat, remounted his horse and rode on."

"And the child lived?"

"The child lived."

"Did you know it?"

Greig puts on his hat and buttons up his coat.

"I did. I still do. Though as you see, he is a child no longer. Goodnight to you now, sergeant."

Inspector Lachlan Greig walks out of the office and the sergeant hears the sound of his footsteps going down the corridor, to the accompaniment of *The Bluebells of Scotland.* Whistled slightly flat.

Finis

Thank you for reading this novel. If you have enjoyed it, why not leave a review on Amazon, and recommend it to your friends?

Printed in Great Britain
by Amazon

15202334R00139